D0090242

THE
RETREAT

THE
RETREAT

ELISABETH
DE MARIAFFI

MULHOLLAND
BOOKS

Little, Brown and Company
New York Boston London

Copyright © 2021 by Elisabeth de Mariaffi

Mulholland Books / Little, Brown and Company
Hachette Book Group
1290 Avenue of the Americas, New York, NY 10104
mulhollandbooks.com

First Edition: July 2021

Mulholland Books is an imprint of Little, Brown and Company, a division of Hachette Book Group, Inc. The Mulholland Books name and logo are trademarks of Hachette Book Group, Inc.

The Hachette Speakers Bureau provides a wide range of authors for speaking events. To find out more, go to hachettespeakersbureau.com or call (866) 376-6591.

ISBN 978-0-316-70630-8
LCCN 2020944370

Printing 1, 2021

LSC-C

Printed in the United States of America

For Bianca.
There's an intersection between grace and fierce:
only a dancer can teach you that.

I can say I hope it will be worth what I give up.
—Santigold, "L.E.S. Artistes"

THE
RETREAT

PROLOGUE: DAY 7

THE DOOR FLIES open against the wind and then Maeve is flying too, her body hurtling out into the cold, the palm of her hand ripped open and bleeding hard. It's still night. Snow swirls up and sprays at her eyes as she stumbles into the dark.

Now what? If there's a moon, it's a thin sliver or hidden away. There's no light and no color, just shadow and snow and more snow, crusted and rising up into drifts that collapse, Maeve knows, like a trap under too much weight.

The hand stings something fierce. There's the howl of the wind and then another sound, the high whine of the door opening again. She can hear him screaming after her, calling her name.

He can't see her here. He can't find her in the dark.

She repeats it like a mantra but only until she sees the sweep of his flashlight skimming across the snow. Searching. There's a flicker from the woods: the fluorescent trailhead marker picking up the beam as it floats past, a guiding light. She gets low and takes off across the field toward it, sinking and stumbling in her boots, trying to guess where the deep snow is packed hard and stable. If she can get to the cabins ahead of him, just get inside her own studio, at least there she'll be safe. She can lock the door. There's no other way in.

He can't stay outside in this weather forever.

Inside the tree line she slips, almost falling, her feet sliding where new ice coats the old. The roots and branches force her to slow down. An injury now is unthinkable. She can feel her heart pounding in her ears: *You can't run on a broken ankle. You can't run on a sprain.*

She knows when he hits the woods behind her, the sheer noise of it propelling her forward again. The sharp crack of falling ice, frozen branches splintering, his voice coming throaty and harsh. He's still calling after her, but she can't make out the words anymore. It all sounds like heavy breath, like the grunt of strenuous labor. Physical. Forcing his way through. It's hard to resist spinning back, just in case, to make sure it's really him and not some animal charging after her. But the stream of light is still there: she can tell he's running, moving fast. The beam jumping around, making surging, flickering shadows ahead.

In the trees, she feels protected. There's a clearing between where she is now and the studio cabin, and she skirts the edge instead of cutting straight across even though it would be faster. She's thinking of the gun in his hand: better off ducking branches, staying in the cover of the woods. She gets as close as she can before darting out into the open. The snow between her and the studio door is hip-deep and ice-crusted and she plows her way through, muscles screaming.

But when she gets there, her heart drops into her belly. She slams her good hand against the lock.

It's iced over. The new storm has coated the door, the handle, everything like a shield. She looks over her shoulder, frantic, scratching at the ice with ragged fingernails, pressing the heat of her hand against it, anything to get inside—but then there's the glimmer of his light and it's already too late.

There's no one to yell for, no help coming. Just Maeve, alone. Wind whips at her ears, her fingers. She realizes that she is shaking.

She looks down to see a new shadow, a dark stain spreading in the snow at her feet. The line of her old scar runs across her palm, now just a broken parallel to this new wound, open and bleeding, her hand slick with it. She knows what the scent of warm blood can attract out here. The thought makes her gag a little bit, but she holds it in her mind.

She needs to find someplace safe, fast.

She can't double back to the center—there are too many doors, too many windows, too many ways he could get in. But a wild idea works its way into her thoughts: There's still one more place. High up on the ridge, where the ledge leans out over the frozen river valley.

One last place to go.

Far to her left, there's a sudden crack, and then the gunshot echoes through the woods around her. A warning?

She can't stay here.

She squeezes her fist and counts to five, waiting to see the stutter of the flashlight beam one more time.

Then she runs.

DAY 1

MAEVE STARTLES AWAKE, her head throbbing.

They've hit a bump or train tracks, and she's jostled roughly against the side of the shuttle bus, her temple smacking the window as the vehicle lurches to a sudden halt. Outside, rain lashes at the ground. A three-hour trip up the mountain from the airport. The last village, High Water, some ten miles below them now.

Maeve is the only passenger left. She's staring out the window into the night, her own reflection just an outline in the glass against all that darkness; her dancer's bone structure, high cheekbones and wide eyes, dark hair lost to the black of outside.

There's a heavy thud of footsteps and then someone is there. She spins to face him.

The driver, a stocky man in his late fifties, stands over her, his stubby fingers gripping her seat in the dark. He gives it a rough shake.

"Better wake up, miss," he says. "We got a washout. You'll have to walk."

Maeve blinks. It's almost two in the morning, the night and weather outside the bus relentless. But the driver doesn't move until she pushes herself to her feet.

She peers out at the way ahead: the road has turned to gravel. They are nowhere, the middle of nowhere. The middle of the night. She pulls her phone out of her pocket and pretends to check the time.

One bar.

"Where are we?" Maeve says, moving her thumbs across the screen. She looks up, feigning indifference. "I just have to text my boyfriend."

The driver glances at the phone, and Maeve wonders if he can read it upside down, if he sees the blank name field and knows she's lying. She's so sick of this, all the lies women have to tell to try and protect themselves.

"Only half a mile, miss. Maybe less. We better get on with it."

Maeve pretends to hit Send all the same.

Outside the bus, the rain is turning into ice pellets, or something worse. She steps down, and her long hair whips against her eyes, instantly soaked. She pulls an elastic off her wrist and ties her hair up high on her head before slinging her pack onto her shoulders. The driver hauls up the cargo door and heaves her duffel bag out and onto the ground, where it lands in the muck. She bends to retrieve it; the bag holds all her dance gear, the whole reason she made this trip in the first place. Two weeks in residence at the High Water Center for the Arts and a dance studio of her very own. Her first real studio time in five years. Her first time away from her children ever.

The bus headlights are still on, casting a slim light out onto the dark road. Up ahead, a sign warns they are in bear country: BE ALERT. ALL WILDLIFE IS DANGEROUS.

Above the words, a bear painted in black and white stares at her head-on, its massive shoulders rising to a hump on its back.

She can't see anything beyond that.

"Gates are that way," the driver says, pointing toward the sign. The bus door closes behind her. He's standing a little too close. They stare at each other.

Then he pulls her duffel out of her hands and heads off into the dark, forcing Maeve to follow, struggling to keep up in the downpour.

"Don't get used to this rain." He's yelling, his voice half lost in the wind. "We had two feet of snow last week. Temperature's already dropping again now." To the side of the road, Maeve can see the ridge of dirty snow, plowed up and frozen and now melting again. The driver calls over his shoulder, "Can't predict nothing anymore, not around here. Nothing's the way it used to be."

At the gate, there's a rusty dead bolt that won't give and he drops her bag again to work at it. Maeve stands to one side, stray hair now plastered to her neck. He's hammering away at the lock with his fist when she hears another sound. Some kind of call. Something moving in the trees.

Apart from a few childhood weeks at a cabin, she's unused to the wild. One reason for choosing this retreat, this place. To challenge herself. To shed old fears.

She takes a step toward the tree line, but her foot slips on an icy patch, and she pulls up quickly, saving herself a fall. The bear warning has left her wary, but this doesn't sound like a bear. It's a kind of blast. A high gripe.

No: a bleat.

At nine, she spent one long night listening to the screams of a far-off deer, run ragged and chased up against a fence by a pack of coyotes. In the morning, they found its remains, the bones still pink and raw and tangled in the tall pickets. Her mother using it as some kind of biology lesson, nudging Maeve forward, forcing her to look.

Now Maeve pulls up her phone and casts a light as she edges her way into the trees.

For a moment, she's a child again, her mother's hand at her back. Then she takes a breath.

It's a fawn.

She can see it now, its leg caught high in the chain-link fence that extends from the gate, trying to follow its mother over. Not quite big enough yet to clear it at a leap. On the other side of the fence, two adult deer dance quietly back and forth in the rain. With her approach, they freeze. They're both does, or anyway, deer without antlers. Maeve stops again and lowers her light, not wanting to frighten them further.

Can she get close? Should she? Try to help somehow, free the thing herself?

Maeve digs her fingernails into her palm.

But with its next yell, the fawn gives a good kick and it's free. It lands, surprised, on the ground and staggers as the two females urge it forward, forcing it to make its joints work. Maeve exhales.

"Hey!"

The driver calling to her from the gravel road. Looking at her like she's crazy.

She follows him through the open gate just as the weather changes— the wind drops, and the first real snowflakes catch in her eyelashes, errant and heavy.

It's four hundred yards up the winding drive, walking blindly in the dark, and then the building is there, looming high overhead. Maeve steps back, surprised by how it seems to have materialized out of the storm. She tilts her chin to look. Six stories. The only light shining through a window is on the ground level, as though a single lamp has been left to guide her. She can see her own reflection, drawing closer, in the glass.

The driver tosses her duffel down at the front entrance. Then he's gone, heading to the road without another word.

She turns back one last time. The deer are still there, motionless. The big doe's eyes on her from the shadows on the wooded side of the fence, and snow suddenly everywhere. Snow coming down all around her.

The door swings open.

"Mommy, I see you!"

Maeve leans into the laptop screen, and back home, her daughter does the same, Talia's long chestnut hair swinging as she shoves her little brother out of view.

Off camera, four-year-old Rudy lets out a howl. "But I want to see Mommy!"

"It's okay—" Maeve starts, but the screen freezes and the image suddenly dissolves, pixelating, as though the little girl in the picture were falling to pieces. There's silence as even the sound cuts. Maeve waits, calling out every few seconds—"Talia? Talia?"—just as if she were sitting at the child's bedside, gently waking her, rather than half-perched on her bed in the bowl of a mountain range two thousand miles away, trying to catch her breath in the thin air.

Jet lag has her upside down. Early November, and the sun not even fully up yet, the first band of light striking a fine note at the ridge of pine that seems to crest like a giant wave, rising up out of the rock face to the east of her. The morning air sharp and clean; the ground, far below, frost-veined.

The connection stays broken and Maeve swirls her finger against the track pad, impatient, then sets the laptop on her desk and pulls on her tights.

There'd been someone waiting up for her when she arrived; the door swung open and a hand pulled at Maeve's, ushering her inside. The sudden contact made Maeve flinch. But it was only a clerk of some kind, an almost severe-looking Asian girl, noticeably young, her blunt black hair cut with razor sharpness. She tugged at Maeve's arm, hand over hand, drawing her closer.

"I was so worried. Are you okay? I've heard—" The girl glanced out at the retreating driver before closing and locking the door. She spun her back against it and looked at Maeve, expectant. "I've heard so much about you."

Facing her in the shadows, Maeve startled: the two women made a sort of mirror image. The same size and height, dark-haired, dark-eyed. But more than that, a tension to the girl that felt too familiar. A nervousness. Small and lithe enough to fit in at audition time, lining up down the long hall with the other junior dancers—and something about the way she held her body. Fierce and anxious, all at once. How Maeve used to look too. But now?

She stiffened. November was the center's off-season, the whole reason she'd scheduled her visit for this time. She'd been told there would be no other dancers on-site, much less someone looking for mentorship. She didn't want to see herself in this girl, in her anxious eyes.

"I'm fine—it's just a little rain." The words coming out more snappish than she'd meant. "And I'm sure you haven't heard everything."

The girl's face went blank and somewhere behind her exhaustion, Maeve felt a ping of guilt. She took the key, found her own way to her room, and collapsed into bed—but then woke in the dark, over and over, with a vivid string of dreams.

First: She is in a garden in winter, everything barren and white, and Iain suddenly beside her, gripping her arm, his spade raised in his hand. Then she dreams that she flies home but forgets the children and goes to a party instead; Iain takes them somewhere and she doesn't know where. She dreams of her old house, the one before they moved back to the city, that she and the children live with Godzilla. This does not seem outlandish in the dream.

Finally, a dream she is being crushed.

In this one, she is in bed, her bed at the center. There's an animal smell— she can smell the thing before she sees it—and then it's through the window, as if the window simply opened to it. Soundless apart from the heave of its breath; the weight of it, enormous. Maeve cannot make it out, cannot seem to open her eyes. Chest-crushing. A darkness pressing down on her.

She woke up then for good, struggling for breath. Her coat like some humpbacked shadow in the corner where it hung, draped and drying, over a chair. She flipped on the light and unpacked.

Now she watches the little loading wheel on her screen going endlessly around and around. Buffering. The nightmares haven't worn off: she just wants to know that her children are safe at home. That they're okay.

But when the image suddenly jolts back to life, Maeve finds that she is looking at her own mother rather than the kids.

"Talia went to watch the TV," her mother says. She shifts her eyes back and forth as though she can somehow peer beyond the screen's limits to see more of Maeve's room. Short-haired and hawk-nosed, she is a tall, broad-shouldered woman.

Maeve takes after her late father; she's quieter and more delicate in her features. She presses her lips together, then forces a smile.

"It's going all right, though?" Her voice is a little flat. This is her first professional time, her first time alone in forever; she resents her mother pushing her way into any of it.

"Of course. What about you? Dancing already? Getting your work done?"

Maeve opens her mouth, about to explain that she just arrived, that the time difference means it's only eight a.m. where she is, that she hasn't even had a chance to meet with the program director, much less get a key to her studio, and that, really, this should all be evident as it's been less than twenty-four hours since she left the kids and drove herself to the airport—but she holds back. "On the agenda for today," she says instead. "I'm barely out of bed. It's early here."

Her mother tips her chin, stern-faced. "Mmm."

Maeve instantly regrets the honesty. Her mother, who'd woken Maeve every day before dawn through childhood, wrapped her ankles a million times, counted out her pre-breakfast workouts, policed her eating and sleeping through twelve years of ballet school, and beyond.

She's silent now, her tight expression pasted in place.

"Look—" Maeve impulsively turns the laptop to face the window, hoping the camera will catch the view. "It's beautiful here." The center is nestled in the backcountry between high ridges; it's like standing in the middle of a crown, jeweled peaks jutting up on all sides.

Her mother's voice cuts through the crisp air. "Maeve! What are you doing? Are you still there? I can't see you anymore."

Maeve takes a breath and swivels the screen back around. She offers a wide, accommodating smile. Camouflage. This call is ostensibly for the kids, but let's face it: it's really for Maeve.

"Sorry," she says. "I thought it would work. Can you call them back? The kids? I really wanted to say hi."

Her mother doesn't even turn her head.

"They don't need you, Maeve," she says. "Let them play. You can say hello tomorrow."

Maeve watches as her mother leans into her iPad, and then the call is over. She stays there a moment, staring at the now-blank screen. Then she takes a deep breath and sticks her tongue out.

Childish? Sure. But it feels good.

She leaves the laptop and goes back to the window, tries to take in the whole view. Allows herself, momentarily, to put aside all the baggage she brought with her: a divorce that left her with nothing, a body that feels like a traitor. She can see the outline of her face, a shadow reflection in the glass. *Maeve Martin, principal dancer.* Who she used to be.

Her last true chance at a career is the grant that paid for this retreat— a transition grant for professional dancers making the leap to directing a company, with a cutoff age of thirty-five.

Maeve is thirty-four.

Put it in a box, she tells herself. *Stick a pin in it. Focus instead on the world stretched before you.*

But even the heavy glass feels like a barrier. Maeve wrestles with the latch, then throws the window open, pops the screen, and leans right out. Her face and shoulders meet the cold air, the snow still falling, steady and gentle, and she has to stop herself from pitching too far; her feet almost leave the safety of the floor. Four stories up, a bird's-eye view. A queen in her castle.

Below, the new snow sweeps off, endless, into the trees. Like a bolt of white cloth spooling out at her feet. Like a blank page set down just for Maeve. She flexes a little higher, up on her toes.

All that white. A new future, just waiting for her to write it.

The director's office is tucked in a corner of the center's wide lobby, giving its occupant a sweeping view of backcountry slope, the tree line ceding to snowcap only a little higher up. The director herself—Karolina Rhys—is struggling with the window blind when Maeve arrives. She knocks on the door frame so as not to surprise her, but it turns out Karolina is not the kind to startle easily.

"You're here!" she says, calling over her shoulder. She's got the look and demeanor of a younger woman, her silver-blond hair cut blunt below her shoulders, jeans tucked into a pair of cowboy boots. She's in her late forties—Maeve has looked her up—the kind of enviable woman who is equally at home on an Oklahoma ranch or at an Oxford riding club. A Czech-born Saskatchewan farm girl; a painter who was once married to a famous playwright.

She gives the blind one more adjustment and turns. "You must be Maeve. My dancing queen!" A quick glance down at the paperwork on her desk. "Maeve Martin Dance Project?" She springs forward, arms outstretched. The greeting is warm and professional: she doesn't shake but closes both hands over Maeve's and looks her right in the eye.

"I'm Karolina. Karo, that's mainly what people call me." Then she's across the office again, rummaging through a cabinet. "Let me just dig up your keys and we'll be off on the grand tour." She pauses, looking over her shoulder again. "You met Sadie already, didn't you?"

Maeve turns, startled to find they're not alone—the clerk from the night before is seated on the couch. Of course. She's the director's assistant. Who else would be asked to stay up half the night waiting for a late arrival?

The girl rises to her feet, but her bearing has changed. Last night's gushing nervousness is gone; Maeve is surprised at how openly the girl seems to assess her, looking her up and down with the distrustful eye of a seamstress or a rival pageant contestant. A rejoinder, she realizes, for the cold shoulder Maeve gave her on arriving.

Karo keeps on. "She's my doctoral student—I found her in Venice, at the Biennale, and coaxed her to come work as my assistant for a year before returning to her dissertation. She tells me you had a rather inauspicious beginning to your time with us."

The girl steps forward and diplomatically extends a hand. "Sadie Kwon," she says. To Karo: "We were…too tired last night for social graces." A practiced smile.

She's neat-looking, and well groomed, but there's not much joy to her. The doctorate makes sense. In the light of day she looks more like a bank teller, Maeve thinks, than a dancer. She takes Sadie's hand and gives it a squeeze, trying to emulate Karo's warmth. Embarrassed now at her frigid reaction the night before. "Yes, I guess I arrived as the weather was turning," she says. "You must love it, being here in the mountains full-time. What a treat—"

But Sadie just nods and breaks her grip. "Every new opportunity sounds exciting in Venice. It's all artists and parties. You know, you're networking all the time." She steps efficiently to the desk and begins sorting through mail on a tray.

"I'm so sorry," Karo says, still searching through her cabinet. "I always fumble the studio keys somehow. Sadie"—her tone sharpens almost imperceptibly—"Sadie, did you not make up Maeve's welcome package?"

Maeve looks around, hoping to extricate herself from the discussion. There's the couch to one side with an aerial-view photo mounted on the wall over it. Black-and-white, a vintage shot, its title in that squared-off 1960s typeface: HIGH WATER CENTER FOR THE ARTS. She swipes a brochure from an end table, turns to sit down, spreads the site map out flat against her lap. Orienting herself.

There are two main doors off the lobby, one leading to the front gate, where she came in the night before, and the other out to the back acreage and the expanse of trees and trails she can see from her own window upstairs. The studios are all cabins set some way off on the north side of the property; the high ridge has been marked on the map with a staggered line, and there's what looks like a ski lift out at the eastern border—the SkyLift. There are two roads in, but only one that's accessible in winter.

The center was constructed in 1922, Maeve reads, *during the heyday of art deco design, and this influence is notable in everything from the vintage light fixtures to the geometric lines and sunburst motif in the lower-level spa area, where visiting artists can enjoy bathing in the natural hot springs for which High Water was named.*

The building has six stories; permanent staff suites are on the second floor and all the artists' rooms staggered on the floors above.

"You'll learn the place quickly enough," Sadie says, crossing the room. She passes a folder to Karo wordlessly, then turns to Maeve. "It's beautiful here, and quiet. I'm sure you'll like it." That same fixed smile. "It's very quiet," she says again.

"You seem so young to be into a doctorate already—" Maeve means it as a compliment. In dance, everyone is young.

"I am."

Maeve waits for her to finish, but Sadie has no more to say.

"Aha! Here we are." Karo pulls a key from the folder, her voice brightening. "Unless there's something else you'd rather do first? Have you eaten?"

But Maeve shakes her head as she rises. She's still got her coat on, ready to go. "I really just want to get to work."

Sadie steps forward as if to go along with them. Standing next to her, Maeve gets that same doppelgänger feeling, a sort of shadow. Something about the girl's posture. It's not a stretch to wonder if Sadie grew up in dance and then switched to academics. Competition is competition, after all.

"It's not far to the cabins," the girl says. She's stepping into her tour-guide role now. "Maybe a ten-minute walk? In the summer, you can sometimes grab a ride on an off-road—" Here she seems to catch herself, speaking more hurriedly. "But not now, not with the weather so unpredictable. Better to stick to the path. We don't want any accidents—"

Karo looks at her sharply, and the girl suddenly hesitates, holding the door for Maeve.

"I'll take Maeve over on my own," Karo says. She tucks the key away again, then slides into a wool wrap and draws up the hood. She turns to Sadie, her voice clipped and quiet: "You have that request to finish up, yes?"

As sophisticated as Karo seems, Maeve sees that she can't be easy to work for. The idea makes her soften, and she tries to brush Sadie's hand, a kind of *Thank you,* as she follows Karo out, but she can't quite catch the girl's eye, and the door shuts behind them.

They cut quickly across the lobby and out the door, then follow the line of the building toward the woods, their reflections rippling in the center's wide windows. About fifty yards out, the shoveled path ends abruptly and they move off through snow that's already almost knee-deep. Ahead of them, a trail marker gleams fluorescent at the border of the trees, and the vestige of a path picks up again, less recently cleared.

The air is crisp and clean. Maeve inhales, and breathes out the obvious tension between Karo and her assistant. Glad to be outside and free of it.

"We had snow early last year too," Karo says. "Almost as bad." She squints up at the sky, as though testing her theory, then corrects herself: "Not this bad."

"When I arrived last night it was raining," Maeve tells her, at a loss for something to say. Her experience of alpine weather is exactly nil. She follows Karo through the trees into a little fairyland of cabins, each set a few hundred feet apart from the others. Somewhere nearby, she can hear a dull echo, the rhythmic *thunk* of a hammer.

"I wondered about bears—" Maeve says. "There was a warning sign on the road—but maybe they're already holing up for the winter?"

"In November? No, I wouldn't say so. Anything's possible, of course: they may be adjusting to the new weather patterns faster than us. But they generally stay higher up in the mountains. This time of year, it's really the elk you have to worry about. Rutting season." Karo thrusts her shoulders back like a girl trying to get some attention at a club. "Mating. It's not their fault." She breaks into a bold smile, pleased with herself. "They're not rational."

The path curves and the rhythmic sound grows louder. Maeve slows, peering into the trees. The forest here is almost all evergreens, tall and spindly lodgepole pines and dense firs; it's hard to see. But there's definitely something there, moving.

She pulls back a little. It's a man.

He's wearing some kind of camouflage gear, a parka in mottled grays and browns, but his hat is orange. The kind hunters use so they don't get shot. He cuts a fine figure among the trees: tall and somehow commanding, even all alone like that. The sound she heard wasn't a hammer. It's an ax. He's chopping wood, setting up logs to split on a wide stump.

"That's Dan," Karo says from a step or two farther up the path. "He's our facilities manager. So you'll see him out and about on the grounds—working."

She pauses. When Dan glances over, Maeve raises a hand in greeting and he stops and regards her a moment before executing a gallant, good-natured salute. Then he hefts the ax and keeps on. Karo steps in closer to Maeve, a proud, almost motherly smile on her face.

"He came to us from the army, so—"

Off in the bush, Dan sets up the next log to be split. The ax falls. *Thunk*. Maeve flinches.

Karo gives a satisfied nod. "He takes his job very seriously." She turns away again, tugging at Maeve's sleeve. A moment later, she's pointing merrily into a clearing ahead: a windowless structure, a round house, just beyond the break in the trees. "Look, here we are."

The key is in a little brown envelope. Karo unlocks the door but allows Maeve to push it open—it's her studio they've come to. They kick off their boots in the doorway. Maeve takes a glide across the floor. It is pristine, immaculate. The cabin itself looks wheel-shaped from the exterior, but inside, she can see it's more of an octagon. The walls are lined with mirrors; light pours in from pie-shaped skylights cut into the ceiling above.

"That's why this one was built in the clearing," Karo says. "You get both worlds: privacy and gorgeous light. No windows at eye level." She raises an eyebrow. "You can dance naked if you want."

Maeve laughs. "I might, if I ever get warm enough."

Karo paces the area efficiently, flipping on lights, opening cupboards hidden in the wall.

"It's meant to be a full-service space: heat and electricity, obviously;

refrigerator, kitchenette, a powder room in the back corner." She swings a tall pantry door open, revealing neatly packed shelves. "We keep the kitchen stocked with dry goods, so you won't have to run back and forth. There's enough food here to sustain you for days—" She pops open the next cupboard door. "And you have everything else you'd need, utensils and plates and bowls. There's a cast-iron soup pot in here big enough to use as a firepit," she says, reaching in and rifling through the pots and pans. "Ah, here it is." She knocks on the pot and it rings like a bell—then she waggles a finger. "I'm joking! No fires indoors, okay?"

Maeve smiles, but she's only half listening. It's all so much to take in. She circles the space, a finger trailing the mirrored walls. Her heart-beat starting to come up quicker. She looks so unprepared, somehow. Hair falling loose, jeans cropped at the ankle by hand.

Two weeks out here by herself? She wonders if she still has the stamina.

"The only thing we ask is that you don't sleep out here but return to your suite at night. The insurance company is quite adamant about that. Liability: we can't guarantee your security on the perimeter like this, and cell service, I'm sure you've already noticed, can be sketchy—especially in the trees and especially with this snow. So we prefer that you come home at night."

Maeve nods, distracted by the many versions of herself in reflection, Maeve upon Maeve in the mirrors. She walks into the center of the room, wanting to somehow take ownership, feel in control of the space, and pushes off on one foot, a controlled spin.

As she turns, Karo's voice sounds smaller, as though she's speaking from somewhere far away.

"It was really designed as a rehearsal space for dance companies. Small troupes, you know, and that's often what we get here—"

Maeve breaks out of her turn.

"I am a dance company." This comes out louder and more suddenly

21

than she'd expected, the acoustics of the empty room changing her voice, expanding it outward. She looks up only to see her own face staring down, distorted in the curved glass of the skylight above. "Or," she says, "or I will be. It just doesn't look like it yet."

When Karolina doesn't respond, Maeve finds herself doing that thing—filling the silence with details.

"That's why I'm here," she says. "To build something new. Not to perform myself anymore, but to direct, to build a company." Standing in the center of the room makes her feel like she's onstage. She steps forward, leaning into it.

"I used to be a principal with Dance Theater Nouvelle Vague. And before that, with the National—"

Karolina nods, suddenly interested.

"I know exactly who you are." She looks at Maeve and there's something new in her eyes, some bit of fire. "I actually know Nouvelle Vague very well. Or I did, years ago. My husband was Gianpietro Conti, the playwright. He did some work with them when Jules Bourassa was the director."

For a moment, Maeve can't breathe. This piece of history is news to her. How much does Karolina really know?

"Before my time," Maeve says quietly.

"Ah." Karolina gives a little shrug. "Well. I hope this new endeavor will make you happy." She seems tauter now, more intense. "I saw you dance once, when you were touring. At the Opera House in Bonn. But then you quit."

"No." Maeve takes a few steps toward her. "No, I never wanted to quit."

"All right—you left."

Karo closes the last cabinet, the latch clicking softly into place.

Neither of them speaks. Maeve, a hand against her thin T-shirt, fingers absently running over the ridged line of the scar across her belly underneath. C-section, her *career-section, ha-ha;* this is Maeve's great joke, but she doesn't say it aloud now. There are no more principal roles for Maeve. Not at her age, and not with this body history. The only realistic goal is the one she's set: start her own company, take the lead in a new way. And to do that, she has to stay focused. No matter what.

Overhead, the light changes. A new wave of snow clouds moving in.

"Quiet out here, isn't it?" Maeve moves back to where Karolina is standing, near the door. She's eager to put the moment behind them.

"Well, you're here at a bit of a strange time—I'm sure I mentioned that in my e-mails." Karolina leans against the door frame and begins to pull her boots back on, her mood easily reset. "We ended a term program last month, so there's only a few of us here. We're quite the little club already! Don't worry, you'll fit right in. I'm here year-round. Our journalism director too. He's a lovely kid, pure fun—Justin Doyle. But as far as artists are concerned, it's really just you out here in the cabins. There's a filmmaker, Anna Barthelmy, from New Orleans; she's a sort of activist, her family is practically Creole royalty. She's working up in the main building. Her second time at High Water in a year! If you like it here, you love it." Karolina switches feet, tugs on her bootstrap. "And Sim Nielssen, have you seen his work before?"

Maeve shakes her head.

"He travels a lot," Karo says. "Shows overseas, mostly—Europe and Asia. He's in residence for the year. Been here since September, working on a great, giant installation. In the gallery, just off the lobby. It's going to be fantastic, you can't imagine how good."

She stamps her foot into the boot, punctuating the very goodness, the greatness of this installation.

Maeve has a shiver suddenly, something on the back of her neck, cold enough to make her flinch. She reaches for it, but it's only water— a bit of snowmelt from her hair. As she moves, she catches herself in the mirror again. For a second, her face hollows out; her lips are black, her eyes only sockets. A trick of the light from above.

She takes a breath. She hasn't begun to put her own boots back on.

"I might stay behind here for a few moments."

The absurdity of this strikes her as she says it. She's dressed in jeans and a leather coat, and she's brought nothing with her, no change of clothes, not even an elastic to tie back her hair. What does she plan to do here, alone in the middle of the woods?

Karolina either doesn't find this strange or hides it if she does.

"We'll have dinner this evening, all of us," she says. "There's only a small group here; no sense in keeping the kitchen open for four hours every night. Seven o'clock? That's not too late?" She opens the door.

Maeve steps forward as though this is her house now, as though she is showing Karo out. "I never would have quit if I'd had the choice," she says. The words trip out of her, awkward and sudden.

Karolina simply looks at her, surprised. Maeve pulls away and brushes again at the back of her neck.

"It's wonderful, I mean. That's what I mean—I'm glad to be out here. I'm here to work." Her hands drop to her sides. "So it's fine with me that there'll only be a handful of us," she says. "The fewer people, the better."

She finds the installation artist by accident. On her way back through the shadowland in the evening; a difficult first day of work, but Maeve forced herself to stick it out. It's already heavy twilight by the time she finally pulls her jeans back on, tucks them down inside her boots against the wet.

Beyond twilight. Later than she thought. She bundles her coat under one arm, despite the snow coming down. She's warm, hot even, from practice—her first extended workout in what feels like forever. It's important to remember what that's like, rehearsing and dancing all day.

When was dinner again? She's likely missed it.

She rummages in her bag as she moves along, finds a granola bar she snagged from the cupboard, and unwraps it. There's an odd pleasure, a delicious feeling, from the emptiness inside her. Familiar. You can get away with a little more in modern companies, but all Maeve's formal training was in the ballet, where size is everything—a blur of cigarettes and Diet Coke.

The path hasn't been cleared since morning, but there's a wide enough swath cut through the brush that she can determine where it would be in summertime, and there's a rough trail, someone else's footsteps, to follow through the snow. Pine and spruce grow up on either side of her, their needles blackening in the dark. A few dim, solar-powered fixtures, well spaced, guide the way.

She's dawdling, lost in her own thoughts. The snap of a twig somewhere close brings her back, and she looks down at the food in her hand, suddenly nervous. Far off, down in the valley, something cries out—an animal cry, it must be—and Maeve jumps a little despite herself.

Remember to bring a flashlight tomorrow, she's thinking when a beam flips on behind her. For a second Maeve freezes, her clothes sweat-damp against her skin.

"Or you could use this one right now." A man's voice.

It's cold and dry and dark, the trail washed out in the new glare, a layer of fresh snow sparkling ahead of her. When she turns to face the light, there's someone there, a silhouette. But no orange hunter's cap, no camouflage. It's not Dan, the woodcutter they saw in the morning.

She brings a hand up to shield her eyes. "I said that out loud?" she says—out loud. "About the flashlight?"

"You did."

"I didn't see you. I didn't know you were there."

He's tall and lean-looking, the shadows catching the contours of his face. She steps out of the light and her eyes adjust. Blond—she can see that much. Hair cropped close at the sides, a full beard. Instead of a jacket, he's wearing a lined flannel shirt, red and black plaid, with snaps.

The light dips a little, and she sees that it's only the torch app from his phone. He tries to catch her eye.

"I didn't expect to hear a voice in the trees," he says. "So we're even."

The cry comes again—a cry and a whistle all at once, dilating—and Maeve spins as though the thing might be right there behind her. Something about it makes her anxious, pulls some cord at her center. She thinks of the deer the night before, but this is different. More piercing. A whittled yelp. High and urgent.

"Elk," the man says, tipping his chin toward the dark. She can see him better now: mid-thirties and good-looking in a groomed way. Like an image out of a mountaineering catalog, at home in his skin. "It's the rut, this time of year. You know what that means?"

"It sounds like a wraith."

He steps closer. "City girl, hey?"

He has an easy smile, a voice that pulls you in. Maeve leans into her hip, and he stays put, just holding the beam on her. Not quite in her eyes; as though she is a thing he is examining. A specimen found in the woods. In his other hand he's holding something, a machine or tool.

Not a tool. An antler?

"It looks like an antler," he says. "Or a piece of one. Doesn't it?"

Maeve steps back. She almost jumps.

"No, you didn't say it out loud, but you were staring. And that is what it looks like, I guess. Plus we're in the woods, you find them lying around sometimes. An antler, right? Deductive reasoning." He holds the thing up and briefly shines the light on it.

Whatever it is—not an antler—it's long and curved and white.

Maeve thinks: *Oh no.*

It's a spear. He's one of those forest guys. Like some kind of medievalist who runs around in the woods pretending to be Robin Hood.

A trickle of sweat runs down her back, and she shifts, uncomfortable. Wondering how she herself must look after her long day. She spent the first hour pacing and staring at herself in the studio mirrors—*Work, damn you! You can't waste a whole day!*—then tentative starts, falling again and again into old traps. Small gestures, the compact sequences that can ghettoize women's work. One eye on the mirror, Iain's voice in her ear: *You have no aggression! You could never direct, Maeve. All you can do is what you're told.*

She gave up, hauled a mat out of the closet, lay down flat, and went to sleep, exhausted by her own anxiety. When she woke, she thought of nothing at all, just stripped down to her underwear and went through a Lester Horton class by memory and on from there, hours of it, worked herself till her hair was slick against her face and the back of her neck. Worked herself better, sore and down to the bone.

She's tired and dirty and standing in the woods without her coat, and now there's a guessing game. "It's bone," she says. "Your whatever you have there. Made of bone, yes? What is it? A spear or something?" She stops short, catching herself, a hint of impatience in her voice shining through. "Sorry, it's just—"

"Don't apologize." He nods and drops the light so that they can really see each other. "I've interrupted you, that's irritating."

That smile again; the more she pushes back, the more he likes her. "It's a rib," he says. "So not *made of* bone. Bone! Just a piece of the rib, the very smallest one. The smallest piece of the smallest rib of a great blue whale. It's what I'm building with: a whale skeleton. These mountains used to be under the ocean, too, you know. That's why I'm out here. Looking for a piece of antler the same shape, to match." The bone flips playfully in his hand, and he gestures to the forest all around them. "Everything," he says, "is in our service."

He aims the light ahead for her, and the pathway reveals itself. "You're the dancer. Is that right?"

"You're Sim," she says.

There's another snap in the trees, and he turns his face to it, deliberate and serious. Something else out there in the shadows. But when he looks back to her, he's more thoughtful than alarmed. Cool. Sure of himself.

Maeve knows she should be wary, but somehow she is rooted in place. Her hair freezing in little tendrils at her temples, the back of her neck. The elk cry comes again, farther away now, lonely and echoed.

He moves closer. A shy gesture, a small step, but his eyes are fixed on Maeve.

"It's the female that makes that call."

His gaze draws her, his eyes blue-black in the dim light. Maeve is mesmerized. In his hand, the bone flips again and turns, an extension of himself, a limb casting forward. She has an impulse to reach for it, take hold.

As though he might use it to reel her in.

DAY 2

IN THE MORNING, Maeve is surprised by the silence. There's no one chattering in the front entrance or sitting around the open-pit fireplace, which is clean and cold, although there's plenty of wood stacked nearby. On the other side of the vacant lobby, a massive set of oak doors stand firmly shut. There is no one at the desk. No one will leave or need welcoming for weeks.

Not *weeks*, she reminds herself. Days. Thirteen more days, at which point someone will need to call the shuttle for Maeve and send her on her merry way. Exit, tiny dancer.

In the dining hall, Maeve tries to imagine what the place must be like in full swing: musicians with their violin cases tucked beneath their chairs, tables full of actors drinking late into the night. She lingers over a small dessert display, looking down at the neat wedges of pecan pie set out on plates, her hands clasped behind her back. Then she drops her shoulders, a little heart-opening stretch.

Her stomach is empty; the stretch makes her feel taut and strong.

"Do you suppose they'll keep the buffet going just for little old us?"

Maeve startles, surprised to find she's not alone after all.

The woman hands her a cup of coffee. "We missed you at dinner last night," she says. "You must be Maeve. I'm Anna."

She's tall and striking—broad shoulders, a deep, tawny complexion, with green eyes and the barest brush of freckles across her nose. Perhaps not quite forty, although she's the sort of woman who probably always looks a little younger than she really is.

"Anna the activist," Maeve says, remembering.

"Ha! Well. Anna Barthelmy."

"I think they'll keep feeding us. They must feel lucky to have us here at all." Maeve wraps her hands around the mug, grateful for it. "When it's off-season."

Anna turns and pops the lever to check progress on a piece of toast, then, impatient, jams it down again. Her fingers are noticeably stained, the nailbeds sallow and the fingertips cracked and dark, almost inky. Maeve wonders if it's actual ink or something else. Karolina said she was working on...what, film? So a reaction to developer or some other chemical.

She turns back to Maeve. "You met the others yet?"

"Just Karolina. Oh, and Sadie." For some reason, she keeps Sim to herself.

Anna nods as though they're agreeing on something and leans to grab a napkin. She seems at home in the space; Maeve remembers that this is Anna's second time at High Water.

"Karo can be cool. And Sadie—you know. She's a kid. She'll be all right."

She turns to the window, and Maeve follows her gaze. Outside, snow is falling in a concentrated way, straight down. In the back field, there's a man navigating some kind of obstacle course. Exercising. In the snow.

"You met Dan?" Anna says without turning away from the view.

Maeve looks a little closer. She hadn't recognized him without the camo gear. "No," she says. "I mean—sort of, yesterday. We weren't introduced."

Outside, Dan is dragging a chain weighted with heavy tires down the field. A military-style workout.

"You'll bump into him if you're out on the grounds—" Anna pauses, lips pursed, as though she means to say something further, but then she changes her mind and just turns and checks the toaster again.

Maeve keeps watching as another man comes into view, a little younger, more compact in build. No coat, but he's shrugged a blazer on over a hoodie, and he's wearing a fine-looking red scarf. She can't hear what he's saying, but it's easy to tell his tone just by the way he holds his body and by Dan's reaction. The younger man is clowning, trying to crack Dan up, make him laugh, and it's almost working.

But then the little guy shifts to one side, and she sees he has a camera. Filming, Maeve realizes, as Dan continues his feats of strength. She watches him close in on Dan and wonders if this is a thing they do, the way she sometimes films herself dancing to see her form later, to see what worked.

Anna looks over again.

"Justin Doyle. You heard of him? He used to do a lot of stuff for *Interview, New York* magazine. But…he was having too much fun. You know what I mean? Took a job in the mountains to clean up. Not sure it's working for him, though." Her nose wrinkles. "Fancies himself a hot little ticket."

Justin glances over his shoulder as though he's heard his name.

"Careful, now," Maeve says. "His ears are burning."

The toast pops up, half black, and Anna takes a knife to it, buttering savagely. "Gay," she says, licking a finger.

Maeve picks a green apple from the buffet. "Got it. Thanks for the heads-up."

But when she looks back, something's gone wrong outside. Dan strides forward and almost rips the camera from Justin's hands. Maybe he didn't realize he was being filmed after all? Maeve stiffens. She can hear him yelling, even through the glass.

Beside her, Anna shakes her head, but she doesn't seem bothered. "Oooooooh, he got in trou-ble!"

Maeve shines her apple thoughtfully on her sweater. Maybe she's too sensitive to conflict after living with Iain for so long. Out in the yard, Dan goes back to what he was doing and Justin composes himself, flexing his shoulders, smoothing his jacket against his chest. He's a stylish kid. Seems a shame for him to be stuck out here in the middle of nowhere.

She's pulling away from the window when Karo walks in, efficient and businesslike in a pom-pom hat.

"So," she says. "And then there were seven."

"That's it? No more arrivals?" Anna says. "All by our lonesome?"

"Skeleton staff will still come in a few days a week. All part of the charm of being here off-season, my dear. Think of it this way: we have an excellent opportunity for ghost stories."

"The shadowy trees outside my studio are an A-plus location if you're looking to be spooked," Maeve says.

"You didn't come to dinner! I wanted to introduce you around." Karo steps to the coffee urn, fills her cup. Then, turning to Anna, her tone conspiratorial: "Did you get your footage?"

Anna shakes her toast.

"I'm hoping it'll turn into a performance piece. I have to sneak up on him." She turns to Maeve. "Her *artiste*—Sim Nielssen. I'm trying to get a peek at his installation." Anna points her thumb out to the lobby, toward the heavy oak doors Maeve noticed on her way in. "He won't let anyone in there to see."

"You have to wait for the surprise," Karo singsongs. She sips her coffee, and her face changes. "It's wonderful, isn't it? To have a secret project." A fleeting sadness to her tone, before she recovers almost as quickly, leaning out to the lobby. "Ah! Here's my boy."

Maeve swivels despite herself, but it's Justin at the front doors, meticulously brushing the snow from his sleeves. He has a skier's sun-bleached streak through his hair. She watches him navigate the ring of chairs in the lobby, heading in their direction. He doesn't look any worse for wear after whatever strange argument just occurred. He's still got the camera in his hands, at chest level.

Then Maeve realizes he's filming—capturing the three women as he walks.

A deep sigh from Anna. "Justin's working on a little doc project," she says. "You should know that, just in case you're shy—"

"Don't make her worry." Karo mugs for the camera now that Justin is within earshot. "It's about the center—our anniversary. We're almost at one hundred years. Most of what he's using, he has to dig up in the archives. But I wanted a little something else. Flavor of the place."

Maeve nods to Anna. "You work in film too. Don't you?"

"We're all fancy filmmakers here—" Justin arrives beside them and the camera drops to his hip. "But Anna's work is more...hands-on. Isn't it, my darling?"

There's a friction to the comment that Maeve doesn't understand, but she's beginning to see that they've all got their loyalties established already—and their tensions too. Anna simply turns and holds up her stained fingers.

"He means I'm *actually* fancy," she says. "Experimental horror; I get my hands dirty." She turns back to Justin, offering him a pointed smile. "That *is* what you meant, right? My darling?"

"No fighting," Karo says, cutting them off. Then, to Maeve: "And no more skipping meals! We're very secluded here; your social time is important—" She steps away, buttoning her coat. "I think this evening, we'll go for a little soak downstairs. After dinner, yes? You know we're sitting on top of a natural spa, right? Shake off your work goals. It's good for you."

Maeve feels a stitch tighten in her stomach.

"I bet Justin'll come," Anna says. "Won't you, Justin?"

"Beauty bar? Hell yes."

"You'll have to strip down to your skivvies," Anna says, fussing over him. "But—keep the scarf, I think. You know, so we can identify the body in case of…accident."

He turns to Maeve. "Don't worry: Anna only pretends to be queen bitch. She's actually in love with me."

Justin winks. He's a little bit full of himself, Maeve can see that. He's also young. Thirty at the outside, if she had to guess. So maybe he's full of himself and rightly so?

"And?" He's still looking at her, at Maeve.

"Maeve Martin," she says. "Here for thirteen more days, less for the spa and—" She wants to wink back, but it doesn't feel natural. Instead, she just shrugs. "More to reinvent my career completely, whichever comes first."

"No, you can't talk like this!" Karo stamps her foot playfully. "A steam will be good for your muscles, you'll see."

"Balance, baby." Justin pulls out a hat and adjusts it on his head. It's a beanie, but in a distinguished charcoal. He gestures to Maeve's apple. "What is that, dancer's rations? The Bolshoi breakfast special."

"Let her be. She knows what she's doing." Karo enjoys seeing herself as the master among apprentices, Maeve thinks: the fearless leader, the sage. Now she reaches to fix Justin's hat for him. "Happy hour down in the hot springs! Okay, yes—" She turns back to Maeve. "So I hope you're not shy. The heat can make you dizzy. What's better for balance than that?"

* * *

Maeve hits the floor, panting—then rolls away and pushes up, falls again. Pushes up. Pulls in to spin. And spin, and spin. Out of the turn, extending, her quads and calves burning, she's in the air and then down again, landing too hard, *Jesus, Maeve!*, arch, lift, pull up straight, wide-turn-step, step-step, ball-change, reach and hold-hold-hold-hold—fall.

The wood floor always rising to meet her, the sound of her own hard breath ruthless over the music.

Where the impulse is to turn in, Maeve opens out. Where the impulse is for small, she wants to make it big, expansive. Powerful. *Women's work tends to explore emotional spaces*—from a review she read in *The New Yorker* on the flight here. Not just women's work—what's designed for women, over and over again, by male choreographers.

Maeve intends only the opposite. Athletic, virtuosic. Bold shapes. Aggression.

Fight.

There's sweat in her eyes. Her hair is tied up in a bun and the bun wrapped in a kerchief to keep strays from distracting her. She pulls up, a doll on a string, and for a moment she's completely still, staring herself down in the mirror. It takes more strength to hang in the air like this, to appear suspended, than to nail the showy, high jumps. This is where the damage of the C-section lays itself bare: without a solid core, she has less control. Everything she does looks impulsive, skewed.

The light lifts, as though a new spot has been trained on her. She spins back and drops again, hitting the ground hard. Too loose, sloppy in her form. She can feel the shock wave in her hip. Why can't she be more careful? When she lifts up again, it's like punishment, hip throbbing, and she's throwing herself through the room. *Why. Can't. You. Be. More. Careful.*

And she comes down, purposely careless, angry, hurtful, her shoulder off the wall. Hard enough to make her cry out. If you hurt yourself, you have to stop.

This time she stops.

The shoulder stings and she's almost afraid to touch it. If she injures herself now, then what? There are no more grants, no other retreats. She gives it a tiny roll, back and then forward again. A test.

Injury is self-sabotage, Maeve. What are you, stupid? It means you give up. You're done. You have to go home with nothing. You left your children for nothing, you came here for nothing.

When she talks to herself like this—derisive, angry, mean—it's Iain's voice she hears. Her husband. *Ex*-husband, ex. Ex, for God's sake.

Still—after all this time.

His voice that leaves her dizzy, leaves her nauseous, spinning. But drives her to get up again.

And again. An old habit she just can't shake.

When she met Iain, he was the artistic director with a company in New York. Maeve was a visiting principal, a classical dancer from Canada—a national company—only there for a month-long intensive. Right away, there was a connection. He knew her so well. Without, it seemed, even trying.

A relief, at first: it's not a life everyone understands. She'd had boyfriends in high school and even after that, nice men who used words like *relax,* who told Maeve that she didn't have to keep getting up, she didn't have to measure herself obsessively, she didn't have to be perfect. But in Maeve's world, none of that was true. They meant well, all of them, but they drove her rageful. They drove her to tears.

Iain wanted her driven and exhausted. He wanted her perfect, too. He loved her best when she was most unhappy, when she was a slave to it. No one else had ever known Maeve inside out. Not like that.

When she didn't return from New York, her company director screamed breach of contract down the phone line. The *LA Times* referred to Iain as a strategist and Maeve as Nouvelle Vague's latest acquisition; *The New Yorker* teasingly called him a poacher, Maeve his trophy. Her photograph in *Rolling Stone.* In *Vogue.*

And suddenly there they were, five years on.

Talia came along, an accident. A happy accident?

Yes, Maeve thinks now. She squats down on the studio floor and rounds her back, feeling the stretch between her shoulder blades, knees hugged into her chest.

Yes. She has thought it over a lot. Despite everything, she is glad to have them, Talia and Rudy both. Despite what they did to her body. Despite the way they tied her down. The way they tied her to Iain. They are a passion.

Such a passion, in fact, that she has to leave them to focus on anything else, and the leaving itself is so sharp and painful that just thinking about them makes it so Maeve can hardly breathe. Iain knew this about her, that love would be her weakness, long before Talia was born. *I know you.* He could sense it in her, he said, the same way he'd known everything else that made her tick.

I know you.

Iain knew, for instance, that what Maeve feared more than anything was an injury. So it was a good threat. Hold her down by the wrist, twisting. Just enough. His weight on those tiny bones. Enough to make her comply. Or her arm, caught up behind her, the pressure on her shoulder. He aimed for the joints.

A bruise, she could live with. Bruises: who cares? Just no sprains. Please. No muscle injury. For God's sake, a bone, even a little one in her hand or foot, would mean she couldn't dance for weeks. Something he leaned on when she proved she could take it without crying out, without waking Talia, toddler-sweet and sleeping in the next room and then, later, Rudy too.

He'd thought, briefly, that he could use her fear of waking the kids as a threat. But Maeve can be silent through just about anything.

She curls against the floor now, the way she used to curl up, protecting herself. The music—mostly drums, improvisation music—comes out of a speaker in the wall and it is relentless. She needs it to stop so that she can think. She needs to stop thinking and get up again.

In the end, the marriage left only two marks on her. One, the surgeon's knife at her belly; and the other, a thin red scar that runs the length of her index finger down into her palm. The wound caused by a shard of a broken mirror.

The mirror from a studio just like this one.

Maeve pulls up and crawls to the corner, slaps the speaker's power button until it finally cuts and there's nothing, quiet, and she sits there on the floor and takes a breath.

Her head hurts, some combination of the new altitude and minimal sleep and acoustics. She's glad of it. It's a sharp pain, steady, something to focus on that's not the pain in her hip, her shoulder. She closes her eyes and breathes out, then opens them again.

It's impossible to avoid yourself in a studio. There's Maeve, sitting against the wall, knees pulled into her chest, wrapping her arms around herself; there she is reflected in twenty different mirrors. Every angle of her. Every line. Whispering to herself through the silence, in the gentlest way. Lovingly.

He's gone, he's gone. He's gone now.

A weird wave of relief washes over her, half euphoria, half endorphins. Like a rush. She opens her hand and traces the scar from fingertip to wrist. *He's gone.*

Her voice growing cold: *Iain is gone.*

Maeve waits in the silence until her breathing is even. Then she turns on the music, and she gets up.

It's snowing more heavily than ever when she finally pulls on her boots and wanders out of the studio, dazed from the work. For a moment she's disoriented. You can see how hikers go missing. She remembers reading how pioneers used to tie one end of a rope to the house, the other to the barn, so they couldn't get lost in a storm. Maeve doesn't have a rope, but someone would come and find her if the weather was really bad, right?

As if on cue, the wind suddenly lets up—the path is dusted with fresh snow but plain to see. It's obviously been cleared sometime during the day, but when, and by whom? Maeve is the only one working out here. At the edge of the woods, she can see the chain of solar lanterns, still unlit at this hour, a trail of little black hats leading to the center.

She's supposed to go to the spa. Karo is right; a hot soak will in fact be good for her muscles. But she suspects that's not her reason for going, and she's chastising herself a little. Sim Nielssen with his whalebone and his steady gaze. The curve of his lips.

His way of addressing her, one artist to another: *Everything is in our service.*

As if to prove something to herself, Maeve detours sharply across the clearing instead of heading straight back. There's still enough light in the sky, and she traces the tree line to where the ridge crops out, bare white, going over the work in her head as she moves along, conjuring up the few, fleeting glimpses of herself from the mirror that satisfied her, pasting them together. She knows she hasn't hit it yet, hasn't found what she's hoping for, but she twists and changes the shapes in her mind. Trying to imagine how it could look in the bodies of younger dancers, dancers with all their muscles intact, with more control and less exertion behind each gesture.

She stops at the boundary of the woods, against the steep edge of the gorge. Far below, there's a shallow river, already frozen, and farther along, an arc of cable extends over the valley to a wide platform. She remembers the attraction she saw marked on the center map— the SkyLift.

A shadow sweeps in, and she turns to look, spooked—but it's just the range, rising higher and higher to all sides, the weight of the shelf looming. A bowl. Maeve feels dizzy inside it.

She toes at a ridge of snow and it lifts up, layered and whole, then suddenly flips and somersaults down over the rock. Perfect fort-making snow. She can picture Rudy, his fleece hat cocked on his head, working to build a wall.

What is she doing here, hiking up a trail two thousand miles away?

From down in the valley, there's a cry. The shadows shift; something else moving in the riverbed.

"Probably not a good idea to stand so close to the edge—"

Maeve spins to find Sadie there, picking her way down the path—on her way back to the center herself.

"There was an accident here a few months ago. A painter—" the girl says, and she stops a good yard away and stays there, as if to make a point. "Elisha Goldman, ever hear that name? Just stepped off the ledge, boom. Couldn't see where the ground ended and the sky began."

Maeve nods but also steps back from the edge and into the trees. "She died?"

Sadie shrugs. "Might as well have. Half paralyzed. I'm sure she has her regrets."

Her tone is flat.

Maeve bites her lip. Every interaction with Sadie is awkward, starting with that first, admittedly lousy, impression Maeve made. It was late, she was exhausted; does she need to apologize now? How much could it really matter?

But there's a softness to Sadie's face in this light and Maeve thinks of the way Anna described her. She really does look like a kid—albeit a kid who's trying too hard. That feels familiar to Maeve.

She takes a breath and tries again.

"I'm wondering if I should be here at all," she says. "I didn't expect this weather, not so early in the year. I have children. They're little." Snow swirls up in a quick gust, the soft, heavy flakes catching in Sadie's hair. "How about you? Don't you feel trapped out here? You're practically a kid yourself—" The words catch in Maeve's throat almost the second they're out.

Too late. Sadie is already gluing on her forced smile.

Maeve holds up a hand, mea culpa–style. "That's unfair. I was dancing professionally by the time I was eighteen years old and I fucking hated it when people talked down to me."

But Sadie shrugs it off.

"It's pretty common," she says. "I'm twenty-three, though, not eighteen. I have a master's degree in art history and an MBA in arts management. I graduated high school when I was fifteen. So I'm used to it." There's a beat, Sadie looking her up and down. Then: "I used to dance too, you know. I guess you could say a lot of girls do."

"Oh, did you?" Maeve hesitates, unsure of what to say. "I'm sure you were very good. You're built for it."

Sadie offers a half smile and for a second Maeve is sure she said the right thing. So much of dance is measurements. Proportions. She steps closer. The girl's hair is pulled back neatly in a satin band, her wool coat cinched at the waist. Her face never changes unless she wants it to. Everything seems purposeful, like she's onstage. That, too, feels recognizable.

But Sadie's smile suddenly sharpens. "Just another high-performance Korean girl, right?"

Maeve sharpens too; her eyes narrow. It feels like she's supposed to apologize again, or maybe curtsy. She does neither. The snow is piling up on her sleeves and she brushes it off.

Sadie turns to head down the path.

"There's some talk about all this new snow," she says, calling back over her shoulder. "We've had a strange year. If it keeps up, they'll orchestrate some explosions." She holds up a hand to catch the snow as it falls. "To manage the snowpack, you know? But not right now—don't worry. Probably not till after you're gone." This feels like Sadie the tour guide again, until she goes off script: "People who live in extreme places like to think they're in control."

The cry echoes in the valley again and Maeve leans out to look. Whatever is down there has come out of the trees. There's an undulation to its movement and it takes her a second to realize it's not one thing, but many. A herd.

Elk.

"We should go," Sadie says, impatient. Maeve realizes this is what she's been doing all along. Not forcing an awkward conversation or waiting for some kind of apology. Of course not. Just doing her job: corralling Maeve.

"Sorry," Maeve says. "I didn't realize—" She hurries along the path to where Sadie is waiting. This seems to please Sadie, a moment of deference.

"I don't really care what you do, but—" Sadie pauses, and a slyness creeps into her tone: "Have you met Dan?"

Maeve looks at her. "You're the second person who's mentioned him to me."

"Oh, who was it? Justin? Or, no—Anna!" She rolls her eyes. "He's attractive, I guess. He's got that cop thing going on, some women really go for that." They skirt along the edge of the trees, where the walking is easier. Maeve nods at Sadie, encouraging her to continue—the girl finally seems to be warming up.

"He won't like you wandering around by yourself. He's—I don't know." Sadie shakes her head. "He reminds me of my father." She leans down and plucks something out of the snow. A stick? No, a piece of antler. The way Sim Nielssen said: you find them lying around sometimes. Sadie's voice lowers a notch: "Always needs to be top gun."

Maeve expects her to tuck the antler away, save it for a collection, but instead she spins and pitches it hard into the trees.

There's a clatter in the distance as it makes contact.

* * *

"What do you mean, you pulled them out of school?" Maeve has her mother on the line, her room phone pressed between ear and shoulder. "I wanted you to stay with them at my house. That's what you said you'd do. That was the plan."

"So what? They're with me at the cabin instead of home."

"You know how I feel about that cabin."

The cabin Maeve has refused to return to since that first visit, the summer she was nine, choosing dance camp, intensives, even summer school if it meant never having to face that high fence where the deer died in the night.

"Just because you hate it doesn't mean they will. They're fine, they're happy. And I thought you decided to be outdoorsy now, up in the mountains? No? It's a failure?"

"That's not the point."

Maeve presses her lips together to stop herself from screaming. She arrived back in her room to find a voice mail from the school secretary: Talia and Rudy hadn't been in school that morning. Could Maeve please remember to call them in as absent? It's school policy.

She knows the fucking school policy.

The principal called her that first year, just after she'd left Iain, and Maeve almost missed the call, her phone set to Do Not Disturb while she toured yet another rental house. She'd wanted to seem confident, professional, as she leaned on the kitchen counter to fill out the application, but when she saw Carter Street Public School flash silently on the phone's screen, she set aside her pen to pick it up. Talia was only four years old.

The call was just a formality, the woman said. *But there's another parent here to get Talia for her dental appointment and—we weren't aware this was a shared-custody situation?*

Maeve threw herself into her car, the engine flooding twice as she rushed to start it up. A red light and a pedestrian ambling across the crosswalk and she leaned on the horn, burned through. At the school's front entrance, the principal unlocked the door. Maeve fell to her knees on the classroom floor, her face in Talia's hair, arms wrapped tight around Talia's skinny little ribs.

That was the first school. After that, Maeve sat down with every new day-care team, every new teacher, and explained there was no shared custody, no matter what he said. She even tried—once—a restraining order. Not that anyone helped enforce it.

Now she catches herself in the vanity mirror, hair in a knot on top of her head, and reaches for a photo that she's wedged into the frame: a photo-booth strip she brought from home, Maeve and Rudy and Talia at the mall, smiling and sticking out their tongues and making kiss-lips. She takes a breath and releases it again, the way those relaxation apps tell you to, a silent four-count in her head, stroking the photo with her thumb.

Rudy always just one step behind, kissy when he ought to be pulling a face.

"Kids like schedules, Mom. They like things to stay the same. And I can't work if I don't know for sure—for sure!—where they are." Her voice is rising, but she can't help herself. "You know what I went through! Do you have any idea how panicked I was when I got that voice mail? Why wouldn't you at least tell me?"

"They're fine," her mother says flatly. "Maeve, you're the only one who still thinks about him. You're the one who can't get past it." Her voice sharpens. "If you can't stop worrying about Iain, then come home. Otherwise, you're just fucking around."

"Are they in the room?"

"Maeve."

"Are they in the room right now? Are Rudy and Talia there, listening to you talk to me like that?"

"Of course not."

Four-count. Breathe in, breathe out.

Maeve wedges the photo strip back into the mirror frame and turns to the window. In the dark, it's hard to see just how much snow is coming down, but the wind sounds stronger than ever. Below, there's the light from the rear door and the path, half buried where it crosses through the pines. No one out walking. She leans close for a better look, then catches herself, suddenly aware who she is looking for.

Sim Nielssen.

But he's not out there looking in. No one is.

That's a good thing, Maeve, she reminds herself. *You don't want that. You don't want a guy that follows you around.*

There's a pause on the other end of the line before her mother begins to breathe noisily. Maeve turns from the window to deal with the problem at hand. "It's just—it's been a long time since I had this kind of space to give to myself, Mom. What I'm trying to do is not small, it's not a small thing. It won't all get done in two weeks. This is just a start. I'm trying to kick-start myself, creatively."

"So start kicking. Go to work."

"I know Iain's gone. But I'm trying to remember to trust myself—"

"Just don't waste your time—"

"—it would be nice if I could trust you too."

There's a silence. Then:

"He's dead, Maeve."

Maeve wants to throw the phone through the window. Her voice shakes: "Put Talia on, will you?"

"Not gone! Dead. Dead! Say it, Maeve. He's dead."

But Maeve doesn't. Her face tightens. She won't respond.

The dining room is dark when Maeve arrives. She wavers at the entrance, checks her phone. It seems odd. Maybe she got the time wrong?

"Hello?" She takes a few cautious steps over the threshold, her voice lost in the big room. To her left, there's a scratching noise—she turns, and the place lights up.

She's not alone after all. Maeve pulls up short. He's got his back to her, checking some kind of lighting panel. She knows it's him because of his size—easily six foot four. That, and he's wearing the orange tuque.

He turns and sees her and removes the hat.

"Sorry about that." He points to the lights, then strides forward, almost too eagerly. Maeve finds herself backing up. "Daniel Darling." He says it proudly—his real name!—reaching out a hand and taking hers to shake, confident but also warm. "Anything you need, anything at all, just ask. I'm the only one here who's actually *from here*, you know?"

"You're from High Water?"

"Born less than two hours away. Spot called Hope Lake." There's a pause before he lets go of her hand. "You can just call me Dan."

"Dan," she repeats, then realizes that she hasn't introduced herself. "I'm Mae—"

He cuts her off. "Maeve. I know. I saw you last night, coming out of the dance studio. I was—" He glances over her shoulder, just long enough that Maeve checks to see if anyone is behind her. But there's no one. "I had some work to do on one of the cabins," he says, refocusing. He'd almost said hello, he says, only he didn't want to startle her.

His brow furrows. "And then Nielssen came along."

Maeve nods, trying to catch up. He didn't want to startle her? He's too big, really, to sneak up on anyone. He keeps on, though, ducking his head as he speaks, almost shy.

"I've got a whole storage room downstairs full of equipment. Whatever you like: skis, snowshoes, you name it. You've only got to ask."

She tries to match his smile.

"Probably won't risk the skis," she says. "Hard to dance on a broken ankle, right?" But this draws his attention down the length of her body and she hurries to think of something else to say. "Do you—make any art yourself?" It's the only polite question she can muster.

He just looks at her, confused, then shakes his head.

There's a hoot, and behind him the kitchen door swings open: Justin, a bottle of wine in each hand.

"Maevy," he says, stopping short. "Maevelicious. You're early—"

But by the time she's registering his surprise, there are already new voices behind her. Anna and Karo appearing from the lobby, deep in conversation. Dan turns back to the panel he was working on, pulls a screwdriver from his pocket, and screws the door shut.

Sim and Sadie arrive last, Sadie trailing him slightly. Maeve can't quite tell if they were together beforehand or just happened to cross the lobby at the same moment. Karo shoots Sadie a look and the girl reluctantly leaves Sim's side and goes to work opening the buffet, pulling lids from the chafing dishes. There must be a cook somewhere. Part of the skeleton staff, Sadie filling in the gaps. It can't be what she was promised as a doctoral candidate making the rounds at the Biennale.

But she's watching, interested, as Karo takes Maeve by the hand.

"I can finally introduce you," she says. "Sim Nielssen, our artist in residence for the year—"

Maeve freezes, unsure of what to do. It will seem odd, now, that she didn't mention meeting him in the forest the night before.

Sim looks at her expectantly. Amused. In the light, she can see how blue his eyes are, that Nordic blue, clear and bright.

"And this is Maeve Martin, you remember I told you—"

"I remember." Sim takes her hand in his, a formal shake, compensating for her paralysis. "I've heard so much about you, Maeve." The trace of a smile still hovering at the corner of his mouth, and she has to break his gaze, look at Karo as she responds. Breath catching in her throat.

"Thanks, of course, yes."

She turns away, relieved—only to find Dan quietly watching them from the corner.

There's the pop of a cork, and then another—Justin cracking into the wine.

"Help me with these, mademoiselle?" Anna holds out a tray of wine-glasses, and Maeve moves down the table at her side, setting them in place. When they're done, she takes Maeve's arm and they peruse the buffet selection: stuffed potatoes, grilled chicken, the usual something-with-beans.

They eat staggered down the length of one long table, Karo at the head, and Dan far away at the other end. He never says a word—but Maeve catches him looking over at her again and again. When she meets his eye, he breaks into a smile like he just can't help himself.

Kind of a country boy. Hope Lake. She wonders if he's getting his hopes up.

"Can I take that?" Sadie leans over Maeve's shoulder, gesturing lightly at her plate.

"I see you get all the glamorous jobs," Maeve says, but the joke falls flat. Sadie stands there, one sullen hand on her hip. "Never mind." Maeve rises to her feet, plate in hand. "I'm still working on it."

She makes her way over to the bar, where Anna has begun prepping a tray of cocktails to ferry down to the spa. With fewer than twenty people on-site, deliveries come only once a week; no mint for mojitos, Anna says, but all the rum and Coke you can swallow. She sets up a row of glasses and drops ice into each one.

Maeve says she can't risk a hangover. Only twelve days left.

"But this is what it's like here." Anna adds a slice of lime to each drink and leans across the bar. "You work and you work and you work all day and it's never enough and at night you don't want to be alone with it."

"If I'm hungover, there'll be no work at all."

"It must be terrible to have to rely on your body." Anna flicks her eyes across the room and Maeve realizes she's watching Dan. He's crouched low, checking the burners under the buffet one by one. "Why is he ignoring me, do you think?"

The question throws Maeve off balance. It takes a moment, but then relief floods in: if Anna and Dan have something going on, she's off the hook. She's just been overreacting. Not unusual for her; not since Iain, anyway.

A kind of vacation fling, Anna says. Not terribly unique at this kind of retreat. But it started in the spring.

"Half the reason I came back. Don't tell Karo—she thinks I'm here for the atmosphere."

Maeve would never have guessed. Anna and Dan haven't talked or touched once since dinner began. What does Anna get out of it?

Anna twists at the wedding ring on her finger as she talks. There's a man back home in New Orleans—a man who calls without fail every night and every morning, sometimes more, she says. Anna holding the phone to her ear and smoking a cigarette out the open window of her room.

"Three, four calls a day to check up on me. *Just checking up.* I need someone who's interested in my body. Who makes me feel nervous in that good way, you know?"

Maeve doesn't. But she thinks back to what Sadie said about Dan on the trail: *He's got that cop thing, some women really go for that.* Only she didn't mean *some* women. She meant Anna.

"Besides, he was fucking with some waitress last year—my husband was. Thought I didn't know. So I guess my business is my own." Anna gives Dan a last look and shakes her head at Maeve. "But why is he ignoring me now?"

"Maybe he's playing with you." Justin slides in next to Maeve and hooks a finger around one of the drinks. "I mean, all's fair in love and war. Wouldn't you say, Anna?" The question seems harmless, an innocuous bit of teasing, but Anna's face changes, hardens.

49

Justin lifts the glass.

"Bottoms up."

There's a sarcasm, an edge to the two of them together that Maeve can't figure out. But she's the newcomer here; maybe it's no surprise that she doesn't get the inside jokes. She shrugs, and then they're interrupted by Karo, anyway. Ready—Maeve assumes—to usher them down to the spa.

Instead, she speaks only to Maeve.

"Sadie says you were out on the trail by yourself."

Maeve glances around for Sadie but finds her standing back, watching from a few feet away. Karo's tone is oddly stern.

"I was in sight of the center the whole time. Do I need to be worried?"

"No, of course not. Not at all. But in the past, we've had residents who were a bit too complacent."

Dan's voice cuts across the room. "It's not the city here, Maeve. Not even close."

Maeve turns back to Karo, troubled. "I'm—" she begins, but then stumbles. What to say? *I'm sorry*?

It was still daylight. She's an athlete. Unlikely to fall off the trail.

Sim hands his dirty plate to Sadie, then catches Karo's arm.

"What are we waiting for?" Glancing to Maeve as he says it. He raises an eyebrow and then a subtle shoulder—more a signal than a shrug, a *This place is crazy* look. He hooks his arm around Karo's elbow. "Come on, Karo. Let's get these people in hot water."

Maeve feels something at her shoulder and realizes that Dan has come to stand beside her. She steps back to give herself some space, but Justin is already lunging over the bar, a bottle of wine in one hand and two in the other. "Wait up there!" Then, looking coquettishly over his shoulder: "Hey, Dan—my hands are full. Why don't you slip that corkscrew in my back pocket?"

But Dan is still watching Sim as he steers Karo away from Maeve and out the door.

* * *

The baths, according to a plaque on the wall, used to be an enclave for men only. When the center was first built.

Now, of course, there's no place women can't go. Deep underground, the spa is more of a hall than a room, and the steam from the baths makes it feel like some kind of luxe grotto. Maeve sinks a little deeper, the water naturally dark with iodine. There are three pools at three different temperatures. Those art deco details again: each pool is edged in smooth, carved stone.

At the entrance, Justin drops his robe, preening, before slipping in hip-deep. Sadie peels her clothes off, folds them neatly into a pile. Consciously unselfconscious as she moves.

Maeve knows that no one is thinking more about Sadie's body than Sadie herself. Twenty-three, and with everything to prove; there must be someone here she's trying to impress. She finds herself watching the girl. The fallout from that walk in the woods surprised her.

It surprises her that Karo more or less has a spy.

It's a wide enough pool, with its nooks and corners, that Maeve's own space seems oddly private. She closes her eyes and when she opens them again, Anna is there, crouched beside a stone lion, water pouring from its mouth, her face obscured by a camera. The lens makes her look one-eyed, a Cyclops. Maeve stares into it, first startled, then steady. It's only after a moment that she thinks to wrap an arm around herself to cover her breasts in her thin lace bra. Her bathing suit forgotten back at home.

"Tell me again what kind of work you do?"

Anna laughs.

"You're deep enough, don't worry." She lowers the camera to her side. "Most people, that's their first instinct—cover up! It took you a moment to even worry about it. I like that."

Maeve lets one shoulder rise and fall. "Dancer, you know. We don't have any privacy. The body is everything. But it's also just a thing. Right? You get used to that idea. This thing to form and reform, push around." Out of the corner of her eye, she can see Dan on the far deck, examining some piece of jutting tile. Karo, her pants cuffed neatly to the knee, sits checking her phone on a bench.

"That's me too." Anna holds up her cracked fingers. "Like you say, form and reform."

"Is that from the chemicals?"

"Nah, just paint, and then paint remover. I'm using a technique called rotoscope, where I draw right on top of the film. Right onto the humans, really, as they move." She zips the camera into its waterproof case and sets it down. "Man, I wish you were staying longer! I'd love to do some work with a dancer."

She strips down to her underclothes and slides into the next pool over but turns back to keep talking across the divide. Maeve is grateful; it's easy to feel alone when you're new. She hasn't had close girlfriends, not since her days in the corps. Her star rose too quickly at Nouvelle Vague, and then of course Iain wanted her to himself.

Anna brings an easy intimacy to everything she does. Insta-pal. She leans her elbows over the pool's edge: "You had the dream yet?"

"Dream?"

"The bear dream. That's the project I'm working on." She scooches up a little higher. "Nature turns to chaos. In New Orleans we have a werewolf, the *rougarou*. But up here, people see a bear in their sleep—"

Maeve shivers. She had so many dreams the night she arrived. She'd almost forgotten—the animal smell, the rush of something coming into her room. She looks to Anna, nodding.

"The first night—" she says. Now that she's talking about it, the dream seems so intimate, so close. Almost sexual. It embarrasses her.

"See? I knew it! Damn, I've been here twice, and nothing! You know, when I was here in the spring, there was one night where everyone had it. Everyone! Except me, goddamn it."

"Maybe it's just part of being an artist," Maeve tries. "Wild dreams. Your brain on overdrive, kinda."

Anna looks skeptical. "The problem is you can't control it," she says. "Go ahead and tell me it's about art when you're crying in your bed." She winks, then slips away to the far side of her own pool, wading along with her camera case in hand.

Maeve turns away herself and stretches out with both arms, heart lifting. There's the murmur of conversation on the deck and high laughter, Anna or Justin putting on a show for Dan; she can hear him laughing too. She pushes up toward the pool's edge, legs trailing—alarmed when her toe brushes something behind her. She sets her feet down in a hurry and spins.

But it's only Sim—and an almost respectable distance away. The raw line of his shoulder rising out of the water. Steam or sweat in beads at his brow.

"Better put those things away," he says, nodding to where her legs are hidden down in the cloudy water. "I don't want to get clobbered. Even by accident."

She crosses her arms over her chest. "Always sneaking up behind me, aren't you?"

He holds a hand up like a shield. "Just trying to avoid injury. Lot of power in a dancer's legs, I'll bet."

She plays at the water with her fingers, the color rising in her cheeks.

"I should really head back," she says. "I feel like every moment out here is a moment wasted. Lazy, you know? Swimming instead of dancing."

"Ah," he says. "A worker bee."

"I'm only here for a short time."

"Don't be so proscriptive." When she doesn't respond, he steps a little closer. "Trust your instincts. You came here, didn't you? It was a choice. You have to honor that."

His body, the line of his collarbone, distracting her.

On the other side of the pool, Dan takes a few steps toward them. Maeve watches him, then she moves closer to Sim. She's not sure why she does it; it's a little coy.

She dips down lower and smiles up at Sim as though he's just said something marvelous.

"I got in trouble," she says. "For going on a walk by myself."

"*Verboten,* don't you know." He leans a bit closer again. "I got in trouble last week for sneaking up to the chairlift. Karo was very upset. That's only allowed in summer."

"Why summer?"

"It's not for skiing. It's for tourists, like a bird's-eye view. They call it the SkyLift—" He gives her a professorial look. It's meant to be charming, and it is. "A way to take it all in without causing habitat destruction."

"But now people will come higher into the mountains," she says slowly. "Won't they? To get on the lift?"

"It's not really good for artists either." His mouth curling, a little roguish. "So much for a secluded retreat in the woods. We renegades have to stick together."

From behind them, there's a splash, laughter, more voices. She glances over her shoulder; Dan is gone now. Up on the deck, Sadie hoists a glass in victory.

"Look out," Justin yells. "Sexy Sadie's back in town."

She turns back to find Sim waiting.

"What are they playing? Beer pong?" She's joking, but he gives her a slight nod.

"Something like that. Only with champagne."

"Wait—really?"

"Brut pong, let's call it."

Dan comes out of a changing room but he's still dressed; like Karo, he's rolled his pants up halfway to the knee. It feels voyeuristic, to gather them all here like this, then simply patrol the decks. Justin leans a hip against the wall and Sadie pushes him off like she owns it, spins and forces a high-five from Dan. She has to step in front of Anna to do it, Anna skidding back a little on the deck. Then she turns, scanning the water before calling out to Sim: "Sim Nielssen, quit wasting my time! You're up!"

Drinking, like poker and kung fu movies, is just another way-in for young women trying to grab a place at the boys' table. Or at least, those were the routes when Maeve was young. Even here, where the boss is a woman, she can see the value that comes from hanging out with the guys. The power.

She turns back to Sim. "Looks like you're supposed to play the winner."

"I'd rather stay over here," he says. Then: "I mean it, about trusting yourself. Any time you say yes to someone else, it's a surrender."

Maeve steps in, one eyebrow raised, closing the gap between them. No more small gestures.

"But you want me to say yes to you."

He's about to answer—is he? She can't tell—when they're interrupted by Sadie cheering, calling again for Sim to come take his turn.

Instead, he leans in, his mouth at Maeve's ear:

"Who says I'm asking?"

"You're interested in him," Karo says, hovering on the deck as Maeve pulls up out of the pool. The moment feels a bit like an ambush.

"He's interesting, all right."

Karo hands her a robe.

"You married young, didn't you?" But she doesn't wait for an answer, turning instead to watch the players, the little ball flitting between them, tossed and caught in plastic champagne flutes. "I married Gianpietro when I was eighteen," she says. "He was forty-four. I had to run away with him, can you believe it?"

"Eighteen is a lifetime ago."

"It is," Karo says. "He died."

"Oh, I didn't mean—"

Karo waves the apology away. Lung cancer, she says. "When I was thirty-two. It's strange to think of him now. So you're right—it's like a different life completely. It's almost as though I didn't live it at all, like it's something I read about once in a book."

Maeve sits with that and doesn't answer right away. She can feel her body tense. Iain does not seem a lifetime ago. "So," she says, a little puzzled by Karo's attention. "You're interested in Sim?"

"Me?" Karo tips her glass. "No," she says. "Not the way you mean. But I don't want him to get distracted." She glances over at the men again, then pulls it back. "Or electrified by something other than his work. He owes me an installation, and I want it done well."

It's not advice. It's an accusation. Maeve feels herself harden in response. She wonders if Sadie has endured this same reproof.

Karo doesn't break her serious look.

"People come here and they suddenly become teenagers. Don't waste your time—"

"Fucking around?" Her mother's phrase: *You're just fucking around.* But Karo only dips a toe in the water and shrugs, as though Maeve is overreacting, before she turns away.

Maeve pulls Anna into the bathroom with her.

"Karo gave me another lecture," she says, through the cubicle wall. "That's two in two hours."

"Oh, fuck her." Anna's feet go pigeon-toed in the next stall. "She gave me a lecture about smoking in my room. What am I, fifteen?" Her foot dances about, trying to get back into its flip-flop. "I wish you'd been here when the place was crowded. It's easier. The truth is she handpicks her artists and then she thinks she owns us. She was a painter, you know, but she stopped making art to do this admin job instead. So now she wants to pretend our work is hers somehow? No, thanks." A pause. "I mean, it's a big job, I guess," Anna says. "In fairness. But still."

There's the rolling thunder of the toilet-paper dispenser.

"I'll tell you what's a big job," Maeve says. "Working your whole life with no easy template, just working blind and hoping something sticks. No pension, no security, nothing. What happens when we're all seventy? Ever think of that?"

"I'm not defending her."

Maeve comes out of her stall and looks at herself in the mirror, the white robe hanging open, her body exposed underneath. The exchange with Karo has left her hostile: a mix of angry and defiant and oddly ashamed, as though she were a much younger Maeve caught with a schoolgirl crush. She pops her hip, testing it, but the damage from her earlier fall is just a bruise. Rolls her hip one way and her shoulder the other. Everything works. Now she only feels the power of her recklessness in the studio. If she can harness that, control those big sequences?

She didn't even get hurt.

"For God's sake, I'm a grown woman," she says to Anna.

Maeve leans against the sink, arms crossed. Anna lets the cubicle door bang shut behind her.

"You're gorgeous. Let me use your lipstick."

Maeve digs through her bag, then passes the whole thing over.

"I don't do this, you know. I mean men. Not since my divorce. Maybe twice. That's it."

"You can do whatever you want," Anna says, correcting the lipstick at the corner of her mouth with a finger. She catches Maeve's eye in the mirror. "What would a dude do, Maeve? Would a dude be skulking around in the bathroom, *Oh no, maybe I'll get in trouble…*" She caps the lipstick, hands it back. "No. Your body, your decision, your time in the mountains."

Maeve gives her own lips a swipe of color—then leans impulsively into the mirror and presses them against the glass.

An open mouth. A kiss.

"I'm only here for twelve more days," she says, admiring the print. "That's no time at all."

Out in the spa, there are accusations.

"Who's the least drunk here? Who?" Justin wants an impartial judge, and it's Maeve who steps forward, bold in lace underwear, before Sexy Sadie gets a chance. She can feel Karo's eyes on her and pulls herself up taller. Sim merely juggling the little ball in his cup, playing innocent.

"He's obviously a shark," Maeve says to Justin. "You should never have put your money against him."

Anna hoots with delight, pouring out a few more glasses of champagne, Dan and Sadie handing them around.

"I say this man's a cheat and a liar!" Justin is having a good old time; he holds his glass high as he calls it out. "Let's all raise a glass to this genius, who has stolen a hundred-dollar bill right out of my hands. He's left me with nothing. Look—" He pulls the wet pocket of his trunks inside out, but it is not quite empty after all—a last, damp twenty flutters toward the floor and Justin catches it with a snap of the wrist. He spins to Maeve, the bill in hand.

"I'll pay you twenty dollars right now to slap that grin off his face."

Sim steps in. He is grinning, it's true.

"You wouldn't." He's talking to Maeve, not Justin.

They're using her, she knows, as a kind of amusement. Justin flickers the bill in his fingers.

"You'd make me immensely happy," he says, sparkling.

"You'd make me immensely sad," Sim says. But he suddenly turns to

Dan. "She'll never do it, she's very nice. Haven't you seen how perfectly nice she is? Can't even get a drink in her."

Dan stiffens, like a man expecting a fight.

But Sim only looks back to Maeve, a new slyness to his smile: "Can we, worker bee?"

There's a beat, his eyes locked on hers, Justin's goading smile, and the weird, hostile stance on Dan behind him. Sadie raises an eyebrow— a dare.

She doesn't want to be the one to look away this time, demure.

Maeve takes the money and smacks him. Open hand. Clean across the face.

The sound of it.

There's a shock of silence, the room gone electric—

(A rush of fear in her throat; for just a flash, it's Iain standing there, Iain whom she's hit; what Iain would have done in return—)

—and then the moment breaks, the high, bright explosion of Anna's laugh, pure glee, leading them all on. The place erupts.

Maeve standing there, a flood of adrenaline down her limbs, right down into the sting of her palm. She takes a breath, surfacing. She can feel the line of her bra against her bare skin. Sim hasn't moved and won't take his eyes off her.

Then he shakes his head, shakes it off, offers a long wolf whistle. A good sport.

"Let me get you some ice for that hand," he says.

Is this why it happens?

Not guilt, but because she's galvanized. The current between them is lit. Skin to skin. She wants more of him.

The rest of the night feels like a blur, everything eclipsed by the lingering burn of her palm, a dull ache right up into her shoulder. Sim holding a cold highball glass to his cheek. The drunks get drunker.

At the end of it, she walks him home, their footsteps echoing in the back stairwell.

"A lot of dangerous people around here," she tells him. "Better not to be alone."

He's got a corner suite on the floor above hers, all windows and exposed concrete where he's rolled back the rugs and set a canvas taller than Maeve against a wall. She presses her back to it, catching her breath—but he's waiting for her to come to him.

"I never do this," she says, almost to herself. The space between them taut as a highwire.

"Never?"

There is no moon or the moon is hidden. Outside there is nothing but snow and more snow and silence and Maeve walks around the whole space and shows him every place she wants him to fuck her.

Here, with her hands and breasts pressed against the cold window glass, and here, up on the counter with her legs high and spread in a V, toes pointed like a good ballerina, and here, where the bedclothes have been thrown down in a corner, this time Maeve holding him hard to the ground and her small body looming over him, the duvet a cushion for her knees.

She cannot risk injury, she tells him. They must think of her knees.

"Don't you have anything you want to do?" she says. "No weird artist stuff? You don't want to dip me in paint and press me up against your sheets or something?"

He says he wants to put his tongue inside her, and he doesn't like the taste of paint.

The room is dark. When she peels her clothes off, he switches on the light.

"What's this?" he says, rising to meet her. She is naked; his fingers trace the scar at her center that cuts her in two. She hesitates, her hand with its own scar unconsciously closing and drawing away from him. Then:

"C-section," Maeve says.

He takes that in silence but spreads a hand over her belly, cradling it. "I thought it might be some crazy stage accident. You have a baby, baby?"

"I have kids. Two."

"Huh. Married?"

"He's dead," Maeve says.

She turns out the light.

Later—it's very late, so late it's early, if it weren't for the time of year and the heavy snow, there would be light in the sky, Maeve thinks—they wind themselves in the bedclothes and rest.

"Do you not sleep in bed at all," she says—they are still on the floor—"or are you a sort of fantastic slob?"

"I like the floor. Especially here. It feels like I'm camping."

From where they are lying, all they can see is the night sky, heavy with snowfall. In the near distance, the eastern ridge. They are surrounded by frozen ridges, as though at the center of some fortress. Nothing but high walls on every side.

He lights a cigarette and holds it out to her. "Don't tell Karo I smoke in here. *Verboten.*"

"Aren't you worried you'll set off the sprinklers?"

"They're disabled."

"You disabled your smoke alarm? On purpose?"

"Problem solved."

She rolls the cigarette in her fingers but doesn't take a draw before passing it back to him.

"No tobacco either?"

"A temple, I say." Maeve pulls aside the sheet to display the temple, then gets up to leave. He shakes his head.

"And she didn't even stay for a nap."

He's languorous, smoking in his bed on the floor. It's a performance. She gathers up her things.

61

"I'm fine," she says. "I have to go. I have to work, I'll sleep later."

He watches as she reconstructs: bra, dress, shoes.

"You aren't wearing panties."

"No." Damp from swimming, they're in a ball at the bottom of her purse.

He stubs out his smoke in a little tin ashtray and sets it aside.

"You leave your children so you can be someone else for a while."

"No," she says again. She pauses, standing there, then slowly goes back to buttoning herself up.

"So you can be yourself, then. Which is it?"

"I don't think that's true. I don't think it's either/or."

"When someone asks if you're a dancer or a mother, what do you say? Don't think! The very first thing that comes to your mind. What are you, Maeve Martin?"

She doesn't say anything, her fingers still playing at the top button of her dress.

"I know what you are," he says. He runs his tongue along the seal of a new cigarette before lighting it up. "Otherwise, why would you be here? You weren't even drunk." He takes a drag and repeats himself: "You weren't even drunk."

"No." She wraps her hair into a bun and pins it. "I told you: a temple. A working temple."

"Most unexpected."

He's drunk himself, but there's a different look to him all of a sudden, something Maeve recognizes but can't quite place. It pricks at her.

"Almost like I was asking for it," she says. "How's your face? Still beautiful?"

She can see the shadow of a bruise where it's coming in, high along his cheekbone, but he doesn't say a word. Only draws on his cigarette and smiles.

DAY 3

THIS TIME SHE plays only deep jazz, women with their mournful songs, and Maeve's body purposefully wild, operating not in time but its opposite. Defining herself in contrast to the long-held notes and low voices: spin-out-lift, lift-go-farther, reach and pull in, contract, release, contract, release, a high jump just to show off, just to show what she can do. She tips the bowl of her pelvis up, a twinge at the old scar whenever she forgets—God, she wants to forget—swing out and back, arch, lift up. There is nothing careless now to the way she's moving; each moment of flight, each landing meant to look visceral, meant to look lush, and she's sticking it with a precision that makes her head spin. Turn, turn, sweep out, slide, and contract, she can hear her own breath, the sweep of her soles against the floor and the music coming even slower now, push up, roll-to-push, roll-to-push, and up now for good—extend-extend—wide into the turn, high leg, hold-it-hold-it and around—

She hits the floorboards. Lands it.

This is the aesthetic: she's almost giddy with it, operating at the intersection of recklessness and control, taming herself and breaking free in return. This. *This.* The way her body moves now, post-age and -injury, is the thing; it's the hook. Directing young, ballet-trained female dancers to mimic it will show up as both experimental and political.

Raging or joyful, depending who's watching, Maeve thinks. Depending on the eye. She's got a burning in her shoulders, forearms, thighs, down her back, and she walks it off in circles. Less a muscle pain than a fire under her skin. She pushes out from the wall, breathing hard—

Who said you're done?

She's not done yet. Not by a long shot.

It's night by the time Maeve wants to leave the studio, or it's dark, anyway, and she has to fight her way out; the door is blocked with new snow. She arrived before dawn, carrying a piece of pie on a plate wrapped in cellophane—pie! The plate selected with purpose from the kitchen pantry, the sugar going straight to her head—and an entire urn of black coffee she brewed herself, pinched from the empty dining hall, while everyone else slept on.

Verboten, she thinks now, swinging the empty urn in one hand as she cuts along the path in her high boots. Maeve is sure coffee urns are not meant to be taken to the forest.

The wind picks up, but she can hear it more than feel it, the sound of it building somewhere far away, down in the river valley, or along the ridge. In the woods she feels shielded. Safe.

She has that high vertiginous feeling you get when you haven't slept. A kind of dizziness, or giddiness, or both. She's had too much coffee and not enough food and her body aches with victory, every piece of it: the small, strong muscles in her feet and hands, the bands of tight ligaments at her ankles and her elbows, the deep sockets of her hips. A good day. A very good working day. A day when Maeve was fully Maeve again, her body a beautiful streak, every line of her a machine that moves and changes, angle to curve, curve to angle, then changes again.

Her neck and her shoulders are stiff; her limbs feel swollen, but not numb. A heat to her skin. She is swelling within herself.

Expanding. Limitless and powerful.

There's a gap in the trees, and a sudden smack of wind almost knocks her back, but she thrusts her way against it. Not just a woman, but a giant. Coming hard through the forest. Hip-deep in snow.

Close to the center she breaks through a snowbank and falls into a new path. Tire tracks, freshly made. There's the hum of an engine nearby and she squints through the growing squall to see a pickup, chains on its tires, rumbling slowly toward the road.

She comes into the building, shaking the snow off her clothes, out of her hair. There's a light in the dining hall and she follows the sound of voices: Anna's mild drawl, Karo's clear inflection, a low murmur that she knows is Sim. She hasn't missed dinner.

Justin raises his camera and trains it on her as she walks in—the ubiquitous documentary.

"Here we have dance impresario Maeve Martin," he says, looking up at her from behind the lens. "Just in time to hear the news."

Karo says, "Where did you get that coffee urn?"

"Must have been up early this morning."

It's Dan who answers, before Maeve can get a word in. He's not at the table with the others but standing apart, back to the wall. She hadn't even seen him there, but he raises his mug now in greeting.

Sadie scrapes her fork across her plate.

"We haven't had an early riser here since Elisha," she says. "Since Elisha left, I mean."

It takes Maeve a moment to remember the name—Elisha Goldman, the painter Sadie mentioned. The woman who had a terrible accident.

The comment would almost feel threatening, except Sadie hasn't aimed it at Maeve. For some reason, she looks pointedly at Sim. Maeve has that new-girl feeling again, like she's always missing something.

Sim doesn't take the bait, or say anything at all; he only shrugs half-heartedly. He holds his gaze on Maeve, though, a long moment of it. The edge of a smile playing at his mouth. As though he's trying to keep his lips closed.

Trying to keep a secret, Maeve thinks.

She's suddenly awkward, fluttering; she takes a seat as far from him as she can, but with six at the table, there's not much distance between anyone. It's only once she's chosen a place that Dan approaches and pulls out the chair beside her.

"Stop it," he says abruptly—but he's talking to Justin, who aims his camera away without switching it off.

"What's going on?" Maeve says, turning brightly to the others. There's a somberness to the whole group and she doesn't want to lose her buzz.

She leans in to scoop food onto her plate. Lasagna, red and steaming in its tray, bread, those tiny foil-wrapped pats of butter hard from the fridge. Anything she can get. Brazen, this desire to eat, to fill herself up.

"Just talking about the weather," Justin says, faux sullen. He lets the camera swing out toward the window, a view of the blowing snow, before finally setting it down. But he and Karo exchange a look before Karo resumes talking in her usual brisk, officious tone.

"I've sent the cook home," she says, gesturing to the table. "And the housekeeper. That's why there's no buffet. They were the only staff members on-site this weekend."

Maeve looks up from her butter. In her hunger, she didn't even notice the buffet wasn't set up. Karo continues without missing a beat.

"Just down into town, not far. The roads are so bad, and sometimes it takes the plows a long time to get up here."

"Almost three feet of snow in the past few days," Dan says, leaning on the table beside her. Maeve shifts to give him a little room. "And it's still coming. People want to see their families. Can't blame them."

At the word *families,* Maeve feels a sudden twinge of guilt. She's missed the window for calling home today; it's past the kids' bedtime back in eastern standard time. *Worth it,* she asserts. *Worth. It. You're here to work, remember?*

But her hand shakes a little as she brings fork to mouth.

Anna, next to her, marks it and drops her voice: "Everything all right, girl?"

Maeve sinks back against the cushioned dining chair; a hollowness, an ache in her bones. For the first time, she realizes how tired she is.

"Just low blood sugar," she says. "I had a big day."

"Really?" Sim leans in. "I had just the opposite. Couldn't get a thing done. Couldn't focus." He plays his fork against the edge of his plate and comes back to Maeve, letting his voice drop a little lower: "Distracted, for some reason."

Maeve fights a smile, then turns away. Karolina looks grim. "I know it's a bit inconvenient—" she begins, but Dan stops her.

"We'll just hunker down for the next few days." He gets to his feet. "Plenty of food in the kitchen."

"Like camp!" Karo brightens. "We'll take turns cooking."

Justin groans and pulls his beanie lower over his ears.

"I hated camp," he says. "Do you know what kind of nightmares camp brings back for me?"

"Was it fat camp?" Anna leans forward with a pretend camera in hand, mocking him.

"Worse," Justin says. "It was the Hamptons."

Karo starts to rise to her feet, but then sinks back down, her plate in hand. The first edge of strain showing at the corner of her eyes, in her smile.

"We were meant to get a delivery today and it never came," she says. It's a quick recovery, her voice resuming its usual confidence. "Who's up for a bit of hiking? I may have to put on my snowshoes and trek down tomorrow to pick up a few things."

There's an abrupt silence. Maeve glances up from her plate and catches Anna's eye; they've paid for the privilege of being here, of focusing only on work. Bad enough they're now being asked to do their own housekeeping, but a supply run?

"Karolina," Anna says. "Everyone can live without champagne and caviar for a few days. Even Justin here."

"You'd be surprised." Justin watches as Dan collects his plate and moves off toward the kitchen. Karo's smile stiffens.

Sim leans across the table.

"Oh, I don't know. Think we could use some bubbles?" At first, Maeve thinks he's speaking only to her, but then he shifts his gaze. "Sadie will go," he says. "Won't you, Sadie? Pick up a few party favors for us?" That slow smile again. "I mean, if we're going to be stuck here, might as well have some fun."

"She can't go down the mountain alone," Anna says. She pushes back from the table, distracted or maybe demoralized. But Sim keeps his eyes on Sadie.

"Of course she can. Soon as there's a break in the weather, any of us could."

Anna glances from Sim to Sadie to Karo again, her brow starting to furrow.

"Sure, I'll go," Sadie puts in. "And I can totally go alone." She turns to Karo. "You don't have to bother yourself with it at all." She gives a carefree shrug to show how easy it all feels.

But Dan calls from the kitchen: "You'll take one of the guys with you, for protection."

Sadie rolls her eyes. "Or for bait."

She rises to follow Dan, plates in hand, and Anna springs up too. She catches Sadie's wrist just as they round Maeve's end of the table.

"Remember that it's Karo you work for," Anna says quietly, still moving toward the kitchen. "You don't have to do what anyone else says."

But Sadie just shakes off Anna's hand. When she speaks, her voice comes up loud enough for the whole table to hear. "It's Karo's errand," she says. But she looks to Sim for approval, and this time Maeve finds it gets her back up, just a little. Is there something here she doesn't know?

She can't figure Sadie out. First effusive, then cold; confessional on the trail, raucous and racy down in the spa. Dutiful with Karo, resentful with Dan. Compliant—

Is that the right word?

No. Eager with Sim.

For his part, Sim gives only the same little shrug, removing himself from the conflict altogether.

Justin picks up his camera to catch the dishwashing brigade. Karo heads back to her office. Everyone else is done and Maeve, latecomer Maeve, finds she's lost her appetite. Exhausted, she wraps a roll into a napkin and tucks it away in case she needs the food later on. She's alone now at the table with Sim, fidgeting in her seat, although she can't put her finger on exactly why. It was a good one-nighter, followed by an excellent day in the studio. Maybe she doesn't want anything to ruin it.

There's a little silence. When she looks up, he's offering her something. His own roll, also wrapped in a napkin. Maeve can't help but laugh.

"Well," she says, "at least it's not us running errands. That's one good thing."

He shakes his head. "It was never going to be you or me."

"It was almost me. You could see Karo expected me to volunteer. I can be pathologically accommodating. I was trained into it, in the ballet."

"You're a pleaser," he says. He leans across the table, his voice a little more conspiratorial. "You have to stop that right now or they'll all take advantage of you."

Maeve starts to laugh again. "You seem to hold them off." She glances into the kitchen: Sadie with a dish towel drying and stacking plates. "But poor Sadie—"

He gets up and slides into the seat next to her.

"It's never going to be Sadie alone either. Dan loves being in charge." He follows Maeve's gaze, watching Sadie now himself. "Gotta be top gun."

It's Sadie's nickname for Dan he's using—the way she described Dan out on the trail. So this must be something they've talked about.

But Sim turns back to Maeve, cheerful.

"Sadie just thinks she's getting in my good graces by stepping up. Dan's the one who'll actually do the job. Mark my words. And you and me? Ten bucks says we get another bottle of Brut out of this."

He picks up a water glass and makes a little *cheers* motion.

Maeve hesitates, her hand on her own glass. Why would Sadie want to get in his good graces?

In the kitchen, the squad is breaking up, and she can see Anna wending her way back through the tables. Maeve leans in toward Sim.

"Except, of course, Anna's onto you." She means it to be her own kind of flirtation. Roguish. But Sim only blinks. For a moment she wonders if he's heard her.

Anna arrives, and Maeve rises to meet her.

"I'll walk you back," she says before Anna has a chance to sit down.

Sim looks up, surprised—then nods in their direction.

"Chivalry! You'll want to be careful, Anna." He raises his glass one more time to Maeve. "A lot of dangerous people around here. Or so I've heard."

He waits until Maeve picks up her own glass, waits for the clink.

* * *

"Did you fuck him?" Anna says when they are up the stairs and away. "Was it crazy? He seems a little crazy. He seems like the kind of guy who has a swing, you know?"

"There was no swing."

Anna trots along next to her, impatient. "But…"

"Honestly, it was fun—" Maeve wonders at her own word choice. Fun is what you have at a picnic. It does not seem the right way to describe Sim Nielssen's quiet intensity. "He takes instruction well," she says finally. "It was good for me. But…"

She slows down a moment, worrying at the key in her pocket.

"But what?"

"I wonder if—I shouldn't have slapped him," she says. "Last night."

"What—in the spa? Maeve, it was a joke. They practically forced you to. We were drinking."

"But I wasn't. He seems to like playing games, and I just think—"

"Don't think. Get over yourself. So what, you got laid." Anna cocks an eyebrow. "People sometimes do that on retreat. Repeat after me: WWADD."

Anna waits for her to get the joke, but Maeve just gives her a puzzled look.

"What would a dude do! Remember?"

She digs a saucy elbow into Maeve's side a few times. It's practically vaudeville.

"All right, all right!" Maeve dodges the elbow, laughing despite herself. They've arrived at Maeve's door. "I mean, I don't want to have a whole thing with the guy. I'm only here for a few days and I have a lot to get done. Today was fantastic." She looks Anna in the eye, electrified. "Today was so good. I want ten more days like that."

She digs in her pocket for the key, leaning a shoulder on the door—

but suddenly the door gives way. Maeve steps back, confused. She prods it with a hand and the door swings into the room.

"I didn't leave this open," she says. "Did I?" She looks at Anna, then back at her room.

"It happens," Anna says. "If you don't pull it really hard into place, the lock doesn't click."

Maeve tries to remember. She stopped by her own room in the early hours, briefly, after leaving Sim's, just to wash and change into her dance clothes. She'd been both tired and buzzing to get to the studio. It's possible that she flew out of the room without noticing that the door failed to latch.

Is it?

"Stupid of me," Maeve says.

Anna turns and walks backward down the hall, toward the stairwell on the other side of the building.

"Meh, who cares?" she calls. "There's no one here but us."

In the room, Maeve collapses onto her bed. She's long past the moment for easy sleep and crossed over into hyper-exhaustion. Awake too long, her heart pounding. She kicks off her boots without sitting up. On her room phone, the voice-mail light is blinking, and she rolls over, hits Speaker, and taps the button to hear the message. She's expecting her mother's voice.

What she's hoping for is an apology or a reluctant admission that Maeve was right after all; they would head back to Maeve's house in the city, and her mother would take the kids to school.

Instead, there's only Talia's small voice on the line.

"Mommy? I miss you. I want you to sing me my nighttime songs—"

Maeve can hear the fight in her voice, how hard she's working not to cry. There's another moment or two, and then her mother in the background, and the message cuts off.

The time stamp marks the call as three hours ago. Maeve squeezes her eyes shut, picturing Talia alone in a strange bedroom in that strange house, those woods.

You're just too tired for this. You'll call her in the morning. But her body hurts and she can't sleep and she wishes she could call back right now. Her heart feels like a violin string pulling tighter and tighter until it might snap.

You're just tired, that's all.

Too tired to sleep.

She finally jumps up and grabs her robe. This time she pulls the room door shut as tightly as she can and double-checks the lock before padding down the hall in her sock feet. A hot soak will be just the thing; she needs to relax, to bring everything down a notch.

In the stairwell, her feet ring a soft echo against the metal steps. It's dark and quiet downstairs. Inside the spa, she turns on one light, then two, the switch making a satisfying *thunk* under her hand. She undresses and sinks into the warmest of the baths, neck-deep, her breathing slow and even.

At home, Maeve sometimes gets in the bath to cry, but she's too drained for that now. Her clothes sit in a rumpled pile to one side. The only break in the silence down here is whatever noise she makes herself. Sound of her breath. The lapping of the water against the pool's edge when she moves, even slightly. She opens her hand and lets it fall below the cloudy surface, waiting for it to disappear.

When she brings it up again, the old scar is still there, reddening in the heat. In her mind, she can still see the broken piece of mirror clattering, bloody, to the floor. *Stem to stern*, she thinks. Fingertip to wrist. Another inch, and it would have hit a vein. She closes the hand into a fist and lets it sink like a stone. As scars go, this one feels like a badge of honor.

She's resting on a kind of bench cut into the stonework, just slightly too low for someone Maeve's size. Her chin grazes the water's surface, then her lips. The water is so warm; she moves her shoulders and her neck, allowing the joints to loll, muscles spreading out. Her anxiety over Talia slows and her breath along with it. Physical exhaustion finally takes over. Her head nods, and she forces her eyes open. She can't fall asleep here. It's deep; she'll drown.

But closing her eyes feels so good. There's a moment of softness, the water just covering her lips, holding her.

Maeve wakes with a jerk. She opens her eyes, panicked. Shakes her head to rouse herself. The water plinks and plunks around her as she moves. She has the strange feeling that she's missed something. That something woke her, something that's no longer there.

Something—or someone. She glances at the deck, the changing room, and her eye falls on the broken tile Dan was examining yesterday, fixed now. She can see the gleam of fresh caulking, shiny and white.

She needs to go back upstairs. She needs to go to bed. The wet tile slips against her fingers as she climbs out of the pool. She's wrapped in her robe, wringing out her hair, when there's a thud from the hall, and she stiffens. Waiting.

Another, a little farther off.

Then nothing. Just the buzzing silence of the empty room. The ceiling arches high over her head. Maeve suddenly feels strange, vulnerable. Too alone, as she picks her way back to the entrance. She's struck by an abrupt fear that she'll find the door locked, be trapped inside for the night—and then she's padding across the floor, faster and faster. Running.

But when she lays a hand on the door, it yields too easily, almost throwing her out into the hall.

She stops there, frozen. The hall is only dimly lit. But just in the moment of the door's wide swing, she caught a shadow. Around the corner, now gone.

The stairwell is to her right. But the shadow disappeared in the opposite direction, the hall's dead end. She blinks, listening. From here, she can just make out a low hum, a murmur. Voices.

Maeve lets the door close softly behind her and heads not toward the stairs but to where the hall turns and cuts off at an old changing room. She goes around the corner, careful, her feet soundless on the carpet.

Ahead, the murmur grows just slightly; a man's voice, low and sure. She stops.

A thin spool of light spills from the changing-room door, open only an inch or two in the darkness. At the frame, there's a figure crouched low. But it's too small to be Dan, or even Justin. Someone quiet and compact, no bigger than Maeve herself.

Sadie.

The girl hovers there, something cradled in her arm. Something black.

Maeve stays frozen. The murmur grows stronger, and she realizes it's not Sadie who is speaking; rather, Sadie is listening to whoever is in that room. Watching them.

More than one voice for sure, a man's and a woman's. Sadie reaches out and prods the door, the lightest touch, and it yawns another inch. Maeve can just make out Anna's voice now, warm and low. There's a bang and then a stifled laugh, and a figure cuts into the light. Tall, bare-shouldered, his cropped hair almost black against his skin.

Dan.

From inside, a hand slaps the door shut, and the hall is newly dark.

Sadie suddenly pushes up to stand and Maeve leaps away, back around the corner so as not to be seen. She turns and pretends to fuss with the door to the spa. Holding her breath.

A moment later, Sadie comes around the turn herself, head down. Seeing Maeve, she halts, and the two women stare at each other. Sadie's face gaunt and young, defensive.

Maeve steps back. Maybe this is somehow not what it seems.

A fleeting moment of fear, or shock, passes through Sadie's eyes—and then she recovers, glancing briskly over her shoulder before brushing past Maeve, as though on her way to finish some official task.

"The spa is closed at this time of night," she says. Her voice is all business, a harsh whisper. As though it's Maeve who should not be there in the dark.

Alone now, Maeve comes up the stairs, then takes a long, wary look down her own hall before leaving the stairwell. The corridor is lit by a few regularly spaced sconces. There is no one else around.

What could Sadie be playing at? Maeve lingers in the silence, trying to recall her own emotions, her mindset when she was twenty-three. Jealousy, ambition, insecurity—nothing fits. What Dan does with Anna is no business of Sadie's. Maeve can't think of how skulking around in the dark, peeping in doorways, would serve her.

Unless—is it possible she was there not for herself but for Karo? To check up on another employee?

It's all a little more than Maeve bargained for when she signed up for this retreat. So much for a relaxing soak. Maeve lets it go, glad to be going to bed alone. She's tired, and she wants another good workday tomorrow, as good or better than today. Best to focus on herself.

She's relieved to find her door still properly latched this time. Before turning off the light, she digs out her phone and turns it over in her hand. No new voice mail, but her mother has sent a photograph, meant to be a salve, Maeve thinks, or, more likely, a negation of the tearful message from earlier in the evening. In the picture, Talia and Rudy are hard at work, decorating cookies with Popsicle sticks, Talia with blue and pink and white icing streaking the tips of her hair, Rudy with his tongue out in concentration.

She's sorry that they are not here. That there's no way to do both at once. She misses the heat of their bodies cuddling in next to her, the smell of their skin. As love goes, she feels this one physically. It hurts like hunger.

She takes a breath, plugs in the phone, and puts it facedown on the nightstand.

But you don't miss the guilt, she reminds herself. It's true: she doesn't miss the harsher feelings, when she just wants them to leave her alone, give her some space. Fuck off for a bit so she can be Maeve again.

Outside, the blizzard has only gained momentum; there's a slam as the wind buffets the window glass. She turns out the light and lies there, listening to the rhythm of her own breath, her muscles tired and sore.

She can still picture Sadie, crouched low. Watching.

Maeve gets up in the dark and peers through the peephole at the vacant hall. She unlocks the door, then locks it again. Listening for the dead bolt to catch.

When it comes this time, she can see it.

Its dark fur. Maeve is sure she must be awake. First, the smell of it, wetness and musk, a bog smell, a sex smell, washing in like a heavy wave. And then it's already there, coming at the window. She can see the blackness in its eyes.

The pressure in the room hurts her head. Maeve tries to pull up in bed, to stand, but she's so tired. Her shoulders burn. Her muscles won't work; her bones won't support her. She is weeping with the effort. If she doesn't get up, she will never get home to Rudy and Talia. She has to get home to save them. The bear is coming for them too—

The dead bolt moves in the latch.

Her door bursts open; a rush of wind pins her down. The little photo strip flutters against her mirror, then flies away. Maeve finds herself pressed flat, trapped, and the bear, the bear is right outside her window, coming at her with the sound of a train.

There's an explosion of shattering glass and then it's on her, its long claws slicing her skin.

Maeve pushes up, gasping for breath.

She's leapt out of bed in her sleep. Disoriented, she looks around.

There's a swirl of white at the window, but the glass is intact. To the other side, the door is closed and locked, just as she left it. The photo strip tucked safe in the mirror frame.

Her arm stings and Maeve sees that she is bleeding; she knocked into the bedside lamp, breaking it on her way down. The jagged edge of a shard of china is still lodged in her skin. She takes hold of it with two fingers and pulls it out, and the room spins.

For a moment she thinks she will vomit, and she bends her head to her knees.

In the bathroom, she stands over the sink, mopping at her arm with a wet facecloth, then she rinses and squeezes it out and presses it to her forehead instead. She takes a drink and looks at herself.

So. That's the dream.

The bathroom light, a soft white over the mirror, flickers a little. She looks pale. She looks like an old-time movie star, harrowed and lit from above.

Then the light blinks out.

Instinctively, Maeve reaches over and toggles the switch. When nothing happens, she gropes her way back to the bedside. The clock radio stares at her blankly; she pushes at the buttons but no numbers come up. On the far side of the bed there is another lamp, but it doesn't work, either. She reaches for her phone: 3:15.

It must be the snow; a wire is down somewhere. She tosses the phone onto the bed and climbs in, but her arm stings, and she can't sleep without knowing what's going on. She rifles through her backpack in the dark for a bandage. What do they call these snow events now? Snowmageddon. Snowpocalypse. She bandages her arm, then sits under the blankets and pulls her knees in to her chest to wait. Every five minutes or so, she leans over and tries the bedside lamp again, but the more time passes, the more she starts to worry. She turns the phone off to save battery life, pulls on a pair of dance tights and a hoodie, and picks her way down to the lobby.

Maybe, by some miracle, there is power down there. At best, Maeve can make herself a cup of tea in the kitchen. At the very least, she can do some stretching by moonlight, maybe a little barre exercise. As long as she's awake, she might as well be working.

But when she swings the stairwell door open, they are all there, shadows in the dark—Anna, Dan, Justin. Maeve almost jumps. Karo, standing to one side, strikes a match and then carries it around the room, lighting candles.

"I—" Maeve is unsure of what to say.

"Woke you up too, huh?" Anna is sitting huddled in an armchair, knees drawn up to her chin.

"The bear?" Maeve says, remembering Anna's story about the spring session, how everyone woke one night with the same dream.

But instead of nodding, Anna frowns, then sits up taller. "Oh, wait, now, that's cool—" she starts.

"Anna," Dan says, giving her a look. He turns to Maeve. "We just had a bit of a jolt." He gets up to help distribute the candles now that there's some light. "Because of the sound. It woke everyone."

"What sound?" Maeve says. Part of her wonders if she is still dreaming.

"There's been an avalanche," Karo says. Her voice is clipped, controlled. "Somewhere off the eastern ridge. Nothing to worry about. But very loud." She glares at Anna. "That's all."

"But what were you dreaming about?" Anna is persistent. "I have to know."

On the couch, Justin wraps his robe a little tighter around himself and sinks into its hood, petulant. "When I say I'm dreaming about *bears,* you never want to know the details—"

Maeve stays on Karo, trying to make sense of what she just said. An avalanche? Her head hurts. The dream already feels far away. "I mean," she says to Anna, "yeah, a bear. I think so. I don't know; it's already cloudy."

Sadie, by the window, traces her finger down the glass, cutting a path through the condensation.

"Anna always needs everything to be magical," she says. "Like some fun fairy tale."

Maeve startles to see her there, remembering, all at once, finding her crouched in the dark earlier the same night. Anna's voice, her soft moan from beyond the door. Did that really happen? She tries to put herself back there, but it feels a million miles away.

Just another dream? A stress dream. It seems a little too gothic to be anything else.

There's a weird silence, cut only when the back door swings open and Sim walks into the room, snow clinging to his jeans and boots. Dan steps up to him.

"Where the hell have you been?"

As the door closes, Sim moves in so Maeve can feel the cold on him.

"The elk are moving down the valley," he says. He turns to Maeve specifically. "You can hear it. They're running away."

She cannot seem to break his stare. She's still standing there, held in place, when the ground starts to move.

The sound rushes in louder than any train, louder than anything in her dream.

"Everybody get down!"

She can hear Dan's voice, but barely, yelling over the noise—he reaches for Karo to steady her, then pushes her into a chair. It's possible that Anna begins to scream. Sim grabs for the desk. Outside, Maeve can hear the crack and groan of the forest coming apart. She drops to her knees, covers her head: earthquake training.

But it's not an earthquake. It's the western ridge, the very nearest tip, collapsing down the slope to where forest meets road.

Closing them in.

DAY 4

NO ONE LEAVES the room again until it's light.

For safety, Dan insists. But dawn is hours away. In the meantime, the temperature in the building begins to drop, and Maeve is itching to get back to her room to see if her cell phone works. In her confusion, she left it behind. Anna sits on one end of the couch, a blanket around her shoulders, staring out the window. Karo surreptitiously checks her own phone but says nothing.

Unable to keep still, Dan hauls new wood in from the pile outside the door, then stacks it into another pile near the fireplace, repeating a list of assurances as he works: There's a generator in an outbuilding. The fact that it hasn't kicked in automatically is troubling, but not a disaster—he's not sure which areas of the center are considered priority. It's possible the lights are on somewhere else.

"What do you mean, you're *not sure?*" Sadie starts toward the fireplace. "Isn't it your job to know? Isn't it your job to be sure?"

Sim, his wet boots and coat now lying in a heap on the floor, shakes his head.

"I didn't see any lights out there—"

Dan interrupts him sharply. "You wouldn't know where to look." He steps over to loom above Sadie, standing barefoot in her pajamas by the fire. "And, yeah, it's my job. There's a manual generator on-site in a shed by the western pass trail. It just needs someone to switch it on. If you keep calm and stay quiet, I'll handle it."

Maeve glances up, startled by his tone. But Karo just moves across the room to Sadie's side, fluid and even.

"Once it's light, we'll tour the property and see where the damage is." Karo's voice is meant to reassure, but her cheeks are pink with tension. "Regardless, it won't be more than a few hours before crews get up here and get us back to normal."

The message is starting to stink of dogma: If you keep saying it, it must be true. Maeve feels more worried rather than less. On the couch, Justin recites a mantra of his own, cut with sarcasm but no less anxious:

"What are the chances? No one on-site? Staff all home for the weekend? What are the chances?"

It's almost eight in the morning before the darkness lifts enough for Dan to declare them safe to leave. Back in her room, Maeve turns on her phone; it lights up in her hands, but there's no service. Wi-Fi dead, cellular dead. The photo her mother sent the day before is still there, but there's no way to reach her children now, no way to make up for being AWOL when Talia called. She switches it off again in frustration and goes to grab a few extra items of clothing out of her bag. It may be cold for a while, a day for layers. Better to have her boots and coat too.

But as she rifles through the zipper compartment of her suitcase for fresh panties, something sharp jabs her hand. She unfolds a bralette to find some kind of—what? a carving? a claw?—nestled in among her lacy things. It must be a claw—curving out from a pale stub of bone, the hook itself is a mottled brown-black and half as long as her own hand.

The thing is not hers; she's never seen it before.

Her stomach flips. She remembers her dream, the bear's long claw. She glances at the bandage on her arm, then moves slowly to the bed and sits down. No dream-creature hid this in her suitcase. A person did. Someone here at the retreat—someone who broke into her room.

She runs the pad of her thumb along the claw's blade edge, then sets it on the bedside table where she can keep an eye on it while she dresses.

She's downstairs and building up the fire again when Sim comes into the lobby. Maeve rises, pulls the claw from her jacket and holds it out.

"Yours?" she says.

"What makes you think that?"

"Is it yours," Maeve says again. The thing's appearance, in with her panties, makes it feel like some kind of taunt. When he doesn't take it from her, she steps closer. "It is, isn't it?"

"Don't know. What is it?"

"You broke into my room."

He shakes his head, confused. "Wishful thinking, Maeve."

She's still standing, her palm outstretched, the claw pointed toward him. "Take it," she says.

"It's not mine."

"Take it. I don't want it."

He clasps his hands behind his back. Quizzical but game to play along.

"Don't be childish," she says just as Karo and Anna walk in.

"What's going on?" Karo looks more herself again, even under all her layers. Like a model for a chalet-wear catalog. Maeve lets her hand drop. The whole thing feels dumb.

"Nothing," she says. "I—I found something in my room. I thought it might belong to Mr. Nielssen here."

Sim raises his hands, hold-up-style. "Mr. Nielssen denies responsibility."

"What is it?" Anna steps up, and Maeve opens her fist to reveal the bear claw. Anna raises an eyebrow and plucks it out of her hand.

There's a noise from the other side of the lobby and then the cool click of Sadie's boots as she crosses from the office to where they are standing. She has the satisfied look of a kid who's arrived just in time to see her sibling catch hell; Maeve realizes she's been watching the whole time.

"It's nothing," Maeve says again, turning to Karo specifically. She's suddenly embarrassed to be making a fuss—like she's the childish one. If Sim won't own up, she doesn't want to stand here arguing about it. She holds her hand out to Anna for the claw. "I found my door unlocked yesterday evening and it gave me a turn. That's all."

"Maybe it's a talisman," Anna says, setting the thing back in Maeve's palm. "Where'd you find it?"

Maeve glances at Sim, then slides the claw into her coat pocket without answering.

"Dan and I are going to take a tour around the property," Karo says, looking each of them in the eye in turn. "Down to the main gate. See if we can fire up the generator or find out what's going on." She adjusts the scarf at her neck and fastens her top coat button. "There may already be a crew there working, for all we know. Sadie will stay here in the office to keep an eye on things in case the phone line comes back." She nods to Sadie, who had been buttoning her coat. Now she begins to neatly unbutton it again. "What is everyone else doing? I think I'd prefer it if we all stay within range of each other while this is ongoing."

Maeve bristles. What exactly does *within range* mean?

Anna says that without light or power, there's not much she can do. There are a few books in the archive she's been meaning to look over—historical accounts of men who went missing, survivors stalked by a giant bear or haunted by terrible dreams—but she can bring them back here and sit by the hearth.

"Cozy," Maeve says. The last thing she wants to do is return to that dream; she blinks it away. Turning to Karo instead, matter-of-fact: "I'm going to the studio for the day."

Karo tilts her chin, surprised. Sim does not seem to hear; he is bent over the fire, adjusting the logs.

"I might as well," Maeve goes on. "You said it yourself, there's probably a crew already working on the power lines. It's not snowing right now, and I'm only here a few days."

What she doesn't say is that working will distract her, will give her a focus, something to keep her grounded. She can already feel her anxiety spiraling up, her cell phone tugging at her back pocket. If she's not working—physically working—she knows she'll end up sitting by the fire, obsessively switching the phone on and off, on and off, driving herself into a panic.

"We don't know what the conditions are like out there," Karo says.

Maeve wraps her coat a little more tightly around herself and ties the belt.

"So I'll be careful. If it feels dangerous, I'll come back and entertain Anna with my choreography." She looks at Sadie when she says that; after last night, she'd like to have a moment alone with Anna, regardless.

Sadie seems unbothered, though, her coat swinging open now that she's been given the order to stay put. Chin jutting a little. She slides into an armchair by the fire and leans in to talk to Sim, who has been playing with the flame.

But when Maeve turns to go, Sim rises and joins her. He's got his cigarettes out. She cannot help but notice that Karo does not offer him the same look of reproof that Maeve herself attracts. Frustrating when women in power get stuck in the same old conventions.

They pass through the rear doors together and then Maeve stops. There's no obvious avalanche damage here, nothing close to the main building. Dan has been out shoveling already, but farther on, she can see where the path has fully disappeared, buried in new snow.

"You'll need a little trail of bread crumbs," Sim says.

Maeve looks out at the white. There is no sound, nothing; not even birds. She turns to him.

"Look—"

He's closer than she thought, his head dipping just slightly as he lights his smoke. She falters, and he's careful to hold his cigarette away from her as he exhales.

"Maybe I'll come with you, hey?"

"What do you mean?" Then, understanding him, she shakes her head. "Worker bee, remember?"

He surprises her by reaching out to wind a piece of her hair in his fingers. It's an intimate gesture but also gentle. Affectionate. The way she herself might reach out to catch Talia's hair, tuck it behind her ear.

Maeve thumbs the bear claw in her pocket; it's possible, of course, that it wasn't him at all. But then who? Justin, joking around? Sadie? Dan?

She stops. Dan. Of course.

Maybe not something she would have suspected before—he seemed so easygoing the first day or two. But the turn in him this morning, since the avalanche? It bothers her.

Dan, the local wildlife expert, whose job is managing the building—who must have a key to every room.

Sim catches her eye.

"Off you go, then," he says. "Just be careful. Don't get chased by wolves or you'll have to call the woodcutter to save you." He draws on his smoke, laughing a little.

In the outdoor light, she can see where the bruise on his cheek is already yellowing. She looks back at the snow and bites her lip.

* * *

86

Why is it that you can never go anywhere or do anything without some man fucking it up?

Maeve grips the claw in her pocket as though she could crack it in two. The lock on her door wasn't broken, it was just open, and who else would have a key? She hadn't pegged Dan for frat-house pranks, but maybe this is his army background coming to the surface. Maybe he thought it was funny.

Or he just thought he could get away with it. This morning, the way he clamped down, acting like he owned the place.

The snow is ridiculous. She's wading in it, eventually pulling her hands out of her warm pockets and using her arms to pump through. It's not a matter of snow getting down inside her boots: her jeans are soaked. There is snow inside her waistband.

At the studio, she finds the door blocked and jumps to pull the shovel down from where it sits in a rack over the transom—now she knows why it's up there instead of leaning on a wall—and begins a rather violent shoveling-out. Her shoulder pings; she has to lift the snow above waist level and with almost no room to maneuver. She turns in circles as she goes, just trying to carve out a space wide enough for both her own body and the arc of the door.

She stops shoveling, breathing hard, and lets herself in with the key, kicking the last bricks of snow away from the entrance. The shovel comes inside with her for now. More snow is moving in and she wants to be sure she can get out later.

Inside, she can see her breath. She strips off her soaked jeans to reveal the damp dance tights underneath; she's sorry now that she didn't think to bring an extra pair. It's cold and she's wet and the whole thing feels like misery. The only light is what filters in from the skylight above, a dingy gray. There is no possibility of music: the stereo won't work and she doesn't want to waste her phone battery. Maeve turns the phone on briefly but there's still no signal, and she switches it off again to start her warm-up.

She tries repeating a silent mantra: *This is not an emergency, just a short-term situation.*

Her muscles are stiff and uncooperative at first. In her hips especially, a tightness from the constant work of pushing through deep snow. When she's warm enough, she gets down on the floor, crosses one knee over the other, and reaches forward in an effort to relieve some of the tension. The stretch makes her wince.

In the stillness of the posture, she can't concentrate; her mind immediately flies back to Rudy and Talia. She hates that they're not safe at home the way she planned. She hates that they're at the cabin, the woods and their hidden dangers rising up dark on all sides.

More than that, Maeve knows how demanding her mother can be. Unforgiving, even. Her own childhood a blur of early-morning rehearsals and evening classes and her mother drilling her over her homework late into every night. No one could have higher expectations of a child.

Talia's voice, shaking, on the phone.

Maeve squeezes her eyes shut and counts to fifteen, breathing, then switches legs and tries it again, with the same result. What do they think has happened to her? How much do they know? Assuming the avalanche has been on the news—

But this, of course, is the question. Can she assume that? Would it make the news back east? Certainly, the record snowfall in this part of the country would be broadcast—and maybe the avalanche where the center has lost contact?

Except they're between terms here. It's the off-season. Maybe no one has tried contacting them at all.

Maeve sticks out her tongue to release the tightness in her jaw, sighs out a big breath. *Come on. Get back on track, girl.*

A short-term situation. That's all.

If she keeps moving, she'll think less. The children are fine. Probably.

Maeve is probably fine too.

She breaks out of the stretch, stands, and rounds over, her head to her knees—then comes up clean, flat back, watching herself in the mirror all the time. She pulls in at her core and tries some isolated movement, hips, ribs, shoulders, but it takes a different kind of focus, a new effort.

A moment later, she's back in the same anxious spin—

An avalanche is guaranteed to make the news only if someone dies. Here's the real question: Is the town of High Water also cut off?

There's a pop and a twinge at her left knee and Maeve pulls up quickly. *Careful, now.* She sighs out again, loud, and shakes out her legs. Frustrated with herself.

Okay.

New plan: Purposely focus on the kids. She steps to the barre and works her left side, pointing and lifting in time with the increasing speed of her own thoughts.

Let's say it's been on the news. There are two options: either her mother has told Talia and Rudy that Maeve is in an avalanche zone, or she has not. This is hard to guess. Maeve's mother is not predictable. And Maeve herself is not sure what she would prefer—

Terrify them—two small children—with the idea that their mom might be in danger? Or shield them from the news and let them think she's simply not calling, that Maeve has forgotten them altogether?

With this, she pushes from a deep squat to a lunge and a sudden, stabbing pain tears through her hamstring.

"Fuck!"

Maeve yells this out loud. It echoes around the room.

"And fuck this fucking snow!"

She crouches, rubbing the underside of her thigh and cursing fiercely. A hamstring pull, a bad one, can really limit your range of movement. It messes things up, easily leads to more injury if you're not careful.

Maeve is not feeling particularly careful, although the irony of having to go outside and fashion a kind of snowpack to ice the muscle under her snow-soaked tights does not escape her. She opens the door, and a burst of white blows in at her.

Oh, good, more snow.

She's standing there in the doorway, freezing in her bare feet, when she catches something—a flash—from the corner of her eye.

Then it's there again: a light in the forest.

A light? Any kind of electric light would be remarkable, considering there's no power, but this one swims back and forth before it finally settles, then stills. Muted. Some kind of heavy-duty utility beam. A flashlight. Maeve shoves her cold feet into her boots and takes a step out from the door, straining to get a better idea of it.

It's not coming from the main building, but from the deeper woods to the south. Not within the trees proper; instead of spreading and thinning over the snow, it seems contained. A glow. A candle? She takes another step, curious.

The light blinks out.

If Karo and Dan are down near the front gate trying to fire up a generator, they can't also be wandering around here.

A candle in a window: she realizes where it's come from. One of the other studio cabins. Where no one else is supposed to be. Only Maeve, Karo told her, would be out here. She waits another moment, the snow block melting in her hand, but the light doesn't come back on.

Maybe it was only a reflection? She squints up at the sky, looking for a streak of sunlight. A pane of glass catching a random beam?

The clouds thin and part, then come back together, as though to prove her theory on the spot. Her leg throbs and she turns her attention to it instead.

It's easy to feel watched when you're alone in the woods.

She crouches down and gathers a new layer of snow. Rolls it, then packs it tight. Her hands are beyond cold now, white and stiff; she tucks her arms closer against her body to retain some heat and squeezes the pack to compress it. She's down there, low to the ground, when some-thing tugs at her again, some kind of sixth sense, and she pivots on the balls of her feet, expecting to see that same light blinking on through the trees. But the other cabin is dark.

Maeve rises, then backs up toward the studio door.

It's not a light that's bothering her. Something less tangible. A scent.

At first, she just wrinkles her nose, but then the smell suddenly hits home. Familiar. A dank smell. Strong, and strange in all this silence, all the clean snow.

Maeve freezes, holding her breath. Listening.

Somewhere to her left, she hears a snap of twigs, a low *huff*. A grunting.

A new chill runs up the back of her neck. She wavers, light-headed. She should get inside, where it's safe.

Her legs feel like cement.

Maeve glances one last time to where she saw the light, back in the trees—this would be a good time to find she's not alone.

But there's nothing there. She backs slowly into the studio, shuts the door, and locks it.

Now she is inside, and the bear is out—somewhere. Because of the construction of the place, the only view is through the skylights, so there is no way for Maeve to see where the bear might be. How big it is, whether it's black or grizzly, and—most important—when it decides to leave. Instead of looking out a window, she is looking only at her own reflection, repeated over and over in a house of mirrors: a stringy thing, she thinks now, in wet clothing. A woman with a limp, holding a snowball to the back of her thigh.

No match for a bear.

She gives it a good few hours. How long do bears usually stay in one place? This is not exactly Maeve's sphere of expertise. It has to be looking for food, she thinks, or it's disoriented by the avalanche. She ices her leg and stretches, ices and stretches again, until she feels like she could run if she really had to. Then she puts on her jeans, and her boots and jacket overtop. At the last minute, she remembers the shovel leaning against the wall. She grabs it to take along with her, half weapon, half shield.

But as she goes for the door, there's a sound, and she pulls up short. A rough thump or a stamping noise. Something just outside.

Maeve waits, listening, her grip a little tighter around the shovel's handle even though there is a door between her and whatever is out there.

Then the scrape of a key. She watches, one hand still on the doorknob, as it seems to turn all by itself.

Not something but someone. Someone outside coming in.

For a moment, she remembers her first walk back through the woods at night. And Sim, lighting her way in the dark.

The door pushes open and Maeve is thrust back a foot or two. But it's not Sim who steps into the fading light.

It's Dan.

There's a moment of silence, each on their own side of the door, Maeve too genuinely surprised to know what to say. Dan pulls the key from the lock and sinks it slowly into his pocket. Behind him, the forest is already growing dark.

"What are you doing out here?" His voice is sharper than it needs to be. "I thought I made myself clear this morning: everyone stays together."

Maeve feels her body contract. She was expecting him to apologize for walking in on her, to make some excuse. Instead, he frowns at the shovel in her hand.

She lets it drop to her side.

"There was—I think there was a bear," she says by way of explanation. Trying to recover. "A couple of hours ago, just outside. I could hear it moving around, and, you know, they have that smell—"

She's tripping over her words, her eyes falling to the tool belt he has strapped to his coat. A utility light dangles there, against his hip. Dan, she reminds herself again, has a key to every door on the property. Cabins too.

"You shouldn't be out here in the first place." It's such a change from the Dan she met only a couple of days ago. His voice is clipped, forceful. "Freaking yourself out."

"No, I mean—it's true, I was outside and—"

He doesn't wait for her to finish.

"Let's go," he says, already turning away. "This is an emergency situation and I want the whole group together. Where it's safe."

"I was leaving anyway. You didn't need to come out here and—"

He spins back to face her.

"*I want the whole group together*. What part of that do you not understand? I'm the one in charge here. I'm the one who's responsible for your ass. So I will go door to door if I have to and make sure you All. Stay. In. One. Place. Get it?"

Maeve just stares.

He steps out of the cabin and gestures for her to do the same, then he locks her door himself and follows behind her as she struggles back through the white.

It's a strange way to collect someone you're worried about. His stride is longer than hers, and she can feel him on her heels as she tries to break her own path, plunging and sliding with every step. Yet more snow coming down.

When she sinks her hands into her pockets to warm them, she finds the claw still there, curved and sharp, and she tries to walk faster.

A bear would leave a trail, and she scans back and forth for signs of it—signs that it's long gone—but once they're out of the clearing and back in the trees, there are too many shadows. Everything looks suspicious, every dip in the snowbank a potential hiding place, every hollow, every tree trunk another dark shape rising to meet her.

* * *

"The good news," Justin says, "is that there's no shortage of ice." He drops what looks like a chunk of icicle into a glass and adds a few splashes of bourbon on top.

The fire is still going in the lobby, tended by the others all day. A kettle sits at one edge of the stone hearth, a pot with a lid on it at the other. Anna hands Maeve a steaming cup of tea.

"The good news is they found a radio," she says, glaring at Justin.

"Yes, and if the radio doesn't work, we can drink ourselves to death before we freeze." Justin is wearing last night's heavy robe, now over his clothes, tied at the waist with a belt. Also what appears to be many pairs of socks. Layers. He raises his mug to Maeve, cheerful. "Win-win," he says.

Maeve, cross-legged by the fire, doesn't raise her own cup in return. She arrived back at the center cold and soaking wet and tired of the feeling of Dan's eyes on her. She still has her hat on, although she's stripped off her jeans again in the hopes that they'll dry, the bear claw from her pocket now tight in her fist. She squeezes at it, a compulsive motion. When she opens her hand, she can see the mark it's left there.

Sim is the only one missing. No one has mentioned him, but his absence is something Maeve noted in the moment before she unzipped her pants. Her tights are warm against her legs now. The hamstring still throbs in the background, but it's muted. Anna has fortified the tea with a single shot of whiskey.

She's already heard the bad news: The automatic generator failed to kick in. This may have something to do with negligence on the part of the company man who inspects it every year, Karo says, or it may just be bad luck. What is certainly bad luck is that the manual generator—the fail-safe—is stored in an equipment shed near the western border, and this shed was buried in the second avalanche. She and Dan hauled themselves out there on an ancient snowmobile to try and retrieve it but found the shed lost to snow and debris. The snowmobile's engine quit halfway back, the track too short for deep powder, and they were left to walk the rest of the way home.

But the radio. The radio is good news.

While Maeve gets warm, Sadie is behind the front desk, working to get the thing set up. It's on a crank charge, like a camp radio, and she pumps the handle around and around—but it sticks and her hands slip when she tries to go faster. She pushes away, frustrated.

"It's just a matter of finding a clear channel," Karo says, standing over her. She looks up, and Maeve can see her baseline confidence is still there, although by now her eyes are tired. She wants to get through to someone in town—anyone, really, she says. Someone who can give them a timeline on the power restoration.

Anna pushes two chairs together and stretches out, singing to herself anxiously, near where Maeve sprawls on the floor. Justin paces, turning his phone on, then off again, then on. The light comes and goes on his screen.

"Anything?" Maeve says. She's done the same thing herself a dozen times in the past twenty minutes. She's itching to do it now, her phone held loosely in her hand.

"Works great." He drops to a crouch next to her, angling the phone and ducking his lips, then snaps a photo of them both. "I mean, there's no signal, obviously. Why, was there a reason you wanted to call some-one?" Maeve rolls her eyes. She hopes he can keep this up, his good humor—hers is already mostly gone.

Dan walks into the room. He's been securing all the exterior doors and windows—*Why?* Maeve wonders. *Against what?*—and checking one more time for damage to the building's structure, but now he slides in beside Karo to look over Sadie's shoulder at the radio.

"Protocol," he says—to the group, ostensibly, but pointedly to Maeve—

"emergency protocol at High Water Center for the Arts states clearly that in the case of natural disaster, center residents are to stay indoors in a common space so that everyone is accounted for—"

He's interrupted by a sharp banging and Karo glances up.

"Someone go in there and tell him to stop that," she says, and for the second time, Maeve registers that Sim is not in the room. No one has mentioned him. Anna gestures to the ballroom next door, the gallery.

Of course. Why stop working just because you don't have power tools?

Out loud, Maeve says, "So why is he allowed to keep working and I'm not?"

Dance—movement, repetition, exertion—is the only way she knows to stay grounded. It was hard enough to keep calm in the studio. How will she possibly cope if she has to spend a whole day just sitting by the fire?

Sadie jumps up and heads for the gallery door, but Dan is already there, rapping sharply on the wall. She hardens, glaring at him.

The banging stops.

"Because," Dan says, turning back to Maeve, "he doesn't have to go outside."

"Well, what about me? Is there someplace I can work, then? What about tomorrow?"

But the question is met with silence; Dan actually turns his back. Finally, Karo looks up.

"This problem will be solved by tomorrow," she says.

She grabs the radio—almost roughly—from where Sadie has left it unattended and begins to crank it herself; the girl stalks out to the chairs and sits down. Maeve watches her. In another world, she might have asked Sadie to help. She's a former dancer, after all—she could have found Maeve some private place on-site, some unused meeting space or boardroom. Maybe if they hadn't gotten off to such a bad start? Maeve frowns. No. Since the episode in the spa, she's reluctant to approach

Sadie at all. Karo's and Dan's controlling demeanor makes sense—they are responsible for the residents. She can find reasons for Dan to be letting himself into each cabin in turn. What was the word Karo used? *Liability*. Liable: that's what they are.

But Sadie just seems abrasive. Mercenary. Maybe even sly.

Dan gets up and pounds on the wall a second time even though Sim's work noise has ceased. It's like the pounding is an outlet for him. The emergency has triggered something, put him on some kind of razor's edge.

A moment later the door opens, and Sim walks out. There's dust in a streak across his face where he's wiped his eyes with a hand. He doesn't say a word but his mood is low, glowering. He locks the big oak doors and pockets the key, then crosses over to the fire, dips a mug into the pot on the hearth, and drinks out of it. Maeve had thought there was some kind of food in there maybe, but of course it's melting snow. No power means no filtration system. Even if the pipes don't freeze, Dan won't allow them to drink what's coming out of the taps.

Sim doesn't sit; he wanders back around the chairs and Maeve understands he's come to stand behind where she is on the floor. She moves so that her back is against the warm stone of the hearth and she can see everyone at once.

Dan lets himself fall into an armchair next to Anna, almost brushing her hand. Maeve notices again the pointed effort he makes to keep space between them. It doesn't feel like discretion. It feels like negging.

She's irritated on Anna's behalf, even if Anna herself doesn't seem to care.

"I have to be honest," he says, oddly pensive. "I thought we'd have power by now."

Maeve plays with her phone, turning it in her hand.

"I'm quite worried," she says suddenly. "I'm worried about my kids at home. How much longer till we get back online?"

Dan shifts in his seat, openly surprised.

"Oh, I don't mean for you to worry," he says. With no task at hand, all he can manage is performative calm. He looks stiff: like a Wikipedia image for normal, unafraid man. "The generator—I mean, that's fucking irritating. But I've been up here in storms before. It's not uncommon to lose power for a day or two. And we'll be just fine without it."

Anna just laughs, rather meanly. Her own pointed effort. Dan's face darkens.

"Not something you put in the brochure," Anna says.

"Sure it is." This is Justin, already half in the bag, his voice growing louder as the evening wears on. "'Research and develop new work in the quiet seclusion of the High Water Center for the Arts.' I mean, Quiet Seclusion Is Us, am I right?" He takes a drink.

Maeve draws her knees in and gives herself a hug.

"I don't mean to complain. I just—" She pauses. "It's hard not to panic."

I Survived the High Water Center for the Arts. She wants it on a T-shirt.

Sim drops down to sit on the edge of the stone hearth. He is not quite touching Maeve, but she can see his arm and hand, still dusty, out of the corner of her eye. He leans toward her.

"Jokes aside," he says, "this is an artist's dream. Avalanche isolation. No possible contact from the dirty world. Now, *that's* for the brochure. Karo, do we have to pay extra?"

Karo stops pumping the radio and shakes out her hand, middle finger lightly extended. Justin reaches under his chair, but whatever he's hoping to find isn't there: he gropes around, then drops to his knees for a better look.

"Where's my camera?" He straightens, scanning the room.

"Where'd you leave it?" Sadie says. She gets down on the floor, imitating him, her voice rising high in feigned horror. "Where's the case?"

He doesn't answer but his brow furrows. Maeve was right—he is drunk. But Sadie's way of mocking him is too catty, childish.

"Maybe Dan took it. Dan hates that camera—" Sadie keeps on, up on her knees now. "Isn't that right? You had, like, a bad interrogation experience or something?"

"Leave it, Sadie—" Dan says, starting to ramp up again. But Justin jumps in, his voice louder still.

"This avalanche is the craziest thing that's happened here in years— it's a real opportunity. Not just, you know, to make some ad for Karo—" He glances over to her as he says it. "But really. Actually."

"You know if you weren't always dragging it around like a toy—" Anna says. She turns her back to him, and focuses on Maeve. "Listen, there's no reason to panic," she says. "I'm from New Orleans, right? You know where I was in Katrina? Not in a tastefully decorated mountain lodge, I'll tell you that."

Sim looks at her, interested.

"Where *were* you in Katrina?"

For once, his tone irritates Anna, and her voice sharpens.

"Evacuated out to Jackson. My whole family." She looks back at Maeve in an effort to ignore him. "But there was no electric in Jackson for five days either, and we didn't know if our house was standing or fallen down or what. You'd just sit and watch the news and see all that water, and the people on the I-10. And bodies. It was the end of the world," she says. Then she leans in, reaching for Maeve's hand. "We're going to be okay here. It's just a matter of time. Time and patience."

"Okay," Maeve says. She stretches her legs out long and folds her body over them, feeling the tug along the back of her hurt thigh and into her hip. Glancing at Dan, she gauges his mood now versus out in the snow. "I think there was a bear," she says—not to him, but to the group. "Outside my studio. I told Dan already. But I thought I should say it again, out loud. In case anyone's walking around."

Karo's head snaps up.

Dan looks annoyed. "I already told you not to worry about that."

But he hadn't. He'd dismissed her or assumed she was making excuses, trying to get out of an awkward situation.

Sim seizes on it.

"What did you see?"

"I didn't actually see it. But—"

Dan's jaw clenches: "*I* didn't see anything, and it's literally my job." At this, Karo gives him a sharp look.

She's embarrassed him, Maeve realizes suddenly. He feels like she's called him out. He rises to his feet.

"That's why I came to get you," he says. "Figured you'd be scared out there. And you were. Not safe for a woman all alone."

Maeve blinks.

"The woods are only scary when someone's following you. If you're alone, it's fine."

Dan stops and cocks his head, looking at her. He wasn't expecting an answer, and Maeve's tone was sharper than she'd meant it to be. There's a taut silence before Justin cuts in—he's still on his knees on the floor.

"Folks, I'm serious. Who took my camera?" He waggles a finger at Maeve. "This is an amazing fight and I'm missing out on recording it for posterity."

Dan goes to leave, then turns back.

"And no one is going to be out just *walking around*," he says, talking to Maeve. "We already covered that."

Maeve is about to argue when a noise distracts her. The banging has resumed, a little more subtly this time. She looks behind her.

Sim is gone. The long argument gave him what he wanted: the opportunity to slip back into the gallery and keep working. No one else seems to have noticed. Across the room, Dan is still staring her down, waiting for a response.

She reaches forward into her fold again.

"Okay," she says.

* * *

When it's night, Karo sends Dan out to set off a few flares. The rest of the group gathers around the window like they're watching fireworks, but it's not like that at all. He fires them off from a flare gun, high into the night sky, the wind ripping at his jacket, and each bright spark just climbs and falls and that's it.

When he pauses to reload the gun, Sim swings the door open and Dan spins to meet him.

"Get back inside."

"Shh—"

"I need everyone to stay indoors while I'm operating the flare gun." Dan cocks his wrist as if he's holding a pistol, not an emergency beacon. "I said get back inside."

"Just give me a second—" Sim raises a hand, then puts a finger to his lips. He's braced himself in the doorway. Maeve can feel the cold of outside whipping into the room and she moves closer to Anna, the two women huddling together against the chill.

There's a moment of silence before Dan moves toward Sim.

"What the fuck are you doing?" Dan says.

"Listening." Sim takes a step, and the door closes a little. He's still got his back against it, and he raises his hand again as though he could stop Dan talking with it. He looks up to the sky. "There's no one up there—we'd be able to hear them. Search-and-Rescue use choppers and the wind's been too high for them to take off today. The weather's too bad right now for them to save anyone from the weather. Know what I mean?" He nods at Dan. "You've already fired three of those things. Better save some for tomorrow."

He steps back inside and the door closes behind him. Dan stares at him a moment longer, then turns and fires off two more flares into the dark.

* * *

By now, it's long past the dinner hour. They heat leftover lasagna in foil packets over the fire and eat it with bread from the freezer. The deep freeze is a walk-in and will stay well below zero, even without power; there's no risk of food spoilage for days, Karo says. Maeve is privately distraught every time someone uses that word, *days*. She wants to pour another shot of whiskey into her mug but doesn't.

She pushes the pasta around in its foil bowl in an effort to interest herself in eating.

"Dancers," Karo says. "Were you always so tiny?"

"Tiny and strong like bull," Maeve says.

She takes a performative bite and chews, but the joke is lost on Karo.

"You'll find it's remarkable how life can change you," she murmurs, and Maeve frowns; a flicker of something, sadness or regret, showing in Karo's eyes. Then she's already turned away, toward the windows and the dark. Listening the way Sim was at the door, the same intent look on her face. But there's no new sound, no light of a vehicle on land or in the sky.

Anna says she's tempted to sleep by the fire in her two chairs pushed together.

"It'll be cold upstairs," she says to Maeve. "Don't you think?"

"How cold? Will the pipes freeze?"

Dan says no, the building should retain enough heat to keep things manageable—

"I know," Maeve says, cutting him off. "For a few *days*."

She hadn't even realized he was listening to them.

Consensus is that the power will be back on in the morning. But Karo can't find a channel on the radio, and there's a decision that if for some reason the power is not back the next day (although this is unlikely, Dan says yet again), they'll hike out to the eastern rim to see the road conditions.

"We can try the radio from there—out in the open," Karo says.

Maeve nods, but she's uneasy: is everything going to be okay in the morning or not? She gives Anna a last smile, picks up her discarded jeans, and heads to bed on her own, looking for a little quiet. Her phone flashlight illuminates the back stairwell as she goes.

She's halfway to her floor when she hears the creak and thud of the steel door below. Another light blinks on. And then footsteps following her up.

At first, she assumes it must be Anna. The sound stops on the landing below. Maeve turns to look down.

"Hey—"

But it's not Anna who's following her up. It's Sim.

Maeve hesitates, startled. It's not that she's unhappy to see him. Not exactly.

"I thought about taking the other set of stairs," he says. "Double time, to surprise you at the top."

"Ah." Maeve leans on the rail. "To scare me?"

"Not to scare you," he says.

For a moment, neither of them moves. Then she steps back on her heel, and he takes it as an invitation and climbs the remaining stairs between them.

Maeve turns to keep going, thinking they can walk up together. But instead, he reaches out to hold her there. His hand on her wrist, pulling her in closer. His other hand at her waist, on her back.

She twists away and moves up to the next step. Then one higher, putting space between them again. It's not that she wouldn't be interested. It's just—timing, maybe?

"Where do you think you're going," he says mildly. As though this is a game and they are both playing.

Maeve shines her light up to the next landing, to the door that leads out to her level. Then down beyond him, the stairs winding back toward the main floor. Anna, she remembers, is curled up by the fire next to Sadie. Justin and Dan and Karolina still trading gibes, well used to one another's company. No one else is coming.

She stops, firm. Two steps below her, he looks up, his mouth curving as though he's trying not to laugh. Like he's allowing her to be taller, and it's funny to see her there, above him.

"Look," she says. "I'm going to bed. Alone."

"So, what, then—" He's still smiling. "We're just going to pretend nothing happened?" He comes up a step, shaking his head thoughtfully. "No," he says. Answering his own question. "No, I'm not doing that."

Maeve backs up toward the landing.

"I'm not pretending nothing happened. It's just, I mean—" How to say this? Maeve feels like wringing her hands. The day has been so long and so strange, and she just wants it to be over. "Nothing really happened? Right? It was super-fun, okay, it was a fun night. But I'm here, I'm trying to work, there's a goddamn avalanche, I'm worried about my kids. Cut me some slack, man."

Something in what she's said—she can't tell what—stops him. The smirk disappears. He nods. "I keep forgetting you have kids."

Maeve leans toward him, relieved that he's finally listening. "I have kids. Two of them, little kids."

He takes that in. She glances up to the door again and then back to where he's standing.

"You must be really worried."

"I am," she says, opting for the full earnest. It feels a little like cracking her heart open: it hurts. "It's really hard for me to think about anything else."

"That makes sense, then."

Maeve is not quite sure what to do with this. She wasn't trying to make excuses or help him understand. She was trying to say *No, thanks.*

From down the stairs, there's a long creak of the lobby door opening and then a new set of footsteps. Maeve looks down between the rails. It really is Anna this time.

"Hello?" Anna stops at the first landing, shining her own phone up at them.

Maeve raises a hand, a kind of wave. Anna climbs another step or two, trying to see. When she lands the thin beam on Sim, it's obvious—she leans back and out again, catches Maeve's eye.

"What's going on up there?"

Maeve looks from Anna back to Sim. There's a beat, his eyes on hers.

"Nothing," Maeve says. "Just having a chat."

But Anna doesn't move. She holds up a pack of cigarettes.

"Think you can give me a hand?" she says. "I was going out for a smoke. Dan's got all the doors locked tight, and I don't feel like arguing. He's a little wired tonight. I thought I could prop this one open for a minute before he notices."

Maeve can see that Sim is less comfortable with this new dynamic. This interruption. There's a moment of silence, and then he calls down to Anna himself:

"I can help you with the door."

"Great," Anna says. "There's a free smoke in it for you."

Sim just nods and reaches up to touch Maeve's arm. He doesn't try to move in any closer, but he gives her a little bow.

"Get some sleep, Queen Bee," he says.

He has a way of talking to her that's disarming. His eyes never break contact.

"Yeah," Maeve says. "Yes. You too." She leaves him there, and he watches her go, with Anna waiting below them, down on the landing. Maeve pulls the door to her own hallway open.

He's still there on the stairs—she turns to look—as the steel door swings closed behind her.

DAY 5

THIS TIME, IN the dream, Talia and Rudy are with her. They are walking together, hand in hand, through the wooded trail to the studio. There is no snow on the ground. Perhaps it is spring. The spruce and pine seem to grow into the path overhead, branches meshing; the ground at their feet sprayed with forget-me-nots and feathery green yarrow. Talia is talking and Maeve looks down at her, but the words seem far away. She can hear Talia's voice but can't make out what she is saying. Rudy pulls at Maeve's hand, urging her on, faster and faster.

As they near the studio, Maeve stops and presses a finger to her lips. She turns slowly, a full circle, squeezing the children's hands tighter in hers.

The scent of the bear is all around them. She thinks she can hear its rough breath back in the trees, but Talia will not stop talking: the sounds muddle. At the studio door, the wood frame has been clawed— long striations mark the entry, shavings in curls rest at her feet.

That's when she notices her hand. Her index finger has been replaced by a long claw, the same claw she found in her luggage. Maeve pats her pocket and finds it empty. The transformation of her hand is ugly but she can't stop admiring it.

She reaches for the children, but they are no longer there.

There is a breeze and it is warm and pleasant. It must be spring. The door is unlocked and bumps gently against its frame. She reaches for the doorknob, although she knows she should not. She knows it's in there.

Light streams out through the crack in the doorway. The light beaming off the mirrors inside is so bright. It's blinding.

The door opens and Maeve goes in.

In the morning, she wakes with a start. The dream is so close. Sunlight— actual sun!—filters through the window and Maeve rolls over and grabs her phone.

Still nothing.

Her battery is at 21 percent. All the on-and-off, on-and-off wearing it down. She holds it a moment longer. The time is 8:06. She turns it off.

She rolls out of bed and twists and flexes her body. Her feet and ankles crackle to life. When she bends over to touch the floor, she feels her spine straighten, a subtle click into place. A series of clicks: *snap, crackle, pop*. From neck to toes, Maeve doesn't have a joint that won't click or crunch after too much stillness. She stays like that, folded over, her arms crossed at the elbows, a little extra weight to help gravity pull her into alignment.

The chiropractor took a thermal image of her spine when she was twenty-six, told her the effect of dance—even then—was damage. That her upper vertebrae would likely fuse together before her sixtieth birthday. A kind of spinal arthritis. Overuse. She thinks about that diagnosis and the picture of her spine in reds and purples and blues every time she hears a pop or crack from her shoulders and neck. Folded over like this, she can see her feet, ropy with abuse; how they've widened, too, at the arch with age and pregnancy. She pulls up again and stands tall. The good news—at least at her core, the most damaged part of her, the muscles feel sore but strong.

Five minutes, maybe ten, she warms up by herself in her room, getting her mind in shape before she has to deal with anyone else. There is still no power, so nothing has changed: another day as the new kid in school, trying to navigate a tight mesh of strangers. Karo, growing increasingly tense; Justin, vaguely hysterical; and Sadie—

Maeve breaks out of her backbend and looks herself in the mirror, hard. At some point today, she must pull Anna aside and talk to her about Sadie. If nothing else, Anna deserves to know that she's been watched.

She throws on a pair of loose jeans over her tights, wool socks, and the bulkiest sweater she owns, an Aran fisherman's knit in pure cream. The bear claw is sitting on her bedside table: she glimpses it there as she's dressing and looks instinctively to her hand, the dream flooding back in a rush.

She hesitates, then slides the claw into her pocket again, safe against her hip.

Downstairs, a plan is going into action. Karo has made coffee using the fireplace kettle. Anna hovers near the window, where Dan is already lacing up his boots. Justin slumps, half asleep in a chair, red-eyed from the night before—but Sadie is watching keenly as Maeve crosses the lobby toward them.

She just wants a coffee. What now?

"There you are," Karo says. She looks at Maeve a moment. "We were beginning to wonder."

Ah—she's late, somehow. She is about to apologize when Sadie jumps in.

"Where's Sim?"

But Maeve doesn't register this as a question for her and pours some hot coffee into her mug. As she takes a sip, she realizes they are all looking at her.

"Sim?" Maeve says. "How should I know?"

Justin and Sadie exchange a glance. Karo brightens a little.

"We just assumed," she says. "Silly of us."

As though on cue, the back door off the lobby swings open and Sim walks in, stamping the snow off his boots. He's carrying wood from the big pile outside the door.

"You were outside?" Dan is unhappy. This is not *emergency protocol*.

"I was up early. Walking," Sim says. He sets the firewood down in a snowy heap. "*Solvitur ambulando*. What's wrong?"

"For one thing, I said I want everyone to stay together. And it's foolish. You could have been locked out." Dan goes over to the door. "You should have been locked out, in fact—these doors are all set to lock on contact. For security."

Sim cracks the door open a few inches.

"Yeah, I rigged this one a little. Anna wanted a smoke last night; I thought it would be handy. See?" He fiddles with the latch for Dan's benefit. "I know what I'm doing."

Maeve watches him demonstrate and slides a hand against her hip pocket. The bear claw is still there.

"Look," Dan says, glancing at Anna in an irritated way before turning back to Sim. "As long as we have no power, I'm responsible here. Do me a favor, don't fuck with the doors."

Sim lets the door fall closed, hands raised.

"I was awake, what else is there to do?" He goes to the fire, and grabs a mug where they sit warming on the hearth. "Temperature's dropping out there," he says. "This thing is going to get worse before it gets better."

Karolina and Dan look at each other.

"Right," Dan says. "I feel like we'll be back in business by the end of the day."

"Do we get to take a vote?" Sadie says. She hasn't moved from her chair, one leg crossed primly over the other. "Because I know who I'm inclined to believe."

Dan glares at her, his mouth set, but Karo catches his eye and he turns abruptly away.

"Keep her away from me," he says as though only Karo can hear.

He's proposed a group hike out to the eastern edge of the property, sort of a long way around to where the grounds meet a secondary road to town. The main gates are buried under snow, but farther out, they may find a whole different situation.

Maeve feels a wave of relief wash over her. If she can't distract herself in the studio, at least she won't have to sit still all day trying to avoid Dan's changing mood and her own constant worry. Getting outside will feel good: moving always makes her feel better, and she can see firsthand just what they're up against.

Sadie gets up and drifts toward the desk. At first Maeve assumes she's going to gather her things, but no, she just rifles through a file drawer as though she's looking for something, then leans there, listening.

"It's possible the access road's been plowed out," Dan says. "And if not, it's a clear day." He gestures brusquely to Sadie at the desk. "Bring that radio along, we should get a channel no problem."

"What if a crew shows up and we're all out on the ridge?" Justin says hazily.

He's gunning to stay behind himself, but it's of course Sadie who gets assigned the task. Keep the fire going, stay near the phone, listen for the *beep-beep* of an emergency road crew. It's the second time she's been left behind in two days. If the unsexiness of the job makes her sour, she hides it well, performing her efficiency with a brisk smile. She sets herself up at the desk as though she could just fire up her laptop and get some work done.

But her nails tap against the desktop as the rest of them bundle up for the outdoors. Dan hauls a load of snowshoes up from the basement storage room and shovels out a space at the back exit, enough room for six bodies, bent at the waist, to buckle them on.

Outside, the sun is high and bright, but Sim's words ring true: there's a new cold, sharp and biting. From the back door, Maeve can't see how bad the road looks where the western avalanche has made it impassable. Now she wonders if she really wants to know. The snowshoes are new and streamlined, and, looking around, Maeve realizes she's been given a child's pair—Dan guessing at her size. She works to lift her knees so the back edges won't catch and trip her up, falling into a strange kind of walking rhythm.

"I mean," she says, as much to herself as to Anna as they tromp through the snow, "it's only really been a day. Since the power went out. Like, a day and a half, but basically a day. It's easy to feel trapped up here, but in the scheme of things, it's not that serious."

Anna gives Maeve's shoulder a squeeze, but the gesture knocks them both off balance, and Maeve recovers by grabbing Anna's arm so she won't fall. They're laughing, and Maeve is grateful for the moment. The temperature has taken a serious dip. Anna flops along in her giant snowshoes, a scarf wound around her face so that just her eyes are showing. Her explanation, that she grew up in the South and never saw a snowflake until she was twenty-five, is a reasonable one. How can anyone be expected to grow used to this kind of cold?

There's a moment of quiet between them, both women relaxing into it. An unstated, easy closeness. Maeve glances up, gauging their privacy. Looking to see if the others are far enough ahead for the two of them to really talk. With Sadie left behind, it feels like the right time to tell Anna about her, how Sadie might get her kicks from spying on others or might have it in for Dan in some crazy way. She'd hate for Anna to get caught in the crossfire.

But it seems a shame to break the moment with something so ugly. She doesn't want to push Anna away.

"Look—" she begins, but Anna cuts her off.

"Hey, I didn't fuck things up for you last night, did I?"

Maeve tries to recalibrate.

"With Nielssen," Anna says. "I wondered if I was, you know. Interrupting. A cockblock. But for girls."

"Oh," Maeve says. "I believe the expression you want is *beaver dam.*"

"Yes. Did I dam your beaver?"

"You did not." Maeve looks ahead to where the others are, checking the distance between them again. She pulls her thin hood a little closer over her ears and gives a comical shrug. "I...just kinda wanted to go to bed. Is that bad?"

"He finds himself irresistible, so why wouldn't you?" Anna waits, but when Maeve doesn't respond right away, she puts on her best high-society accent: "Ohhhh—he thinks it's an affair."

"I don't know what he thinks," Maeve says. "Maybe I'm just thrown off by"—she gestures around them—"the unexpected winter wonderland. I thought it was a one-nighter! With a goddamn sculptor! Aren't artists supposed to be promiscuous loners?" She's laughing now. "I mean, *Gawd.*"

"Well, we weren't expecting to be up here playing Swiss Family Robinson in the snow," Anna says. "Maybe he's just bored."

Maeve nods and watches Sim walking up ahead.

Iain, in the first days she'd known him, seemed almost not to notice she was there. It was only later she learned he'd been watching her, taking her in, making decisions. On the fourth day, rehearsal was almost constantly interrupted—a dozen deliveries from a dozen different florists, the bouquets arriving every twenty minutes until she was apologizing to the rest of the dancers, the choreographer, the pianist, everyone. The little cards all blank. Who could have done this? It was over the top, embarrassing, but ultimately flattering. The flowers filled a whole corner of the room.

He was waiting in her dressing room at the end of day, leaning against the vanity when she opened the door. Almost shy. A last bouquet held out to her. Roses.

You're the prima here—I wanted to make sure everyone knew it.

She doesn't see any of that in Sim Nielssen. He was open and interested from the first moment. Honestly so.

She wonders now what might have happened if she'd told Iain no that first day. Or even after the first week. If she'd told him the flowers had actually made things difficult, had hardened the other dancers against her. By the time she tried to set a boundary, everything was going too fast; he'd convinced her to move cities, jump companies. He was her director and her lover, governing every minute of her every day.

Although last night, it seemed to be the no that was difficult for Sim.

Not that that makes him so different from any number of men she's known, of course. The years she spent with Iain swallowed her up, she sometimes thinks. She is always fighting her way out of them.

She turns back to Anna. "Look," she says again. "About you and Dan—"

But Anna's eyes flash a warning; Maeve, her head still turned, almost crashes into Karo from behind. Where the trail—if you could see the trail—splits off along the ridge, the others have stopped for a breath. Dan comes to stand between them, his attention flickering between the trail map and the hikers, setting the course for the next leg.

Too late now to mention Sadie. Again.

She snowshoes awkwardly aside, hoping to give herself some space. Near the ledge, she holds on to a branch for balance and peers down to the river below as she did that first day. The landscape has changed. The elk are no longer down there, the frozen river now buried deep in snow. She can see the cable of the SkyLift—they're so much closer now. She follows it with her eyes, back to where it begins, a wide platform set high up the ridge where the forest beds into rock. Like a ski lift, or one of those rides that carry you to the other side of the amusement park.

The snow slides slightly at her feet and she pulls herself back—remembering, suddenly, the woman who fell.

Someone calls to her and she turns. Karo is carrying the radio and a few Toblerone in a backpack, and she hands around the chocolate now. They can't stop for long; the cold is sharp and surprising. It hurts to breathe.

Maeve tries holding a hand over her face to warm the air before it enters her lungs. When the sugar is gone, they start walking again. The wind whips at them. There are no trees here, just open sky and rock—somewhere under all the snow.

They're only five minutes farther along when Dan stops cold.

There is no path anymore—they are making the path. But here, there's a wider swath that intersects it and cuts off northward. Another trail, left by a larger animal, and a depression in the snow where the thing paused. You could almost imagine that it was an elk—two or three elk together, maybe—except for what it's left behind.

The scat is large and fresh enough and would be sitting in the center of the path if the path still existed.

"Fur," Dan murmurs to himself, crouching to get a better look.

Maeve leans in to see for herself. Not just fur but bits of bone: it must have gotten a deer, or even an elk, somehow fallen away from the herd.

She feels winded, like she's been hit from behind. It's hard to speak.

"It's a good size." Dan rises to standing, still staring down at the thing.

"What does that mean," Anna says. Her voice comes up, agitated. "A good size? The bear or the poop?"

"It's hard to predict the size of the bear exactly." His tone is purposely casual, but he's surveying the woods to the north of them with a sharp eye. "It's a good size. I wouldn't normally say this is a black bear. But I lead a tracking expedition every year: we don't get grizzlies usually, not so close in."

Anna backs up to where Maeve is standing.

"At home, we don't even go for a picnic without a shotgun in the trunk of the car," she says. "Just in case an alligator shows up."

Maeve keeps her eye on Dan, thinking of the claw in her hip pocket. He's used to tracking bears in these mountains? That's something she didn't know.

"I thought there was a bear near my studio." Her shoulder brushes Anna's now, but she's speaking loud enough for everyone to hear. "Yesterday. Remember? I told you."

Dan looks put out.

"I told you," she says again, this time under her breath.

It takes all of Maeve's will to leave it there. Her stomach hurts. The day before, the bear was inside the tree line, close to human activity. What's strange here is how open the landscape is. There's no easy cover where they are, no place for an animal to shelter, nowhere to get out of the snow.

"Still nothing to worry about?" Anna says. "They're more afraid of us than we are of them?"

Justin tugs at the zipper of his parka. "I'd like to see the numbers on that," he says. "I'd like to read the interview where an actual bear states that to be the case."

Karo takes a few steps out, scanning the way ahead. There's no other sign of life, but the wind whipping at the top layer of snow has already covered their own tracks.

"Well, we're out here now," Sim says.

Karo's jaw tenses and she looks from Dan to Sim and back again.

"It's true," she says finally. "If the road is open, then problem solved."

Anna reaches into her pocket, pulls out a bell. "And here I thought I was being neurotic."

"Oh, handy," Justin says. "A dinner bell."

"We're a large group, we're making plenty of noise—" Sim says.

But Dan steps over to where Maeve and Anna are standing close. "Go ahead and wear the bell if it makes you feel better."

Sim turns and stalks past him, farther up the trail.

Dan pauses, but then he unclips the can of bear spray from his belt and tosses it to Karo. He takes a new one out of his pack.

"Front and rear guard," he says, pushing past Sim again.

They keep on, Anna's bell marking time now as they go, the three men in front and the women behind.

Maeve keeps her eyes on the horizon ahead and says nothing, but inside her mittens, her hands are curled into fists. Justin spins around, casual, as though he's just being social and not really looking behind them, but maybe just a little. His red scarf flutters slightly in the wind. For a moment he walks backward, narrating.

"It was only their snow pants that saved them—six overdressed *artistes* mauled at mountain colony," he says. "News at eleven."

He turns to face forward, tripping and recovering as he goes but making it stylish all the same.

It's another half hour of slogging before they finally come to where Dan thinks there should be a road.

There is no road.

"Okay," Dan breathes, and it's the first time his voice wavers. Maeve feels a hard squeeze in the center of her chest.

The western ridge snowpack, when it came down, sounded closest. The more immediate worry.

"And it was closer," Dan says now. "We know that's true. It's just that the trigger point of the avalanche here on the eastern side—"

"Trigger point?" Anna cuts in. "You mean they detonated? On purpose? I thought that never happened. You said next week—"

She looks to Karo, who answers in a grim voice.

"No. Nobody caused this. The trigger point is just the place where stress on the underlying layer becomes too much. Once one piece gives way—"

"It's where the avalanche begins," Dan says.

He says he'd thought it was farther off.

From here they can see the path the slab took down the side of the mountain, maybe a mile wide. Much bigger than any of them had imagined, a trail of ice and debris that rises up ahead where they'd expected the valley to dip low.

"Okay," Dan says again, and he moves automatically to Karolina's side, unzips her pack, and draws the radio out.

Maeve turns and looks back the way they came rather than out at the damage ahead. The center, she knows, lies far below them now: too far away to see and hidden, anyway, by the woods between. She can hear Dan and Karolina conferring over the radio, the hand crank turning jerkily around. Dan already doubling-down on his detached calm, his *Father Knows Best* bullshit. Maeve pulls her sweater up over her chin against the cold. She holds her mittens over her nose.

There is no road. There is no crew working on the power lines. There aren't even utility poles anymore.

"Let me see your face."

She turns to find Sim standing beside her, squinting down against the snow's glare. There's a high sun but the cold is brutal now. Maeve, lost in the anxiety of the moment, lets her hands drop to her sides.

"Here." He pulls the fur-lined hat off his own head and holds it out, but Maeve can't move. She just looks at him. "Here," he says again, and this time he tugs her hood down himself and fits the hat snugly over her ears, tucking the fur trim deep into the neckline of her coat. The difference is immediate: Maeve melts into it, relief running through her in response to the new warmth. It's a kind gesture, and he moves more gently than she expects. But then he turns and shouts over his shoulder: "We need to head back, Maeve can't be out here any longer."

"What's going on?" Anna looks over from where she is watching the radio trials.

"She's not built for this, she'll have frostbite if we stay out here."

Maeve only shrugs a little deeper into her coat. She is cold. She is not sure if she is in danger. How do you know? She watches as Anna kicks through the snow toward them, her bell chiming merrily.

"What are you, Dr. Nielssen now?"

"It's not a fucking joke." He turns back to Maeve, but Anna keeps coming.

"It's not a fucking joke, man—" His words, her own mocking tone.

Maeve can see Sim bristle, but it's Dan who cuts her off, yelling from behind them: "Anna! Cool it."

Maeve looks to her, surprised. Anna slowly turns around, but Karo calls out before either of them have a chance to respond.

"We just need a bit more time! The cold is making it difficult to charge."

Dan says nothing more now. He's crouched low in the snow, focused on cranking the radio.

"It's a goddamn emergency radio," Sim says under his breath. "What do you mean it doesn't work in the cold?" Then, louder: "I'll take Maeve back to the center myself."

Dan jerks to his feet.

"No. We stay together."

"I'm really fine," Maeve says. "I'll be fine. I'd rather give them some time—"

"Can you give them five fucking minutes?" Justin has had his back to everyone, looking out to where the road should have been, but now he whips around. His face is buried inside his hood, the red scarf cutting a line at his chin. He's lost his customary flippancy: the change is stark. "Give them five minutes to figure out if anyone even remembers we're out here?"

Karolina marks the edge in his voice and steps in.

"Of course they know we're up here. That's not even an issue. It's just a matter of getting a timeline on the road being dug out." But she's cold too; Maeve can see that her hands are trembling.

"Let me see now," Anna says, hooking a finger into the edge of the hat where it comes in at Maeve's cheek. She pulls it aside and gives her face a quick scan. "You look fine," she says. Then, turning to Sim: "But this was a nice touch, Dr. Nielssen, very chivalrous."

If Maeve wasn't so numb, she'd say something. Crack a joke, even, on Justin's behalf. Break the tension. But she just tugs the hat on more securely and turns away.

"Fine," Sim says. "We'll just let the next person freeze."

Dan has his gloves off, trying to hold the heat of his skin to the radio crank.

"It's no good," he says finally. "Nielssen's right, we should get back before anyone loses a toe."

Maeve thinks Sim must be pleased, at least, that he's been vindicated, but he doesn't say a word to her or anyone.

The way back is marked by silence. They move faster, in part to stay warm, in part just to put the disappointment behind them. The sunshine that buoyed her spirits on waking is long gone, replaced by a new and dense bank of low cloud. Maeve can't shake the feeling that there is something there, behind them—a shifting darkness, unstoppable. But when she finally turns to look, there's nothing. Only the mountain itself.

Wind rips at them. She can see in the distance where the new storm is closing in, already on their heels. The snowshoes catch and flap and she wonders if she could run with them on, how long it would take to get the damn things off if she needed to.

The snow starts blowing as they approach the river valley; this time, Dan leads them into the trees. There's no path, anyway, he says. They need to take a more sheltered route.

Anna stops.

"What about the bear?"

The group slows around her. Maeve checks over her shoulder, then ahead into the trees. Too many branches, too close together to see much at all. And something else: it takes Maeve a moment to put her finger on it. The usual chatter of the forest, birds or squirrels or other little animals, is missing. The place is marked by a terrible stillness, the only sound the creak of trees in the wind.

"We're just as unlikely to meet a bear in the woods as out of it," Karo says. "Isn't that true, Dan?"

Dan says he wouldn't suggest anything he didn't think was safe. He says they're a big, noisy group—as though Sim hadn't said exactly the same thing earlier. She wonders if he likes this plan only because he's the one putting it forward.

Anna hesitates, and Maeve holds out a hand to her.

"It's faster," Maeve says. "We'll be able to think more clearly once we get back, when we're inside."

This has the ring of good sense to it, although even Maeve is not sure she believes it. She knows she is cold and getting colder, and there's a rising panic she can feel in her chest. Anna looks from Dan to Karo, then back to Dan, waiting for him to give her a nod before she begins to move again.

Maeve keeps her eyes on the ground, struggling through deep snow that is mined with bush hazards. If she focuses on making a path, she won't worry about what's going to happen next. Or what won't happen.

No road, no radio, no radio, no road. It's the wrong mantra, unhelpful, but she keeps coming back to it.

They're only a few hundred yards into the trees when she feels Anna pull up and freeze in front of her. The bell gives a dull clank. Anna's reaction is so sudden, Maeve's stomach drops. She looks up.

"No one move," Dan says.

Elk. There are elk all around them, still as the trees. Where the branches have been swept of snow, they camouflage the herd, and Maeve struggles to count them all, her eyes moving from cow to cow. The females are big enough on their own—but she's looking for antlers. Early snow or not, it's still the rut. You don't want to get caught between a bull and a cow. An elk bull can be almost as big as a young moose.

There are three cows all within arm's length to Maeve's left, and more ahead. How did they get so far into the forest without noticing them? The one closest flares her nostrils, her breath a puff of steam. She steps forward. Maeve steps back.

"We can make it through."

This is Sim, quietly.

"No," Dan says.

"We're already almost through."

"No."

Maeve checks behind her. There are a scattered few cows to each side, but their path, the path they forged through the snow, is still clear.

"It's just a bunch of females, there's nothing to worry about." Sim starts moving again, trying to force them to press on. "We'll be in more trouble out in the open if the storm catches us."

But when she looks ahead, Maeve sees one bull, and then a second one, up higher in the forest. Antlers disguised among the branches.

"It's both herds," Karo says. She's remarkably still, her hands wedged in her pockets, arms tight at her sides. "I can't believe how many."

"Best not to turn around. Move backward," Dan says.

"It's three times as far if we go back," Sim says. He strides forward a step and one of the cows snorts, then stamps the ground nervously.

"You need to stop arguing." Dan doesn't turn his head as he speaks, focused on the herd, his jaw set.

Anna is already backing up. From somewhere to their right comes the high, haunted call—like a wraith, Maeve had said that first night. Now it sounds more painful than that, sharper. She moves lightly backward, high-stepping so that the snowshoes won't trip her up.

Sim is the last one to follow.

He's right, in a way: by the time they retrace their steps and find their old path back to the center, the light is failing. It's a long walk, and deeply cold.

When they reach the center's back exit, it's clear that Karo expects Sadie to be there to let them in—but she's not. There's a beat, Karo knocking on the glass, before Sim reaches out and simply pulls the door open himself. He turns to Dan.

"Glad enough I rigged it now."

He holds it open for Maeve and she is first inside—which is why she is the only one to actually see Sadie before the others pile in behind her. Sadie in profile, the soft click of Sim's gallery door as she exits, tension showing on her face. She turns the key in the lock and then she's skittering to the doorway to greet them, the others all crowding in behind Maeve. Her worried look evaporating into a staged smile.

But there's no time to process it; Karo already has five tasks lined up for Sadie. The two women hurry off to the kitchen and Sim bends over the fire, building it higher. Anna and Justin crash around at the door, trying to help Dan organize the snowshoes in sets and get them back down to storage, leaving Maeve alone, her fingers white with cold. She glances one more time at the gallery door and then heads slowly upstairs for a change of socks and a new sweater.

The fire is burning high and hot by the time she gets back. There's a bottle of whiskey and they pass it around. No one makes tea now, although there's soup, excavated from the freezer and set in the pot by the fire, and more bread thawing out on the hot stonework next to it.

Maeve watches the others drink and thinks crazy thoughts.

She knows they must be crazy, but it's hard to stop them coming. The debris field is too wide, the avalanche too close, the lack of contact with the town below too strange. There's been some kind of annihilation. The disaster caused not by extreme weather but by an explosion.

If this—whatever it is, a war? a terrorist attack of some kind?—has reached the middle of nowhere, then what is happening in the cities? Did her mother ever bring the kids back home?

Maeve finds herself holding her breath. It's essential for her to picture life going on as usual, the subway running, school lunch being served at noon on reusable plastic, and she works hard to imagine just this: Talia eating a plate of macaroni at a table of little girls set up in a grade-school gym. Rudy putting on his snow pants for kindergarten play.

She refocuses, forcing herself to come back to the moment and the room of—what should she call them? Her companions? Survivors?

They're still talking about the elk.

"So strange," Karo says. Her voice is cloudy. Exhausted. "For there to be so many all in one place. How they even climbed out of the valley with so much snow..." They usually don't come so high into the forest, not in winter, she says.

The radio is at her feet, but she's stopped trying for a channel. She hasn't touched it since they got back.

Beside her, Sadie plays with Justin's camera. She pokes at him, teasing: It was just sitting under the chair where he'd left it, she says. After all that fuss. Why can't men ever find things?

"Say cheese!" She spins toward Anna. "It's a snow-day miracle!"

But Sadie was warm and dry by the fire all afternoon. The rest of them aren't in the mood for games.

Or, not by the fire after all—but skulking around in the gallery and who knows where else. Maeve checks for the bear claw in her hip pocket. Still there. She wonders now if it could have been Sadie who snuck into her room? To what end?

And the gallery key—is it her own, given to her, or did she take it from the desk? Maeve shakes her head; she's starting to sound paranoid even to herself. Maybe Sadie is just on the hook to clean the space now that the housekeepers are no longer here. Another drudgery job inflicted on her by Karo.

But that wouldn't explain what she was doing down in the spa, peering through doorways. There's still no easy answer for that.

"Animals do weird things after—" Dan starts, but he falters, trying to find the right word. Maeve brings her attention back to the group: Not *"disaster."* *Don't start using words like that.* "After an event like this," he says finally.

"Nature turns to chaos," Sim says, looking at Anna. The theme of her project, her werewolf film. He goes to refill his mug but finds the bottle empty and gets up to retrieve a new one.

"This isn't chaos. It's predictable." Justin slings his legs over the arm of his chair and settles in. "My first job, like, as an intern? Climatology beat—"

"You mean weather boy," Anna says.

More sniping. Maeve reaches for the radio to try it herself, but her fingertips barely graze the handle before Karo skims it with her foot, moving it deftly under her own chair.

"Leave it alone." She doesn't even turn to look at Maeve as she speaks.

Verboten. Sim mouths the word from where he's standing with the new bottle, behind Anna's chair. Maeve just nods, confused.

"I mean, they were talking about this kind of extreme weather long before my time. Way long. Thirty years ago, easy," Justin says. "When you think of it that way, nothing the animals might do feels weird—"

"Even sneaking down the mountain, right, Maeve?" Dan stumbles a little as he rises to his feet.

She doesn't know why he's singling her out. Because she insisted on talking about the bear outside her studio? Because she didn't give him the reaction he wanted when he surprised her there, letting himself in with his own key? She wonders now what his expectation had been.

"Next thing you know, we'll be tracking prints right into your room—" He lurches forward, drawing the flashlight off his tool belt like a pistol and flicking it on. "There it is! Under your bed! Hiding in your suitcase!" The light glares in her eyes.

She pulls back. In her suitcase?

Still in her seat, Anna blanches. "Stop being an idiot, Dan. You're blinding her."

A prickle rises on Maeve's arms, the back of her neck. If Dan leads tracking expeditions, he probably has his share of souvenirs—even a bear claw or two. Maeve feels her throat tighten.

But he switches off the light and turns to the others, only looking for a laugh. He stumbles again, and there's something of the lumberyard in it—not so much the woodcutter, but the falling tree.

She tries to shake it off. He's drunk. They're all drunk.

Except Maeve.

She stands and walks to the far end of the lobby. At first, she just wants some space: she's afraid she might scream and wants to remove herself before it happens. She extends an arm to rest on the back of a chair and squeezes her eyes shut.

She doesn't want to cry, not here. All she can see are Talia and Rudy: Rudy's small face in a rearview mirror. Talia's fingers tight around Maeve's arm, reaching for her from the back seat as Maeve drives down a highway at night. They didn't go through all of that, everything it took to leave Iain, to finally be free, only for her to die up here in the mountains and abandon them.

When she opens her eyes again, she can see herself reflected in the plate-glass window. Pale, a silhouette. She pulls up straight, as though she is not lost in the center foyer but standing at the barre. Far behind her, there is the flicker of the fire, the others grouped around it.

She begins to warm up.

"What are you doing," Anna calls.

Maeve keeps her eyes locked on her own reflection, her pelvis tucked. Toe pointed, calf tight, *tendu-tendu-tendu.*

"I'm going to work," she says. "They won't let me leave, so I'll do it here." Out into second position, down into a plié, up into a rise. "If Sim can work, then so can I."

She keeps the warm-up sequence brief, just getting herself in order before moving into the open and taking up space.

At first, the others are silent, uncomfortable, but after a moment Maeve can hear the murmurs of conversation start up again behind her. The clink of the ladle in the soup pot.

She tries to pick up where she left off on the day of the avalanche, working to remember short bursts, stringing together one little series after another. The more physically demanding she makes it, the more likely she can clear her mind. There's no music and no beat. She keeps the count in her head, punctuating with staccato movements, heel-drop-dig-dig-dig-and-lunge, and from there working out wider, moving down to the floor and pressing up again, then letting herself fall. Up on her feet, contract-release-contract-release. And suddenly, she's ecstatic: the sequence—what she can see of it—is radically unpretty. It looks like work, it looks just the way she wants it to. There's sweat in her eyes and she drops to the floor again.

On the ground, she notices something new in the glass: they've shifted, all of them, to watch her. A quick burst of energy through her muscles, a spark of power. She rises to her knees, spins and arches, turns to face them but then sharply away again. *Don't get distracted. Stay here, stay with this.* The next time she spins back, Sadie is slumped in her chair, and Anna, glaring at her, has Justin's camera in hand. She signals to Maeve, then gets down on one knee, filming.

So there'll be a record of this, Maeve thinks. *If I ever get home to use it.*

Sadie now trying to pretend to look elsewhere, but Dan and Sim, not at all. Karo, head tilted in stern appraisal. Anna's words: *She handpicks*

126

her artists and then she thinks she owns us. Like Maeve's mother from the wings.

Maeve closes her eyes to shut them all out. She's used to an audience at rehearsals, she knows how to use this energy when she needs it. She also knows when it's time to focus and pretend she's alone in the room.

Her leg extends, pulls in, extends: she pushes up on her hands and drags her body across the floor.

She flicks her head up. When she looks back, Sim is on his feet, moving slowly around the edge of the room toward her. But this isn't the same as a remote audience: it feels invasive, as though he might step in or cut her off. She rises and turns away but on her next spin, Maeve finds herself growing wilder, faster, more athletic. Punchy. No—punched up.

He draws closer. She can see him coming in the window glass and for a moment she cannot look away. She is watching him get near, grow larger in reflection. From the corner of her eye, she sees the others in their seats, glued to this new spectacle. Anna on her feet now, changing her angle—Maeve realizes that it is no longer herself alone but the two of them, Maeve and Sim together, on display.

The spell breaks. Maeve turns away—arch and extend, lift, arch—she pours forward at a run, spins, starts again.

Sim paces along the wall now, back and forth, watching her. *Why the fuck doesn't someone tell him to sit down?* Her foot flexed and lifting high, out, down, back, a compass turn, the leg coming in sharply and propelling her around. She falls and pushes up. For a minute, she gets lost in herself again and it feels good—he's gone from her line of sight.

Then, as she's springing up into a leap, she catches him, up on the open staircase now—looking down at her from above.

Maeve lands hard and stumbles, then falls for real, the same hip and shoulder slamming the ground, and she swears out loud. When she gets up again, she curves over, hands resting on knees. She is panting. Overhead, Sim stares down at her, the beginning of a smile.

From the other side of the room, a slow clap starts up. Justin rises to his feet.

"Oh, fuck off," Maeve says.

"A tremendous effort," Justin says. "I'll file my review in the morning."

She feels flushed and drops into a low squat, hugging herself, eyes shut, while she catches her breath. She opens them when someone touches her arm. Anna. Offering water.

Back in her chair, Sadie has picked up Justin's camera again and hunches over it, the camera cradled in her arms. Something about it tugs at Maeve, but she's light-headed and only squints vaguely in her direction, trying to figure out what. Dan gestures solemnly to Anna to rejoin the group, but she turns away and gets down on her haunches instead.

"You don't look well," Anna says.

Maeve takes the mug and drinks, then hands it back.

"I want to go to bed."

Sim comes down the stairs. Anna cracks a new bottle of bourbon and pours a few shots into the mug. She glances at Dan before turning back to Maeve.

"I'll walk you," she says.

Upstairs, Maeve pauses at her door.

"What do you think happens next?" she says.

"We go home," Anna says.

"Are you sure?"

Maeve glances down the hall in each direction. An odd feeling they aren't alone, but maybe she's just spooked by the shadows; it's always so dark in the halls now. She brings her phone up a little higher, shining the flashlight first one way, then the other.

Maybe it's just the leftover effect of their eyes on her, all of them, when she was working to focus on herself.

"Your kids," Anna says. "They're with your parents? What about Dad?"

"He's gone."

Anna thinks on that.

"He was the AD for a big company," Maeve says. "Artistic director. Iain. Everything was fine when he was working. When he was home—" That pins-and-needles prickle at her temples, her wrists. She shakes her head. "When I left him, I thought he might kill me."

She looks down at the scar along her hand. For a second, she's back in that studio, shards of broken mirror lying on the floor.

I fell in love with your dancing, Maeve. How are you going to dance now?

"I used to try and fight back. That was the problem. I was all muscle in those days, you'd think I'd be able to hold my own. Wouldn't you? Think I'd stand a chance?"

For once, Anna has lost her spirit. Her mouth is set, grim.

"Baby, no—"

"Spoiler: It wasn't even a tie. It wasn't even close."

"But he's not there now?" The grim expression turning to alarm.

"No." Maeve plays with the key in her hand. "No, he's dead."

Anna raises her eyebrows.

"That's what I mean. I did leave him, finally. Three years ago," Maeve says. She's talking quickly now. "But it didn't solve anything. He wouldn't agree to a divorce. The kids and I had to move every few months just to get away, and he'd always follow. He used to sit outside my house, look in the windows. Just to scare me." Maeve presses her lips together. "People think that only happens in bad neighborhoods."

She lifts her shoulders, takes a breath: she didn't know she needed to tell this story, not in the midst of all this. The chaos of the avalanche opening the door to old fear.

"But then he died—" she says. "Four months ago. And now everything is solved. It's weird, to be honest."

Anna shakes her head, taking the story in.

"I'm sorry," she says. "I think?"

"I don't know how to feel. He died in a shooting. Just coincidence," Maeve says. "I mean, it's crazy if you think about it. All those years I couldn't get away."

She takes a breath. Holds up her hand, flashes the scar on her palm.

"The day after I left him. I had just started working again, secretly, and he followed me to the studio. Knocked me around a bunch. But then—" She pauses. "Then he kicked a mirror in. The whole thing shattered. And for a second, everything stopped. Glass everywhere, like daggers. I could see myself in the mirror, from across the room, just lying there. I had a piece of it in my hand. It was like he'd given me a weapon."

She shakes her head.

"But I got scared and waited a moment too long. I was going to, I don't know—" She's only ever talked about this in bits and pieces—to her lawyer, her therapist. Now, the whole thing in one go: it feels like a wave. "Stab him, I guess," she says. Then, harsher: "Stab him in the throat." She holds out her scarred palm again. "I got this instead."

Maeve shrugs.

"After all that, he goes on tour and dies in a hotel bar."

"Nature turns to chaos," Anna says. "Always."

They both stand there in the hall without moving. Maeve doesn't open her door.

"How'd you ever manage to leave?" Anna asks finally.

"Most people only ask why I stayed."

"That's a garbage question." Anna reaches for Maeve's hand and Maeve suddenly wonders about the husband back home—the insistent, twice-daily calls and why Anna might need a break. Might need whatever she has going with Dan.

"Hey." Anna gives the hand a squeeze. "Listen. Want me to sleep over?" She breaks into the beginnings of a smile. "Come on, I could just take the room next to you. So you're not alone."

It's a perfect offer, but Maeve hesitates. She wants to be fine, to believe they will be fine. She's about to be a grown-up and say *No* for real when they hear the creak of the stairwell door. Maeve glances to the dark hall. She looks back at Anna.

"This can't be him again? Like last night—" Her brow furrows. "Can it?"

But she's right: it's Sim who appears, his face a carved shadow in the light of his own lantern. He's carrying the whiskey bottle in his other hand.

"Everything all right, ladies?"

He's talking to Maeve, his eyes on her.

"I'll get my things," Anna says. She looks at Sim oddly, then at Maeve, before heading off to the stairs. Her own room is one floor up.

There's a brief, awkward silence as they both watch her go. When the stairwell door closes behind her, Sim turns back to Maeve.

"Here. You left this downstairs." He gestures to his coat pocket: the hat she borrowed peeks out of it, just the fur trim. "Go on," he says. "Take it, my hands are full." When she doesn't immediately reach for him, he steps closer. "Go on."

It's uncomfortable just standing there. After a moment, Maeve draws the hat from his pocket.

"I don't really need it," she says.

"Hang it on the knob," Sim says. "If you leave your door unlocked."

There's a pause as she takes this in. She moves back, thinking to put a little distance between them, but her heel hits the wall behind her, and he steps closer.

"I'm pretty tired," Maeve says.

"Are you?" He's probably a full ten inches taller, but he dips his head to meet her eyes. The effect is the opposite of equalizing. She feels, if anything, shorter, more obviously tiny in comparison. "I was watching you today," he says.

"I—" Maeve drops her gaze, smiling a little despite herself. Not sure what to say. "I know, I saw that."

"No. Not just now. Out in the snow, I mean. Even like that, when you're in three layers of clothes, I can see the dancer in you. It's mesmerizing." He sets the lantern down, and the light flares up from their feet. "There's no time you're not aware of your body, is there? All your moving parts. That piece you were working on downstairs—"

"I was just fooling around. Trying to stay warm."

"No—"

"Yeah—"

He cuts her off. "No, I don't think so. It looked like something. It looked like a fight. Like you were tethered, you know? God, I'd love to use it somehow."

"Use it?" She can almost feel the heat of his body. That's how close they're standing. She has to tilt her chin up to look at him, but it somehow makes her nervous, embarrassed, something. She's not sure.

"In the gallery." He keeps on, gesturing with his free hand, the long fingers hovering, gripping some object in his mind. "Roped to the ground, but fighting like a goddamn wild thing. You could work that in: a big rope, big braid of sailing cord. And there's you, fighting against it. Like some fierce little animal. Staring down the barrel of a gun."

He's standing there with an instructive look, as though he's really considering art and not just forcing her to imagine being tied up.

"That's what you should call it," he says. *Trigger Point.* He relaxes, flicks the hat with a finger. "I'm glad we saved your pretty face."

She wants to look away but doesn't. She can feel her jaw tighten, her tongue against the back of her teeth.

"I'm tired," she says again. Her eyes steady on his. "I'm tired, Sim. I need a break tonight. From this."

They're standing there like that when the stairwell door opens again. Maeve turns her head, relieved. Anna, coming back along the hall. She's got her backpack on one shoulder, the mug of booze still in one hand. In the other, she brandishes the key to the next room.

"Success!"

Sim steps back and watches her open the room next door. To Maeve: "Too nervous to sleep alone?"

Anna swings out from the door, her backpack swaying. "And what do you think has made her so nervous, hey? I mean, can you think of anything? No? How about anyone?"

Maeve hands the hat back to Sim.

"It's fine, Anna." She ducks a little to get around him to her own door. "The last thing any of us needs is midnight drama in the Overlook Hotel." She's cracking wise to get things over with. She looks back to Sim. "Right, sir?"

He bends to retrieve his lantern.

"Everything goes into the work, Maeve. Everything. You and I are the only ones who really understand that." He turns to Anna, raising the bottle in her direction. "Chin-chin."

"Go to sleep, Nielssen," Anna says.

He nods to Maeve just once before turning to walk back down the hall.

"*Trigger Point,*" he calls. "Don't forget I gave you that. It's a good name."

Anna cocks her head at this, questioning. When he's gone, she breaks the silence:

"What was that about?"

But Maeve just shakes her head. She'd rather forget the whole thing.

There's an adjoining door between the rooms, and for a little while, it feels like a slumber party: Anna pacing around in a long nightgown, her coat thrown over her shoulders like a shawl; Maeve gesturing with her toothbrush as they talk. A storm lantern on the floor spills light like a campfire. Outside, snow is blowing in heavy and wet, the world only white. Even on the sill it's piled up ten inches deep. There is less window than there used to be.

No new sounds from the hallway. Sim's room is on the floor above, where Anna has been sleeping; the permanent staff are all two floors below.

"I'll grab that footage of you off Justin's camera tomorrow," Anna says. "Maybe we'll get to work together after all." She does a few dance moves of her own. "That fluidity—that kind of feeling in my transformation scene—I mean, if you're down, obviously."

"Transformation?" How easily they all move into collaboration here.

Anna stops and strikes a pose.

"Remember? I told you! I'm trying to use the bear dreams as a werewolf narrative. Mostly I keep the camera on Dan. You know. When we're—" She bites her lip. Maeve drops her jaw in mock surprise, and Anna laughs. "He's a specimen, that's all I'm saying. Not hard to turn him into an animal."

"He's your werewolf." Maeve nods, suddenly getting it. Then something occurs to her: "Wait—and he lets you?"

"He doesn't—" She pauses, reconsidering her words. "He doesn't love it. That's why he's so touchy about Justin's camera—kind of takes it out on him, I guess." Anna shrugs. "He'll get over it," she says. "They both will."

But her tone seems unconvincing. Maeve stalls on that, wondering if Dan really knows. Is this what Sadie was doing there—helping Anna somehow? Or keeping track, for Karo?

She rifles through the pocket of her jeans, now discarded on the floor, and fishes out the bear claw. "Look, I'm not sure about Dan," she says. "I'm not sure he's safe. Remember this?"

"Uh—" Anna's shoulders come up slightly.

"I think Dan broke into my room. I think he put this into my suitcase."

"Oh, Maeve, no—"

"He's been following me around. The way he came to the studio, and even the first night—"

"No, I mean—" Anna stops, then flops onto the floor, cross-legged. "I did that."

There's a beat, and then Maeve drops to her knees beside her.

"What?"

"I did it. I put it in your bag." Anna puts her hands together as if in prayer, pleading. "I'm sorry? I mean, yeah, Dan knew—I got him to let me have the master key. That's why he made that shitty joke tonight. But I had to beg him! You were having those dreams, and I just wanted to see if it would, you know—trigger something for you. An image, something cool. Something I could use? I really didn't think—"

But Maeve is whirling with relief.

"Holy fuck. I've been driving myself crazy."

"To be honest, I thought—" Anna pauses, trying to find the words. "I guess I thought you'd see the gag right away. Then when you didn't, I don't know. I just let it play out?"

Maeve puts her face in her hands, then looks up. She starts to laugh.

"No, it's fine. It's good, actually. I built this up into a huge thing. So stupid of me. Like I said, my ex—Iain—" She shakes her head. "I'm just used to things being scary, I guess."

"I'm so sorry," Anna says again. "We've got to get you used to something better. It was a dumb prank." She gets up to go, then changes her mind, hovering there. "You've been through a lot, huh?"

Maeve moves up onto the bed.

"Iain? I only wish—" She glances away and then back again, meeting Anna's eye. It's been a long time since she had a girlfriend like this. "The real truth is I'm just sorry I didn't kill him myself."

There's a silence and Maeve wonders if the admission was a mistake. Too much. But Anna comes close again, perches on the edge of the mattress.

"Just remember," she says, "you got yourself out. That's the person you are: you got yourself out." She stays there a moment longer, then nods to Maeve. "You sure you don't want me to bunk right in with you?"

Maeve says no. She needs to feel like an adult. She needs to feel at home in her skin.

"We're getting out of here tomorrow," Anna says. "I promise. But tonight, take this—" She hands Maeve her mug of whiskey, still half full. "I don't need any more. And you could use some sleep."

She douses the lantern before she goes, closing the door between their rooms softly behind her. Maeve sips the whiskey in bed, the buzz reaching her cheekbones. Just as she's drifting off, there's a knock or some sound from next door.

"Anna?" She lifts her head a little, but her eyes are heavy. There's no other noise. Maeve thinks, *It's the bear, outside.* A nonsense thought.

She knocks on the wall, shave-and-a-haircut.

"Good night," she calls to Anna, or to no one, since Anna is already asleep. She sets the empty mug aside and sinks down into her duvet, wrapping herself up. Safe.

Sim's wrong about her. She didn't get frostbite. No tether can hold her down.

She's built for whatever comes.

DAY 6

IN THE MORNING, there is still no change—no signal and no road crew blasting up the hill in a high-powered plow. Maeve doesn't wake to any sound of rescue. She wakes up because it's cold.

This is the first thing Maeve notices and it's the first morning she's woken like this: shivering under her extra blankets, under the feather duvet. Her breath hangs in the air. Not a puff, but pure mist.

Karolina is up and by the fire, so the lobby is warm when Maeve comes down. Dan with a serious look to him, drinking tea but not speaking. Karo looks like she hasn't slept. She wants to call a meeting, but the others are still straggling in: Sim, carrying a piece of whalebone he's whittling into some small detail, his own fingers bone white with cold. Justin still in his robe. Sadie, silently trucking hot water from the fire to the kitchen to wash some cups, then crouching by the hearth to make coffee. When nine o'clock rolls around, Maeve runs up to get Anna—it's strange that she's not down here yet. Every other morning, she's been up and around long before nine.

"Anna?" Maeve leans on the door in the hallway, knocking. When there's no answer, she tries going into her own room and knocking on the adjoining door. "Anna! It's late."

When there is still no answer, Maeve wonders if she can just barge in.

She hesitates at the door. What if it's just that Anna couldn't sleep last night, or she's finally lost her nerve? Maybe she hasn't overslept. Maybe she wants to be alone. There's a part of Maeve that gets it. Why not just stay in bed until this is all over?

"Oh, Anna, for God's sake," she says, opening the adjoining door and swinging into the room.

But Anna is not in bed. The bed, in fact, is barely rumpled, as though she'd gotten up and thrown the covers back into place to keep her spot warm while she—what? Went to pee? Got a drink of water?

The bathroom door stands open, but Anna is not in there either. Maeve hesitates for a moment and then, childishly, pulls the wardrobe door open. But there's only Anna's winter coat hanging in there, alone among the empty hangers, and the boots she wore the day before on the hike.

Maeve crosses back, passing through her own room again—as though Anna could somehow have snuck by her, a game—and then goes downstairs, expecting to find her there now, drinking the last of the coffee by the fire. But in the lobby, Sadie is the only one by the hearth, stirring her own cup with a tinkling spoon. Karo looks up.

"Well?"

"She isn't here?" Maeve says.

"Where?"

"I mean, she didn't come down while I was gone?"

Karo gets to her feet.

"She isn't up there," Maeve says. "So she must be down here somewhere."

"Christ," Dan says. "How many times do I have to say everyone stays together till this is over?"

Karo doesn't say a word to this but simply turns and walks into the dining room, the heels of her boots clicking against the wood floor. Justin looks up from where he's been relacing his own boots by the fire.

"I haven't seen her since last night," he says. "Sadie? How about you?"

Sadie taps her spoon against the rim of her mug a final time before answering.

"I think she was planning to sleep somewhere else. If you know what I mean."

Karo arrives back from her quick tour of the kitchen just in time to hear this.

"What *do* you mean?" she says. She glances sharply at Dan.

"She came down and got an extra key—"

Maeve cuts in. "She wanted to keep me company. I was anxious," she says. "Anna slept in the room next to mine."

Sadie's face changes on hearing this— less smug, more stung. It's not what she was expecting. Karo pulls the master key from the desk.

"So you didn't really check her room at all," she snaps. "You just checked your own and the one next to it."

She starts for the stairwell, but when Maeve jumps up to join her, she spins around.

"No," she says. "Everyone else waits here."

Maeve stays put, but her heart is ringing in her chest. Stupid of her not to check Anna's usual room. She turns slowly back to the fire. Sim meets her eye from where he's working, knife in hand. Then he looks away, goes back to it.

After a minute, they hear Karo's steps echoing down the stairs. She's running.

"She's not in either room. She's not in the common room on any floor. Are there any other rooms she has a key to?" She looks at each of the men in turn.

"Why am I a suspect?" Justin says.

"It's not funny," Karo says. "What if she went outside?"

"Why would she go outside?" Justin stomps a foot heavily into his boot. "To make sure the wasteland is still intact? To play damsel in distress?"

"Her coat is still—" Maeve starts, but Dan speaks over her.

"She sleepwalks sometimes."

Karo's face stiffens, but she doesn't turn or acknowledge him. To Justin: "She smokes," she says tautly.

There's a moment when no one says anything.

"Even if she did go out, Nielssen screwed up the lock," Dan says. His voice is calm and even, meant to restore order. "I looked at it yesterday afternoon, couldn't fix it. You wouldn't have any trouble getting back in." But he's already on his feet. "Right. For once, we split up—everyone take a floor, that way there's no possibility of missing her. Meet back here in twenty."

Maeve takes the back stairwell on her own, the soft clang of her footsteps echoing against the walls. It's quiet and she wishes she'd thought to check for Anna's bag when she was still up in the room, her cigarettes, any hint of where she might have gone. It crosses her mind, briefly, that this might all be a game: hide-and-seek, a great joke on Anna's part. That they will return to the lobby to find her there, feet up by the fire, laughing. *Y'all need to lighten up.*

She's in the second-floor hallway calling Anna's name when Sim comes around the corner from the other stairs. Before he can say anything, she holds a hand up and pulls back.

"Not now."

He slows down, and then he surprises her.

"Of course. Maeve—"

She's already turning to go but he reaches out and brushes her arm, gently, then lets his hand fall to his side. She looks back over her shoulder, wary.

"I wanted to apologize, actually."

This isn't what she's expecting and it catches her off guard. She stays there, mid-turn, a protective stance.

"For last night," he says. He comes a little closer, but not much. "I was drunk, and pushy. I was an asshole. You don't need that."

Maeve has an urge to scan the hall, to see if this is for someone else's benefit. After a moment, she lets herself glance to her other side, but they are alone.

"It's all right," she says finally. "Thank you. Thanks for saying that."

"Everything is—it's just a lot right now, and I shouldn't have pushed you like that."

"Okay."

It occurs to her that they were all supposed to split up and search for Anna, but he has come searching for Maeve instead.

"I should go—" she begins, meaning to break away.

"So we're all right, then?"

She's about to say, *Yes, whatever, just go back to looking for Anna,* when she hears the shouting.

At first, she thinks it is good news.

Maeve spins, leaving Sim to jog behind her as she goes flying down the stairs and arrives breathless in the lobby. Not only shouting. A pounding noise—Dan is kicking at the glass, the whole door shuddering with the effort. Anna's frozen body in his arms.

The lock has engaged after all. Sadie has to push the door open from the inside to let him in.

"We need blankets!" He's cursing as he rushes inside: "Move! Where the fuck was everybody?"

He saw something from the third-floor window, he says—the words pouring out almost too fast for them to catch. A shadow or some weird chunk of ice. He ran outside and that's where he found her: Anna, half burrowed against the wall, almost out of sight. Her knees curled tight into her chest.

Dan lays her down by the fire to start CPR, but her legs are still half pulled into her body, and he has to try and straighten them to give himself room. Close by, Sadie sinks to the ground as though her own legs have given out.

She is not wearing a coat. Anna. Her hair and shoulders frosted with the night's snow.

Maeve stares, stunned. Maybe Karo was right—Anna went for a smoke. But then something happened. Something went wrong.

Dan is already pounding on Anna's chest, counting under his breath. The violence of it: fingers splayed, arms and shoulders rigid with exertion. Hard enough that Maeve is afraid he'll break Anna's ribs. His face twists. *One-two-three-four—*

No one is running for blankets.

Karo drops to her knees beside him.

"Dan—" She wraps one hand around Anna's wrist and lays the other at her throat, waiting for the throb of a pulse, even a weak one.

But Anna is beyond blue. Her limbs flex stiffly under each thrust, like she's made of hard plastic, a CPR practice mannequin he's throwing around.

"Dan," Karo says again. Less gently this time.

It doesn't register; he just pounds and pounds and pounds, still counting.

"Dan!" Karo pulls back. Her hand on Anna's wrist loosens; her other hand, at Anna's throat, has a tremor in it. "Dan, it's too late. It's too late, she's gone. She must have been dead for hours. Dan!"

But he still goes on as though he hasn't heard. It seems to Maeve he really hasn't, that he can't hear anything but his own voice.

"Stop!" Maeve yells. Her hands are clenched tight.

Justin lunges in from somewhere and grabs him by the shoulder, but

Dan pushes him off. When Justin drops to his haunches and tries again, Dan wheels around on one knee and punches him, hard, his fist connecting to Justin's jaw with enough force to send the other man reeling onto his back. From the edge of the room, Sadie screams.

Sim leaps between the two men, and Maeve finds herself on the ground, shielding Anna's body with her own, as he wrestles Dan away and finally shoves him against the couch and holds him there.

"She's dead, okay?" Justin's voice, cracking, as he pushes up from where he's sprawled on the ground. He spits into the fire. His saliva is bloody: a tooth has come through his lip where Dan hit him. "She's dead," he says again. He wipes at his mouth and then his eyes with the back of a hand. "You don't have to break her apart! She's gone. It's too fucking late."

He spits again, and the tooth comes free, hitting the stone hearth like a thrown pebble. Justin brings the hand back to his mouth—like he's checking that this has really happened, he's not seeing things.

"Holy shit, you knocked my tooth out—I lost my tooth!" He surges toward Dan again, but Sim pushes him back, keeping the two men apart.

"Stop fighting!" Sadie rises on her knees, the final syllable extending into a high-pitched shriek as though the sheer sound will call them off. But it's Karo who stops it, shouting hoarsely over everyone—"No! No more!"—until the room rings with new silence.

Maeve pulls up from where she's crouched over Anna and looks down. Anna's eyes are open and unmoving. Maeve waits, staring back at her purposefully. Willing Anna to blink, her lips to tremble. *Blink, goddamn it!* Anything, anything at all to prove them wrong, show she's still there. A hum rises in Maeve's ears, the swoosh of her own pulse. There's a long moment where it feels as though she is in a room of her own: glassed in, separate. Then she hears something behind her and turns to see it's Sadie—rigid with fear, alone and weeping. Finally showing her youth. Maeve almost reaches out to her, thinking of the first strange moment they saw each other. What she needed was kindness—it's what she needs now, but Maeve has failed at it all, every chance. She turns back to Anna.

A few yards away, Dan pushes Sim off and pounds a fist back against the couch—once, twice—but it all seems remote. Like something she can see from a distance, out of the corner of her eye, through water.

Anna does not blink.

When she feels Karo's hand on her arm, Maeve raises her head, but Karo barely blinks herself. Just looks at Maeve, nods. Behind them, Sadie sobbing low: "I hate this place."

Karo takes Sadie's hand and tugs her away.

The door is still standing open and snow swirls into the room.

Maeve gets to her feet, wooden, to close it. At the couch, Dan rises to meet her. Sim stops him again, a hand on his chest, but Dan shakes him off.

"Fuck off." He reaches the door at the same moment as Maeve and goes to shove her aside.

But Maeve just stands in the cold and thumbs the latch. "It works now," she says. Quietly: "You fixed it after all."

She steps out of his way. Dan pushes the door closed and it locks, and he opens it again. Closed, open, closed. Open. Trying to understand.

Sim lifts his face to hers and their eyes meet before she looks away again. She's shivering. Dan's shoulders tighten, but he doesn't turn around.

The cold feels like the only thing. Maeve moves closer to the window. Outside, she can see a trail in the new layer of snow leading around toward the front of the building. The path is packed down hard, almost into ice, as though Anna tried the doors over and over again, pacing between them to keep warm.

When she can't stand it anymore, Maeve turns to find they've all moved back, away from Anna—Karo, Sadie, Justin, Sim—all of them now sitting with their knees drawn in, keeping warm, their eyes fixed anywhere but on her body.

For a few minutes nobody speaks.

"She must have made noise," Maeve says suddenly. "She must have banged on the doors, she must have yelled out." The words burst out of her, hateful. "I mean, you can see where she went back and forth. You can see it."

From the doorway, Dan glances down at Anna, then anywhere else. The back of the lobby. The front desk. The ceiling. Sim picks up his piece of bone and goes back to carving, the knife grinding a coarse dust that catches on his clothes. Karo plays with her necklace.

Maeve keeps on, louder.

"But no one heard her. None of us. We just slept through it all. Like fucking monsters."

She grows cold at the thought and tries to push it away. Her eyes flick to each of them in turn, from Karo to Sadie to Sim to Dan. Then back to Justin, nursing his wound.

An accident. But really? No one heard her out there in the night? No one heard her knocking or calling out for help?

No one?

As if in response, the wind outside picks up, howling its way into the room, and with it a wash of new snow. Dan fights to get the door closed a final time. The only one focused on Anna is Justin, his face swollen now, and a furious sorrow in his eyes.

Dan moves heavily toward the fire.

"Where would you like me to put her," he says. Slow and even.

Karo drops the necklace back against her collarbone.

"I don't know. My office or some other room. Someplace safe."

"You can't just leave her lying on a bed," Justin says. "We have to put her where it's really cold."

Karo blanches.

"For God's sake—" Maeve says.

But Dan nods.

"The walk-in," he says.

There's a beat. He means the freezer, Maeve realizes. The walk-in deep freeze back in the kitchen. She turns, appealing to Karo rather than Dan.

"No," she says. "No. You cannot leave her to freeze again. You can't. It's inhuman."

"Where else are we going to put her?" Justin's voice is growing louder. He's almost shouting. "What if we're here for three more days? You know what will happen—"

"That won't happen, someone is coming for us," Maeve says, cutting him off, her own voice rising to meet his.

"—she'll rot." Justin finishes, and there's a hard silence. "She'll rot anywhere it's even a little bit warm. You think you can live with that?" he says. "I can't."

Sadie's eyes well up again and Maeve turns, helpless, searching for any other support. Sim looks over, but he doesn't rush to intercede. He flips the knife in his hand, twice, then sets it down.

Back to business.

"Justin's right," Sim says. "Even with the power cut, it's still cold enough in there. It'll be subzero for days. And it's safe." Then, to Justin: "But you don't have to be an asshole about it."

"Everyone was thinking it. Everyone was—"

"All right," Karo cuts in finally.

A hand on Maeve's arm. It's Dan; the hand is meant to be a comfort. No—to quiet her. It's too heavy, his grip too tight. She shakes him off and turns away.

It is Sim and Dan who actually move her. Anna.

Maeve corrects herself: Anna's body. Karolina's instruction is to lay her

146

out on a low shelf in the freezer, where it will be coldest, not on the floor. She sends Sadie to fetch a bedsheet, clean and white, to cover the length of the body. For whatever kind of dignity might be possible. They wrap her up before lifting and carrying her away, and for a moment there's only the muted shuffling of their feet. Their voices, a low murmur.

Then they shut the door.

"Now what?" Justin flicks his eyes briefly to Maeve before moving on to glare at Dan. He's got a notebook in his lap but he's not writing in it, just gripping the pen with a taut hand. Maeve sits, playing softly at Anna's bear claw in her palm; she can't seem to let it go or put it away. Not yet.

At least he's not filming anymore.

The fire gives a loud pop—a damp spot, the bark bursting with heat. They've sat together in silence for almost an hour.

Maeve holds out for someone else to answer him. She sees the same tamped-down energy frothing in Justin—anger, impatience, a long howl—that she's working to control in herself. She needs a way to burn it off: to sob, or run, or beat her fists into something. Sadie curls rigidly at the other end of the couch, plucking at her own arm. Everyone fighting to stay contained.

But neither Karo nor Dan volunteer a solution. Justin shakes his head, caustic.

"Right. There's nothing to drink." He throws the notebook to one side so hard that it smacks off the wall. "I'm going upstairs. There's a full minibar somewhere with my name on it."

"No."

It's Dan who says it. He doesn't move as he speaks, just stares straight ahead. Justin pauses, then turns to him.

"Uh, I'm sorry, Dad? Did you say 'No'?"

This time Dan looks over, both dull and stern. "No. We all stay together."

Justin's expression hardens. "My face hurts."

Dan turns away again. "I already apologized for that."

"My face hurts and I want some bourbon."

Sadie twists to glance at Maeve. Looking for help or hoping for a drink herself? Maeve just shakes her head, a signal to stay out of it, for whatever that's worth. Instead, Sadie moves to the edge of her seat.

Dan takes a breath. "I'm not going to say it again. We all stay together."

"Not going to say it again?" Justin is up on his feet now. "You're like a goddamn broken record."

Dan looks to Karo, expecting something, but she just stretches and flexes her hand, as though she has a cramp. She's got the radio in her lap, and she goes back to turning the dial, slowly. Trying to find a voice somewhere.

He stands up to meet Justin. "Not broken enough," Dan says. "If we'd all stayed in the same damn room like I said, this wouldn't have happened. Anna would be alive now. So quit playing and sit the fuck down."

At this, Justin lets out a whoop. "Me? I'm playing? I'm not the fucking player here. I'm not the one playing around." He turns to Karolina. "Karo—I thought you were in charge. Who's in charge here?"

Maeve looks from the two men to Karo and back again. She can see what's coming next, recognizes Justin's stance, his hands clenched into fists. He's already winding up.

Karo gives in and sets the radio aside, her face and neck tense with the drawn look of someone who's been up all night, although in fact they all slept well—too well—and the day has barely begun.

"Listen—" she begins, but it's not fast or furious enough for Justin and he cuts her off, turning to face Dan head-on.

"Nothing's going to happen if I go upstairs for five minutes. Nothing!" He steps right up into Dan's face, pushing for a fight. "We all know why Anna died. She died because this genius fucked with the door lock so she thought she was safe to go outside—" Justin spins to

Sim. "Right, Picasso? Like, we all know that. She thought she was safe. Because of you."

Sim stops his whittling and looks up, not at Justin, but Dan. His hand paused, his hand with the knife in it. There's a moment of silence. Then:

"We're not animals."

His voice is calm. Relaxed, even. Something ardent, but earnest, always in his look: his eyes are so blue. Some kind of James Dean thing. There's a beat, all of them waiting for him to say something else, to keep on. But he just goes back to the work in his hands. Justin starts to laugh.

It's Dan who steps away, Dan who takes the bait.

"What's that supposed to mean?"

Sim just shakes his head.

"No, answer me," Dan says. "He's right—if you hadn't messed with the lock, if you hadn't fooled with it—"

"We're not animals," Sim repeats. He sets the bone and the knife aside. "There's no good reason to keep the doors locked all the time. Why? Why are they locked? To keep out the rescue team?"

For the first time, Karo looks wary. Wired. Maeve can see that she's bracing, ready to rise and put herself between the two men. But Sim is still on the ground, legs splayed out in front. Aggressively relaxed. He leans back on his hands.

"You weren't trying to keep danger out. You were trying to keep us in. Like a pen at the zoo. Why?" He looks around briefly, trying to draw the others in. "You know why? Because you're scared, and locks make you feel safe. Except we're not animals. See?" Sim rises slowly to his feet and it's a reminder of how tall he is, how big his hands are, how long his reach. "You can't keep people locked up," he says. "It doesn't make anyone safer—"

Sadie cuts in from her place on the couch: "It just makes you a control freak."

Dan points at her. "Stay the fuck out of this." He spins back to Sim, closing in on him now. "Everyone would have been safer. Anna would be alive."

"No, she wouldn't, because Anna liked to smoke and she was a goddamn human being and she wanted to go outside."

"Great, she went outside! The last time I touched that goddamn door it couldn't lock, you understand? Do you get me, Nielssen? I *couldn't* fix it. So what happened? A fucking miracle?" Dan gives him a shove, just lightly, a tap on the shoulder, but Sim's whole body hardens.

"So you say."

"What the fuck does that mean?"

"It means you say you couldn't fix it—but clearly you did. You just didn't tell anyone," Sim looks around a second time, like he's taking a poll. "Did you? You sure didn't tell Anna. And now you're the one making excuses. Way to blame the victim—she *sleepwalked* her way right out into the cold? Come on."

Maeve glances at Karo.

"You know what I think?" Dan sputters, obviously taken aback. "I think you did it. I think you fucked the door up and then you fixed it and it's you that didn't tell anyone, and now you're too much of a coward—"

"Okay—" Karo stands up and moves between them, glaring at Justin for starting this.

Maeve and Sadie suddenly the only ones left seated. Maeve is lost in a thought of her own: Anna often smoked out her open window. She'd said Karo caught her at it more than once. So why did she choose last night to go out by herself in the dark?

Unless she wasn't by herself. Unless she slipped out to meet someone, as she often did at night.

She forces the question from her mind and gets up on her feet, pulls a chair between herself and the action. She knows how these things can go.

But Sadie rises to stand behind Sim. "How did Elisha Goldman fall? We didn't have a whole argument about it. Accidents happen."

She's been so quiet that everyone turns to look at her. After a moment, Maeve remembers: Goldman was the painter Sadie told her about. The woman who stepped off the ledge. Paraplegic ever since.

Justin starts laughing again.

"Well, I guess if anyone knows what happened to Elisha, it would be Nielssen. Wouldn't it?"

Sadie looks flushed, almost ill. She steps toward Sim, unsteady, as though someone has pushed her.

"You still talk to her?"

Karo steps between them.

"It doesn't matter who did what." She is furious, shaking. "Anna went outside. Okay? She went outside. Arguing about it now won't help anyone, least of all Anna."

"Least of all us," Justin says.

Karo wheels around to face him. "Go."

"Sorry?"

"I said go. You wanted to go upstairs so badly, right? That's what you want? You want a drink? Go upstairs. We're not arguing anymore. Now we're making a plan. You can be part of it, or you can get drunk. I don't care."

Justin hesitates, but only for a second. He flicks his gaze to Dan, then steps back and strides off toward the stairwell. The door shuts behind him with a slam.

There's a silence and for a minute no one moves or says anything. The question of the door lock is uncomfortable; it puts the blame on someone other than Anna. On Sim for touching it in the first place, on Dan for trying to fix it. As accidents go, it's horrific. Almost unbelievable.

As soon as she thinks that, Maeve gets a sharp twinge again. *Almost?*

151

"Everyone take a moment—" Dan begins.

"What happened to 'everyone stay together'?" This is Sadie, reverting to her usual insolence.

"Everyone take a moment," Dan repeats, ignoring her. "So that we can think."

But almost immediately, he's lacing up his boots, the *moment to think* extended to a group splintering. Dan, Maeve thinks, is always sure he is the only one who should be allowed outdoors. The Elisha Goldman story eats at her. Two bad accidents in a matter of months? If it's not negligent, then it's sinister. Those are the choices.

She does not say this out loud.

"I'll take that moment," she says instead to nobody in particular. "I need it."

Karo hesitates, chewing on her lip, before nodding curtly. She looks uncomfortable in her skin, as though something is making her itch; she picks up the radio from where she left it on the floor and hugs it to her hip. Sadie just seems restless, on her feet and pacing the rim of chairs near the fire, eager to get away.

Sim gives Maeve a final glance and then turns and goes back to the gallery, his own locked door, and slips quietly inside.

Maeve climbs slowly to the fourth floor, meaning to go back to her own room. But just as she swings the stairwell door open, something stops her—an echo of some kind. She pauses, hovering there. The sound of another door yawning open, from the other stairwell, at the opposite end of the hall. She hangs back. Footsteps; the jangling of a set of keys or a zippered jacket. A blunt noise, then a bang.

Then nothing.

Silence. She can feel her heart kicking hard against her ribs. She's expecting Sim—it's always Sim.

But there are no more footsteps, and after a moment, no other sounds at all. Maeve leans out into the hall. For a second, she wonders if she imagined it. The corridor is empty and dark.

No—no, that's not quite true. A slim arc of light makes a dent in the shadows about halfway down. Someone's door is open. Not someone's: Maeve's own door, she realizes. She takes a step farther, letting the stairwell door fall closed, gently and silently, behind her.

She's most of the way there before she realizes it's not actually her door that's open; it's the one next to it. The adjoining room, where Anna slept the night before. She stops and looks behind her. There's no one else in the hall. But a rustling and then that muted jangle again, this time from inside the room, the sound too dull and heavy to be just a zipper, or even a key ring. But what else would make that noise?

A tool belt.

Maeve feels a rush of loyalty and sadness come up into her throat. Dan. Doing what? She lunges forward and pushes the door wide, letting it bang against the inside wall.

But it's Sadie who spins to face her. Furious.

Maeve steps back, surprised. She takes a quick glance around the room. The bedcovers have been pulled off and thrown to the floor, and the wardrobe is wide open. Anna's unzipped knapsack is in Sadie's hands.

Maeve doesn't say anything, just stares.

"Justin's camera is missing, his video camera," Sadie says. She's not surprised she got caught; she's defiant. Her eyes red-rimmed from crying. "The whole thing—the carry bag, all the SD cards. The hard drive. It's all gone."

"That doesn't explain why you're here."

"I was playing with it last night. Remember? But Anna took it from me when you were dancing."

Maeve nods slowly, still staring her down. She seems to remember that Sadie had the camera last. Didn't she? She tries to picture the scene as they left the lobby, but she was so exhausted by everything last night.

153

Maybe Anna came back for the camera later, while Maeve was dealing with Sim in the hall?

"Did you look under your chair?" She's recalling Sadie's own reproach the day before, when it was Justin looking for the camera.

"I know I shouldn't be in here." Sadie sinks back against the bed, a steady new resolve in her demeanor. "But Justin is already asking me for it. He's going to kill me."

Maeve shakes her head. How can this be the priority today?

Sadie starts again: "I use that camera a lot. So I had...footage on it. Stuff. Okay? Things I want to keep. Things I want to keep private."

"So why not ask about it downstairs? Why just come up here?" *Or, better: Why not use your own damn camera?* Maeve cannot figure this out; she doesn't even want to.

"*Private,* Maeve. You know what that means? And Justin—he doesn't know yet. That I lost it."

"And you think this morning is the best time to break in—"

"This morning went to hell pretty damn quickly, don't you think?" Just like that, Sadie is on her feet again, coming at her like a bulldog. "And I told you, Anna must have taken it. She must have."

Maeve holds her ground. "I should get Karolina," she says. "Or the others, Dan—"

But the mention of Dan's name seems to pull Sadie back. Her voice drops. "Look, Maeve—"

Maeve feels her surprise turn to rage. "She's dead! Anna died last night and you're rooting through her stuff—"

"I just really need that camera, okay? You don't understand." Sadie's body buzzing with tension, her voice rising to match. Maeve can practically see the adrenaline moving through her. "I'm—I'm working on something. Like a project. All right?"

Maeve narrows her eyes. "What do you mean?"

"It's hard to explain."

154

Sadie seems suddenly exhausted, like she can barely stand up. The mood swings here verge on performance. Maeve chides herself for the thought: that can't be true. Maybe the girl is in shock? She was so emotional only an hour ago, weeping over Anna's death.

Unless that was some kind of act too.

"Try me," Maeve says.

Sadie sucks on her lower lip.

"It's part of Sim's installation," she says finally. "I wasn't supposed to tell anyone. He asked me to help him with something, and I've been using Justin's camera."

Maeve feels herself pull in a little. "If this is for Sim, why didn't he give you a camera himself?"

"Because the stealth—"

"You mean stealing."

"—it's all part of it. It's part of the conceit of the project, it's important to it." She looks desperate, like she might cry again at any moment. "It's not just for him. This is good for me too, Maeve. I left Europe for this place. For—" She throws her hands out, indicating the empty room. "For—this. All I did in school was write essays about art, and all I do here is clean up after artists. I've never had the chance to do anything— to make anything myself. Please don't ruin this. Sim says it's like—like a mentorship. He's going to bring me along when the installation tours. Being a part of this could really open doors for me."

Maeve presses her lips together, then runs a hand through her hair.

"That's what he told you?"

"I can't explain it, okay? It's a secret." Sadie crosses her arms, locking the secret inside. It's like dealing with a teenager.

"Sadie—" Maeve steps closer. She's trying to remember how it feels to be so young and so ambitious. Tries to come up with something to say; what she wishes someone—anyone—had told her when she was twenty-three herself: "I know it can be really hard—at your age, I mean.

I get it. I was there once too." She softens her voice; downstairs, she'd told herself the girl needed kindness. Maybe it's not too late? "Especially when men who are older—men who are accomplished—ask things of you. We're kind of trained to say yes. We're trained to feel like it's a coup, somehow, a triumph to be the one who gets asked. Even if they're really just using you." Maeve takes a breath. "And they almost always are, Sadie."

Sadie nods slowly, like she's really thinking about it. "Just—just don't tell anyone. Okay?"

Maeve blinks. Something doesn't jibe; there's a blankness to her, as if she's only trying to read Maeve and respond, to feed Maeve the right line.

"What were you filming?"

Another long silence. Then: "I'll put everything back the way it was. I know it's terrible that I'm in here, I know—"

"That night I saw you downstairs. In the spa." Maeve comes in closer still. Something, some object cradled in Sadie's arm that night. Something black. "In the hallway, you remember?"

But Sadie's face changes again. "Spare me the life lessons, okay? Tell Dan if you want. I don't care. We're doomed here, that's obvious. Whatever. Do whatever you want."

Maeve looks around the room, destroyed by Sadie's search efforts. What the hell could be on that camera?

Sadie steps in close, her finger in Maeve's face. "You're not special, you know. Before you, it was Elisha, and before her, just someone else. So don't think you're more important than me."

Maeve stiffens. It's a dig—and not even an elegant one—meant to provoke her, she knows that. And so what? He's a player. Why should she care about that? She only wanted a one-night stand in the first place.

Still. There's a sting to it.

"Anna did not have that camera last night. I watched her unpack."

Sadie nods again, but this time it's curt, impatient. "And she never left the room again?"

Maeve feels her neck tense. Why won't she leave this alone?

Sadie waves her own question away; she can see she's gone too far. "I'm sorry—"

But Maeve is tired of the show. She cuts her off: "We need to get out of here. I'll walk you down."

She goes to the door and waits for Sadie to pass through before turning to shut it behind them.

Downstairs, Sadie walks briskly to the office and shuts the door. Maeve stares after her, unsure which Sadie is the real one: the emotional young woman who wept over Anna's body or this impulsive, ruthless version. Combing through a dead woman's room for—for what, exactly? Approbation from Sim?

Or just to save herself, destroy some footage that will no doubt reflect poorly on her, in the wake of Anna's death.

Justin emerges from the stairwell behind her, carrying a tote bag of mini-bar bottles that clink as he walks. His mood is unchanged: the first empty bottle, fist-size, already firmly in his grip. He heads straight for Dan, but Dan turns and moves off to the back door, taking up his shovel as he goes.

The door swings shut. Justin spins to watch it happen, then tosses the bag of booze down on the big desk with a flourish.

"You're welcome," he says to Maeve.

Sim has disappeared, for the moment or for the day, into his gallery. Maeve and Justin the only two people left in the room.

There's a pause, and he downs the rest of the minibottle in his hand like it's a shot.

"Not filming this part, I notice," Maeve says. It's a feeler: she wants to know if the camera is really missing or if Sadie was lying about her reasons for going through Anna's things.

"We'll want to skip this part of the promo." But he glances quickly around the room, suddenly interested in the chairs by the fire, the couch. It's clear he is looking for something. "I know it just seems like some dumb project, but—it was giving me something to focus on." He pulls the rolling chair away from the front desk to peek underneath. "Sadie probably has the camera anyway."

Maeve would like to get her hands on that camera herself.

Justin throws himself glumly into the desk chair. When he looks up, she notices that his lip has started bleeding again.

"Your mouth—" she says.

"I know, I know." He dabs at the split lip with a tentative finger. "Dan—" He glances toward the back windows, lost in thought, then starts over.

"Someday," he says, "some man will run a thumb over this scar and ask me how I got so beautiful." He lets the hand hover over his mouth, hiding the missing front tooth. "We only hurt the ones we love." It comes out as a weird singsong.

He shakes his head.

There's something Maeve recognizes in his posture, something wounded and wistful, but it takes her a moment to land on it.

"Oh," Maeve says. "Oh."

"Yeah." He nods. "Yeah, I always think I can turn them around."

He sucks at the hurt place inside, where his tooth is missing. There's a little silence, awkward, while Maeve thinks of what else to say.

"That's why he can't apologize." Justin thumbs at his lip. "For hitting me. Not in public. Not in any real way. He can't apologize because he thinks we were a secret. Like no one knew."

Maeve nods slowly. She really didn't know, still is not sure how much there might be *to* know, but she doesn't say this. What exactly is he telling her? That he's been sleeping with Dan? Or is it only a flirtation, a game on Dan's part?

The whole place a minefield of secrets.

"Anna—" Maeve begins. "Anna had a…thing with him too. Did you know that?"

"Did I know? We had a little contest going. Anna and me. Fuck, it's terrible, I know. It was just for fun. Or that's how it started. Anyway." He leans over to his bag, cracks the seal on a second flask, tosses the cap onto the floor. "The funny part," he says. "The funny part is I thought I'd won. Until she showed up again last month." He takes a slug from the bottle and sniffs. "Sorry. It's a shitty thing to talk about now. Today, I mean. It's just—like I said, I always think I can turn them around."

Maeve nods again, as though she understands. In fact, she feels like she's been run over by a train. She can't bring herself to say what she's thinking, what so many people said to her:

But he hits you. He pushes you around. Why do you want him?

She thinks back to Anna and Justin's banter that first night. Their only good night—Anna mixing drinks and wondering aloud why Dan had suddenly pulled away, Justin's little dig at her tactics. Even Anna's dismissal of Justin, the way she'd cut him down. *Fancies himself a hot little ticket.*

But it also lays bare some different version of that morning. Justin's sudden defense of Anna's body, the way he stepped in and pulled Dan off her, now smacks of a weird jealousy. He took a punch for his trouble. And even—

Even the way he redirected the blame from Dan to Sim. The crippled door lock versus the repaired door lock. What do you point to?

You point to whatever made Anna think she could go out into the night and get safely back inside.

"I guess you could say I've won now," Justin says. It's maybe meant to be funny, but Maeve blanches, and a wash of regret crosses his face.

Maeve looks up to see more snow coming down, her reflection just a ghostly outline in the glass. Was it only last night she used that same window as a mirror, still somehow dancing, still trying to salvage some piece of this place? Stupid to come to the mountains; stupid to want to be anywhere but home.

She feels numb.

"No one has eaten anything," she says. It's true: no one has eaten at all that morning, and they barely ate the night before. She moves off toward the kitchen by herself.

Justin throws his feet up onto the desk next to the booze.

Narcissist, she thinks.

She's glad to leave him there.

In the kitchen, there's not much fresh food left. A single loaf of bread, poorly sealed, in the bread bin. Some basic dry goods in the cupboards: sacks of flour, salt, sugar, raisins. The double-wide refrigerator with a sour smell when she opens the door. It's cold, but not cold enough. She pulls out a foil-sealed brick of butter and closes the door again.

But as it swings shut, she catches the reflection of something behind her—a shadow, almost, looming in the doorway. Her mind catches up a moment too late: she's already spinning around, defensive, and she lets out a yelp of surprise.

Sim stands there, eyes wide.

"Sorry," she says reflexively. Although why should she be? "I must be jumpy."

He reaches for a roll of paper towels on the counter.

"It's understandable. Hell of a morning." He pulls a sheet off the roll, wipes his face and hands, then squeezes the towel until it disappears in his fist.

She nods in a vague way. It's uncomfortable, the kitchen with its echo of silence, industrial. A space big enough to swallow sound. She's still got the butter in one hand and she gestures with it inelegantly.

"No one's eaten anything," she says. "I came in here—I'm not even sure there *is* anything to eat. The fridge is full of spoiled milk."

"Karo put most of what could be saved into the walk-in freezer." He looks around for the garbage and lobs the balled-up paper towel toward the bin. "The first morning," he says. "She was careful about it."

"Oh." Maeve nods again. Her mouth is dry. "Oh, that makes sense."

Anna, blue-white with cold, when Dan brought her inside. Not just frost, but an ice filigree framing her lashes, her lips.

Maeve would prefer not to go into the freezer.

"I'll do it," Sim volunteers. "I'll go in if you want. Or you can, and I'll hold the door for you. So you don't feel scared."

"It's just weird," she says. Then: "Christ, I wish you'd never fucked with that door."

He shakes his head. "Oh, now. You too, hey?" He moves in closer. "She would have gone out anyway, Maeve. Or someone would have. It was inevitable; anyone can see that." He turns to glance behind himself as though making sure they're alone. "Look at the control in this place," he says. "Only Dan gets to tell us where to go. Only Karo is allowed to touch the radio. You noticed that last night, didn't you? Try picking it up again. See what happens."

Maeve nods, uncomfortable to find herself agreeing with him. The thing with the radio had seemed weird, it's true. She'd almost forgotten it. But he's also echoing her own thought, that Dan likes to be the only one allowed outdoors. Likes to do the allowing. And Karo, of course, setting Sadie to spy on everyone else, keep them in line—

Maeve catches herself. That's only what she thought Sadie was doing, spying and reporting back. But it's not true. How much has this colored what she thinks of Karolina?

Now she's not sure who Karo is at all.

"It was an accident," Sim says. "Everyone knew Anna liked to go for a smoke before bed. Everyone knew that. It was safer having one unlocked door. It's crazy to have doors on auto-lock in a situation like this. Totally crazy."

She doesn't answer. She doesn't say: *But the door* did *lock somehow.*
Whatever you did didn't work. It didn't work at all.

"I'm sorry it happened," he says.

"Me too," Maeve says. "Understatement of the year." She glances over
at the freezer. "I'll hold the door for you."

"Okay," he says, and he leaves it at that.

"Okay." She breaks away and moves to the deep freeze, but she's relieved, or at least reassured. She wonders how much of her nervousness
is just anxiety, her past life kicking in, not the situation. If he reached for
her now, she realizes, she'd let him.

She's not sure whom to talk to or whom to trust. He reaches for the
freezer door, but she stops him, her hand on his shoulder.

"Did you—" she starts.

He raises an eyebrow. She takes a breath and tries again. "What do
you have Sadie working on?"

"Sadie? Working?"

"She says you gave her some kind of assignment, some film project
related to your work in there." She points toward the lobby and the
gallery door.

"Oh, that." Sim turns his head like he's already weary of the topic.
"When I first got here, she was dogging around after me. It was annoying. So I gave her a little make-work thing to do to keep her out of my
hair." He rubs his forehead. "I wanted some film to cut up, something
I could make abstract, for a projection. Something that can run on the
floor, that visitors will literally walk on, but that feels secretive, like a
whisper. Underfoot, you know? Lots of meaning there. She liked the
idea of a camera and secrets, so I said great, go do that."

His tone, blasé, stands in stark contrast to Sadie's burst of emotion at
the same story. She seemed frantic, whereas the mention of Sadie makes
him look, if anything, bored.

"But why target Anna?"

162

Sim looks down at her oddly. "Anna? What do you mean?"

There's no performance in the question; he seems genuinely confused. Maeve suddenly finds she wants to keep the story to herself. She shakes her head.

"I think you should be more careful with her, that's all. Sadie. She's younger than she seems."

Sim shifts his weight.

"I wasn't going to tell you this." He glances out at the empty lobby and back to Maeve. "But Sadie—she's not that innocent. She's had it in for you this whole time. Since you arrived." He leans into the kitchen island and looks at her more directly. Eye to eye. "She used to dance. Did she tell you that? It was her dream when she was a kid, but her father wouldn't let her. Didn't want her onstage for everyone to see. So everything about you, literally everything—your career, your reputation, this new company you're building—" He pauses for a second, and his voice drops. "Your connection to me," he says. "She's jealous. At one point, she told me she wanted to sneak into your studio and grease the floor so you'd have an accident. Break something." He pulls back, his whole body registering the severity of this threat. Maeve frowns.

It's uncomfortable, a gut punch. The way she felt guilty, watching Sadie try to cope that morning. Then finding her rifling through Anna's room—

So you'd have an accident. All at once she thinks of the way Sadie keeps circling back to Elisha Goldman. She's the only one who keeps bringing her up.

Maeve shakes her head and reaches for the long handle on the freezer door. "Here—" She draws the bolt back, opens the door, and sets her body against the inside panel, like a brace.

Sim walks into the freezer and roots through the stores. There's a stepladder, but most things—taped cardboard boxes, slabs of meat wrapped in freezer paper—are stacked at eye level or below. On the wall beside the door is the emergency release, and next to it, someone has hung a small ax. *In case the release button doesn't work,* Maeve thinks. *Or the power goes out, and you get trapped.*

On the back wall, there's the white bedsheet hanging crisply over the edge of its low shelf. Maeve's stomach turns, but she finds she cannot look away.

Sim rises to his feet, having retrieved more bread and two large, foil-wrapped trays.

"Joker's wild," he says, nodding at the trays. "At least whatever's in here will already have been cooked."

"Breakfast surprise," Maeve says. She shifts to let him by, but the door starts to close, and she has to put her arm out to catch it again. Sim moves past her, out of the walk-in, and wends his way back to the kitchen proper to set things down.

Maeve stays where she is just a moment longer. The subtle movement of the door, that half swing before she caught it, pushed a little current of air through the freezer. Anna's sheet flutters just at one edge. This is what catches Maeve's eye. The corner of the sheet, lifting and falling, over the curved arch of Anna's blue toes.

Anna's feet are bare.

If she'd meant to go out for a smoke, even just for a moment, she would have put on her boots. Wouldn't she? Or something. Sneakers. Slippers, even.

Even if she were planning to step just outside the door. In the moment of crisis, with Anna's legs curled up in her long nightgown, it's not something anyone noticed. But now Maeve stares. She tries out a few rushed excuses: Anna was drunk and forgot, then didn't want to climb all the stairs back to retrieve her boots. Or, as Dan suggested, Anna was sleepwalking.

What comes back to her again is the sound she heard last night just as she turned out the light. Something she wishes she could forget. Half asleep with half a mug of whiskey in her, and then the heavy sleep that followed. A kind of bang, or a knock.

Anna's door?

She recalls her own silly knock in response. How after that, there was no sound at all. She'd assumed Anna was already asleep. Anna only sleeping there in the first place to make Maeve more comfortable. She glances over to where Sim is waiting for her in the kitchen.

Just an accident.

No one would step out into the snow in bare feet. No one. Not in this weather. Not on purpose.

She shuts the freezer door behind her.

Karo is waiting for them in the lobby. She's holding a long cardboard tube, and she draws out the roll of heavy paper housed inside. It's the thing she was searching for—a proper survey, she says.

"I wanted something better than a map." She hands the roll to Sadie and watches as the younger woman lays it out on the desk, then leans over it to smooth the page flat. "We can't wait here any longer. Someone needs to go down the mountain for help."

"Someone?" Maeve says. She can't stop her mind cycling on Anna's bare feet and tries to calm herself down. Sadie seems to have lost her earlier agitation and stands, stone-faced, on the other side of the desk. Her lip twitches as though she wants to bite it. Perhaps Karo has spoken to her; she seems corralled, brought in line.

Justin gets up to take a closer look, leaning on the back of a chair. Dan already has his boots on.

"We're running out of time," Karo says. "It doesn't feel prudent to stay here anymore without at least trying."

Maeve can't help but notice that Karo's hand is still shaking slightly; there's a note of panic to her voice. Sim sets the foil trays down to one side.

"Why can't we all go?"

Dan shoots him a look. "All of us trying to get down over the lower ridge would just be foolish." He shakes his head, as if the decision has already been made. "Too risky."

"Wait—" Maeve's breath catches. In her mind, she is already halfway down the slope, heels digging into the ice, elbows drawn in tight for balance, away-away-away and home. Desperate to leave this place. "Slow down. No one wants to be left behind."

But Dan is glued to the survey, trying to figure out a route down, what supplies they'll need to bring. She's not sure he's heard her. Karo just looks relieved.

"Fine," Karo says, speaking only to Dan now. "Then who? Let's get a team together."

Maeve is jarred by her response; this is all happening too quickly.

"If we can get down there, even close to the village," Dan says, mostly to himself. "Set off some flares. Get some attention. Something to alert the emergency crews."

What used to be an easy hike just a few miles down the road is now going to require a different kind of travel altogether. The debris field to either side of them is bound to be unstable. Dan raps the desk with a knuckle as he thinks.

"The best plan would be to circumvent the worst of it somehow."

"Go around?" Justin says. "Around where? Around how?" He brushes at his face, jittery.

"Go up." Sim traces the survey with a finger, looking at the topography. "You'd have to go up and then down a different way."

Dan shakes his head again. "That doesn't work, either." The issue is the instability, he says, of the slab.

The issue is that it hasn't ever stopped snowing.

"I think we'd need to count on eight hours, maybe longer, to cut along the outer edges safely."

"So we can't leave until tomorrow morning anyway," Maeve says, insisting on the *we*.

But the words are barely out of her mouth before Karo interrupts: "Tomorrow is too late."

She seems to be riding an edge; she's not her usual self but some different, urgent version.

"Okay, so we bring shelter and supplies, just in case," Dan says. "I'd rather go now. I feel useless here."

Sadie pulls a notebook from the desk drawer.

"I, for one, am dying to get out of here," she says to the room at large. "What do we need? I'll make a list."

Maeve blinks, then looks around, trying to gauge the others' reactions. What Dan's proposing seems crazy to her—heading down the mountain with darkness falling and no idea what lies ahead. If Anna's death has shown them anything, isn't it how dangerous exposure really is?

But Karo doesn't argue with the idea. She looks gaunt; she's drawn her hands behind her back.

If Anna's death has shown them anything, it's that someone here isn't really what they seem. Maeve is damned if she's going to walk out into the storm with any of them. With someone who left Anna to die in the cold.

But the only alternative is to stay behind at the center. Trapped. Is that really any better?

"Devil's advocate—" Maeve begins.

Justin sighs loudly. "Here we go."

"I thought you were done being an asshole," Sim says. "No? Not yet?"

Maeve takes a breath and tries again: "If it's only a matter of hours to reach the village, then why hasn't any help arrived so far?" She rocks back a little as though she's already anticipating a fight. "What if the situation is worse than we've imagined? What if High Water village is—"

Justin gestures for her to spit it out.

"What?"

"Buried," Maeve says finally. "I don't think we'd want to find ourselves stranded out there in the dark."

Dan cracks his neck, impatient. It irritates her.

"Lots of good reasons we haven't had a crew up here yet," he says. "Maybe the road is blocked down at the village too and they're waiting for help themselves. We'd be next in line."

He pauses just long enough for Maeve to open her mouth to respond—then he cuts her off again.

"Or it could mean they were evacuated."

"Still a better chance of a radio signal down there," Karo says, her tone rising. "Or cell service, even. Or—"

"Or we keep going farther down," Dan says. Smooth and even. "We go until we find someone."

Sadie sighs audibly, pen still poised in hand. "We're wasting time," she says. "And daylight."

"If we can get down, we can get help back up here," Dan says. He turns to Karo as though the conversation with Maeve never happened. "I'll guide them myself."

There's a bristling energy among them all. Everyone wants to be first to see that rescue crew. First off the mountain. Justin almost bouncing on his feet. Only Sim has gone quiet: he's looking down at the map curiously, as if he's picking out some detail that no one else sees.

Maeve weighs the possible outcomes, reversing her position over and over. What if she's overreacting? At least heading down the mountain is *movement*. Action.

But what if the village is evacuated when they get there? She corrects herself: *If* they get there. And there's no signal after all. A night in an icebound tent, or two nights.

And one of them—maybe—Anna's killer.

It feels as though her heart is not beating inside her, but trembling. Like she might throw up. She takes a deep breath and expels it slowly.

Sadie taps her pen, starting to lose her cool.

Karo reaches over to pat her hand, stilling it.

"Dan's right," Karo says. "I never meant to suggest we should all go. It's too much of a risk, especially once it gets dark."

"Two of us," Dan says. "I really think it's better."

Safer to go or safer to stay here? It's not about getting home faster. It's about getting home at all. At least the center is a kind of shelter.

A shelter with doors that lock.

"I'll stay behind," Maeve says. Her voice wavers: the words pushed out before she can change her mind. The others pause. Sim, his focus back on Maeve now, gives her a slow nod.

Dan turns to Karo. "You see? Maeve gets it. It makes more sense." He glances at the survey again. "Karo and I will go."

"No—" Justin smacks the table. "No way, you're not going alone."

"I always get left behind—" Sadie flicks her pen across the table, hostile.

But even Karo is noticeably shaken. It occurs to Maeve that Karo doesn't want to make the trek herself, she simply wants *someone* to do it.

Or maybe Karo knows something, and she wants someone—but who?—gone.

A hand on her back. Surprised, Maeve turns to find Sim sliding in next to her, too close. He nods at her again and it's weirdly intimate. Like he's responding to a question she didn't ask.

She steps to one side, shaky. If Karo and Dan leave, the four of them will be alone here—just Maeve and Sim playing house, forced to manage petulant Sadie and spurned Justin. Glancing over at Justin now, Maeve sees the same weird energy coursing through him—angry, anxious. He can't keep still. If she didn't know better, she'd say he was coked up. Maybe he is.

Maeve focuses on the survey instead, the elevation marked in uneven, wobbly rings. *You can't be afraid of everyone,* she thinks. *There must be someone you can trust.*

"Well, I'm not staying," Justin says.

Everyone looks up.

"See?" Sadie throws an arm up and lets it fall, exasperated.

"I'm not staying here," Justin says again. "Why should I? Why? To freeze, like Anna? No. If someone's going down the mountain, I'm going too. We should all go. Why just you, Dan? Fuck that."

Karo steps back, ready to take him on, but Sim speaks first.

"It's okay. The four of you go down, then. I'll stay with Maeve."

He touches Maeve's hand and her stomach tightens. Karo is watching her. There's something deliberate in her eyes, something sharp and mindful.

"I don't actually need anyone to stay with me," Maeve says. "If you're going to send help up here, I'll wait, I can wait alone. I just can't risk an accident, or—or anything, really. Whatever happened to Anna." As soon as the name is out of her mouth, Maeve regrets it. She starts again, playing it as earnestly as she can: "I have kids waiting for me at home, and as much as I want to get out of here—believe me, I do—I just can't take any risks. I can't." She turns to Sim. "But that doesn't mean you should stay here too. I'm sure you'll be an asset on the trip."

Sim just stares her down. Calm. His hand over hers on the table.

"I'm fine to stay," Sim says. "I'll keep working. I'm the one who wanted to include *avalanche isolation* in the brochure. Remember?"

Maeve's head spins a little and she feels herself straighten, as though being taller will help her stay in control. She asks herself again: *Is it safer to go or safer to stay here?* She's about to give up when Karo surprises her.

"No. No, I'll stay with Maeve."

Sim looks up sharply. Karo shakes her head at him.

"I'm the director. I can't possibly leave anyone up here. I can't leave at all. I'm responsible for the center," she says. "And for Anna, for that matter." She turns to Dan. "Sim will go down with you. You'll go in pairs, Sim and Justin, Sadie and Dan—"

Dan cuts her off. "Sadie, no—"

"You don't get a choice, Dan." Sadie stands up, gathering her papers and the map. Defiant in that same way. "You're not in charge. Do you get it? You're not a soldier anymore, and this isn't the army." She gains confidence as she goes, ramping up. "You're just a high-priced handyman now. Karo is the boss—"

"—absolutely, yes," Karo says. "And I need Sadie to act as my proxy."

But then she turns to Sadie herself. "Stop provoking—we all have to get along." It's a weak reaction, and even as Sadie swallows her *yes,* Dan is stepping in front of her again.

"We can't leave two women up here alone."

Maeve watches him. Something's changed. He doesn't turn, doesn't lash out at Sadie as he has in the past. His jaw is clenched; there's a stiff fury burning in him now, just under his skin.

Karolina smiles her professional smile.

"Of course you can. Don't be stupid about this. You're a fine team— go for help. It's the smartest thing."

"I want to stay," Sim says. "I already said I'm staying here." He's speaking to Dan.

It's Karo who answers him.

"No." Her smile cuts off. "You can't. We need you out there on the trail."

She gives the survey a final glance, then walks toward her office, gesturing to Sadie to follow behind.

"I have two boxes of tools. You can take one of them. Plus whatever else we have on-site. There's tarps and more flares down in storage, I'm sure."

Maeve steals a look at Sim, expecting him to keep insisting, but he's remarkably quiet. He looks thoughtful but restless.

"Okay, then," is all he says. "Let me get my pack."

* * *

Karo is in her office, leaning hard on the desk, when Maeve comes in. She pulls up stiffly.

"I didn't mean to surprise you," Maeve says. Karo adjusts the candles on her desk and gestures for her to close the door. Behind her, Sadie shuffles a few papers out of an envelope, then stares at Maeve in silence.

Or arrogance. Daring Maeve to tell.

Maeve cannot wait to be rid of her. Sadie and Dan can tear each other to pieces out in the snow for all she cares.

Karo lowers herself onto the couch by the window.

"You know," Maeve says, "if you'd rather go, I can manage, I can—"

"You can't." There's a beat. "And I can't," Karo says.

She's sitting tensely, as though the very action of sitting is work; she looks like every muscle is in slight contraction.

Maeve glances at Sadie, trying to gauge whether she also finds this strange—but Sadie just looks on, impassive, shifting the papers in her hands.

"I'm upset about Anna too—" Maeve is not sure what else to say.

"Yes." Karo squeezes the arm of the couch with taut fingers.

"But I think we need to stay focused, even us, staying here. Maybe especially because we're staying here. You don't seem like yourself, Karo. Maybe a cup of sweet tea or a shot of something—"

"Oh, not you too with the booze." Karo pushes rigidly to her feet again. "You mean this." Her voice drops to a harsh whisper, as though there might be someone outside the door, listening. She holds out her hands, which tremble in the air.

Maeve sees suddenly how pronounced it is. How much, in fact, Karo has been keeping it under control.

Karo turns her hands over, watching them shake, then lets her arms drop. She looks over to Sadie, who finally steps out from behind the desk.

"She has a condition. That's why I'm really going down to the village—for help."

Karo scowls at the word.

"She's going for drugs. I control it with medication. It's not usually a problem. I mean, you see that—you would never have guessed before today." She's unused to confidences, uncomfortable. "I missed a delivery, remember? The day before the avalanche. But—"

"What sort of condition?" It's a dumb question. Maeve is struggling to catch up.

"An illness," Sadie says, matter-of-fact. "Kind of like Parkinson's. Most people aren't diagnosed until they're older."

She takes Karolina's arm and leads her around to the big chair behind the desk, modestly assisting. Sadie's entire role here rapidly shifts in Maeve's mind: she thinks back to when she first saw the tremble in Karo's fingers. Yesterday?

"And the medication—" she begins.

Karolina eases herself down into the chair.

"For the first day or so, I didn't worry too much. I tried just stretching out the time between doses. But it's sensitive stuff. Normally I take it every four hours, day and night."

"Do you have any left at all?"

"No, not anymore."

"Does Dan know?"

"No one knows."

Maeve blanches. She looks at Sadie again, but the girl won't meet her gaze. Instead, she finishes sorting through her papers.

"I don't think—"

"If they knew, they would look at me differently. I manage it extremely well—"

"But this is an emergency."

"I won't die from it. It's not an illness that kills you. Not quickly like that. It's just—without the drugs—" She stops, at a loss.

Maeve turns to Sadie, responsibility nagging at her.

"And you're comfortable with this? With Dan?"

A flash of vulnerability passes over Sadie's face—grim, frightened. Then it's gone.

But Karo slams a tight fist against the desk.

"Dan is a professional. A veteran! With on-the-ground experience. And they'll be safer all together than if two of them go alone." She takes a breath, trying to calm herself down. "I'm asking you not to say anything. Not a word. Just let them go, do you understand? The faster we get a rescue team up here, the better."

She reaches for Sadie's papers—the forms that will allow her to pick up the medication in Karolina's stead—and adds her signature to each one.

They're ready to go before one o'clock. This still leaves them only four hours of daylight: Maeve wonders at the audacity of the plan, but they all seem galvanized. Giddy. Dan has a set of snowshoes for each of them and some overnighting equipment he's dug out of storage: tarps and headlamps, a hatchet, fire starters. He's also got a gun, a .44, which surprises Maeve. She watches him carefully loading it.

"I thought you weren't worried," she says.

At the sound of the barrel clicking into place, Sim lifts his head from his own packing.

"A gun's nowhere near as useful as bear spray," he says. His voice is calm. Casual, even. "I mean, if a bear is what you're worried about. You know that."

Dan just nods. There's a pause, and then Sim goes at him again, harder this time. "So what do you need a gun for?"

"There's a can of spray for each of us." Dan sets the safety and slides the pistol into a holster at his hip. "I'd rather hold on to the gun myself than leave it here," he says. "If it's all the same to you."

"It's not the same to me at all. Is it the same to you, Maeve?"

But Maeve just turns away. The last thing they need now is a pissing contest.

Sim's eyes steady on Dan. "Don't forget you're *ex*-military for a reason—"

Karo glances over, her face rigid, and signals to Sim to let it go.

Sadie is the first one ready. She sits by the door, impulsive-looking, on her pack, snow pants and parka on, hood pulled up, a ridge of dark fur framing her face. She has an air of the impostor about her, or the ingénue. Maeve thinks again how well she'd fit in, lining up in the audition hall: small and lithe, sharp-tongued and insecure. Cruising for a fight. Maeve doesn't know whether to wish her good luck or good riddance.

Dan is assembling the last tool pack when Karo comes out of her office and catches his arm.

"Not everything. You need to leave two tarps behind and two cans of bear spray. And the extra flares."

"You have your own toolbox—"

"I have a toolbox of my own, but I want a few extras. You can't leave us up here high and dry."

He stops moving, his hand curled around a flare.

"Best if you don't go outside, Karo."

He tucks the flare into an inner pocket of the backpack and cinches the bag tight, Karo's hand still on his arm, her fingers digging into the plush of his jacket.

Sadie steps up, jittery with adrenaline.

"What if she has to? We can't just take everything."

Dan pauses, resentful that his authority is being questioned. He rolls his shoulder back, making it clear he's trying hard not to turn to Sadie and put her in her place.

"You're the one who wanted to stay here," he says to Karo. He pulls out the surplus flares and bear spray and a single tarp and tosses them peevishly at Karo's feet. But then he looks at Maeve and starts to laugh. "What, are you two planning to run away before I get back?"

He tugs the waterproof flap back over the top of his bag, fastens it, slings the pack onto his back, and turns away. Justin and Sim are waiting by the door now too, Justin with his red scarf still jaunty around his neck but shifting his weight from foot to foot with a manic energy. Sadie, Maeve can't help but notice, pulling up closer to Sim.

Karo catches Maeve's eye, tension lining her face.

"Right, got it, stay inside," Karo says now. "We're on our honor."

She crouches jerkily to retrieve the unused equipment, bundling it together in the tarp as best she can. Maeve wonders that no one else has noticed this change in her. Hard to ignore. But the men are busy.

From the doorway, Sim calls out: "Remember your pretty face, Maeve." He brushes a gloved hand across his nose and cheeks. "Dan's right—stay inside, out of the cold."

Maeve's brow furrows. It's a reminder of their last hike together—but what she remembers now is the way he argued with Anna. The two of them going at it: Anna facetious and almost silly, Sim unable to drop it, taking it all too seriously.

"We'll be back here tomorrow," Dan says. "With the goddamn army if that's what it takes."

Sim flinches at the word, and even Karo pauses down on her haunches before rising slowly back to her feet. But it's Sadie she locks eyes on when she responds.

"That's what I'm hoping for. Good luck. All of you."

Sadie raises a hand in salute and then they're gone, out the door and away. An immediate, vacant silence fills the room. When Karo walks to the window, her steps ring out, echoey. Maeve follows a moment later, then checks the door to make sure it's secure. The damn door, she thinks.

She turns back to the room, cavernous and noiseless aside from the crackle of the fire. Instead of feeling abandoned, she feels light, almost light-headed, as though there's suddenly not enough oxygen. A slight tremor in her muscles, the feeling you get after a long, hard workout. She remembers now what Sim said to Anna out on the ice.

We'll just let the next person freeze.

They pass the afternoon efficiently, each independent of the other, and without much discussion, as though there were no avalanche and no crisis, as though Anna were merely in another room, working away, and the others off on a day trip somewhere.

Maeve is absently tidying when she finds the tote bag of minibar loot that Justin brought downstairs on the floor by the leg of an armchair. For the best, she thinks. It must have been too heavy or cumbersome to cram into his backpack for the hike downhill. She tucks the bag under the desk for safekeeping and turns to check on Karo, who is reviewing a gallery catalog by the fire, assiduously working to regain her usual confidence. When she looks up, it's like a warning shot. She doesn't want to talk about it.

"About Dan," Maeve says instead. "I didn't realize he and Justin—that Justin had a thing for him. Or they have a thing? I couldn't tell."

Karo's face relaxes. "Oh, Dan has a thing with everyone. That's just the way he is."

Maeve's eyebrows lift. "Everyone?"

"Well. Frequently, let's say. I told you, people become teenagers." She half turns back to the book of color plates in her lap as though she is trying to decide which is more important, the paintings or Maeve. "I think that's why some men choose to work in places like this. Resorts or retreats. Everything is ephemeral, everything is possibility."

Maeve shakes her head and drops into a chair.

"I met my husband at a residency. My ex-husband," she corrects herself quickly. Why does she still do that? *He's gone, he's gone. Ex, ex, ex.* "My ex-husband, my ex."

"So you know. You know what these places are like."

"Anna was hoping she was special, I guess—"

Karo sets the book aside with a quivering hand.

"Anna was naive, then."

This comes out abruptly. Maeve wonders who she could be angry with—Anna? Dan? Herself for letting any of it happen?

Maeve, for bringing it up.

"I'm sorry," Karo says. "It's just—I don't know how I'm going to explain it to her husband. Her mother." She turns and leans into the arm of the couch. "This was her second time here—so I knew her a little bit. She was quite lovely. Energetic, as you know. Brazen." She looks to Maeve. "I liked her very much."

"Me too," Maeve says.

It must be cold enough now upstairs that they didn't need to hide her body away in the freezer, Maeve thinks. It was Justin who made such a fuss about it—and now Justin not even here. She doesn't say any of this out loud, but she can feel it burning in her.

"They fear death," she says instead. "Men—"

"Everybody fears death."

There's a curtness, or impatience, to Karo's manner that Maeve cannot seem to escape. She changes course.

"He never came on to me. Dan, I mean. But I wondered about him a few times. I found him—intrusive." It's a polite way to say what she really means.

Karo almost laughs.

"I saw him trailing you around campus. Dan can be quite competitive. But at a certain point, I suspect he decided you were already taken."

"Gross," Maeve says. "Gross—that is not at all what I wanted to hear."

"You asked. I'm sure it bruised his ego. He thinks of himself as some kind of alpine playboy."

Maeve closes her eyes and opens them again. Debating.

"What about Sadie?"

Karo thinks about that.

"I think Sadie is rather too single-minded for him. Argumentative. That would be too much for Dan in a girl her age."

"No, I mean—you're quite sure you can trust her?"

"Sadie?"

It's the wrong question, or the wrong timing. Nevertheless.

"Sadie's a pleaser," Karo says, casually flipping a page in her catalog. "An achiever. It's what makes her an excellent assistant—she gets a real buzz from praise. I imagine it makes her an excellent doctoral candidate."

"This morning—" Maeve stops, then starts again. "The reason I asked—this morning, upstairs, I found her going through Anna's things. She said she was looking for Justin's camera. She'd been using it for something, some kind of secret. Something to do with Sim—"

Being a pleaser, she thinks, also makes you easy to groom.

But Karo just stares at her blankly and doesn't offer anything in reply. Maeve stumbles on: "I thought it was strange," she says. "I mean, for her to be there at all."

"We all have things we'd rather others didn't see."

Maeve pulls up short. This isn't the response she's expecting.

She stands and begins to brush off her jeans as though they've become ashy. Really, she just has an urge to wipe the slate, wipe herself clean. "For the record, my thing with Sim—it was meant to be easy and quick. A bit of fun. That's all I wanted."

"Men never think we're capable of that." Karo gives a brisk nod and turns back to her catalog. "And, *for the record,* you're right, of course: Sadie shouldn't have been going through Anna's things." She looks up again. "I took the camera. I have it now. It was causing too much trouble, all that sniping, back and forth—and I have absolutely no interest in a disaster documentary for High Water. I thought it would be best to remove it from the mix."

Maeve stands there, a little stunned. Karo struggles to her feet. When she goes into her office and shuts the door, Maeve is relieved to be alone.

At first, she thinks of using the upstairs hallway as a practice space, somewhere she can refocus without a witness. Karo is unlikely to brave the stairs in her condition. Maeve hasn't been able to shake off the desperate urge to hit things, to smash her knuckles into a wall. Using her body will feel good: the extra adrenaline still buzzes in her limbs.

But anywhere outside the lobby is settled in its cold now. Upstairs, it feels not so much like the thermostat has been set too low but like the frigid interior of a log cabin shut up for the winter. She paces the hall a few times, trying to make it work, but eventually just takes the opportunity to move her things downstairs. Extra layers, all her dance gear, every sweater and pair of socks she brought along with her—she packs it all up. She slips into an old plaid button-up, for comfort, pulls on a pair of fleece-lined leggings, then her jeans. Last, she slings the duvet off her bed across her shoulders.

They won't be able to sleep upstairs, away from the fire. Not anymore.

The photo-booth image of herself and the kids: this, she won't cram into her suitcase or risk losing in among the gear in her dance bag. She pauses in the icy room, looking down at their faces, playing the smooth finish between her finger and her thumb. Anna's bear claw with its razor edge still sits in its place, in the pocket at her hip. She slides the little photo strip into her breast pocket instead, to carry close to her skin.

Turns her phone on: No service. Turns it off again.

Before she leaves, she crosses back into Anna's room and stands there. Whereas the rest of the building feels vast, so empty it echoes, in here, the walls feel too close. Maeve takes a deep breath and tries to push it all away—then sets about tidying the mess that Sadie left behind. The bag and its contents, the clothing, strewn over the floor.

She makes up the bed last, a morning habit, the way she would for Talia or Rudy. This time the act of pulling the covers up over the mattress, smoothing them out, feels like ceremony.

Back in the lobby, Maeve works up a sweat by the mezzanine stairs, focusing on whatever burns: a lot of planking, then barre work at the rail. Karo in her office, no audience watching from the fireside this time.

With no witness but herself, she can concentrate on drills, hard athletic work, repetition. If performing is storytelling, then practice is meditation. She starts with her mind spinning out and her muscles stiff, but there's a rug that keeps her hands off the cold ground and makes the floorwork easier, and her instinct is borne out. An hour, then two hours, and the adrenaline is finally gone, replaced by a radiant warmth in her working limbs. She can think again.

It's hard not to keep checking the window while she works, though. Maeve catches herself casting a regular, furtive glance to the white expanse of outdoors, snow and trees and more trees. When she's done, she gives in and takes a long hard look out, both front and back. Realizing, now, that she's been worried the others would give up and return. They haven't.

Outside, the light thins and fades. Karolina comes out of her office and Maeve stokes the fire, adding a few logs and hauling wood closer in from the pile near the back door.

The sun goes down.

"Do you know," Karo says, lighting an oil lamp, "I've lived here for five years, in this place. But I've never been here alone."

She gives her wrist a painful snap, and the match snuffs out. The new flame flickers in its glass cage.

"Just tell yourself it's the last night of this," Maeve says. "A matter of hours."

But Karo's hand still hovers over the flame, the tremor in it unmistakable. The foil trays that Sim and Maeve retrieved in the morning are still stacked on the main desk and she unwraps a corner of each, one by one, to figure out what's in there, but it all seems too fussy. In the end Maeve digs an unopened package of hot dogs out of the back of the refrigerator. The kitchen itself must be cold enough now to keep things fresh. She skewers a few hot dogs with the longer, unbroken sticks of kindling to hold over the fire.

It's quiet and almost cozy with just the two of them. They go to pull the couch up closer to the fire, but Karo falters and then backs away. Maeve waits for her to take up her side again, but when the other woman doesn't—only standing there, gripping her hands together as if in prayer—she adjusts it herself. They curl up, each at one end, holding their hot dogs over the flames.

For a long moment, neither of them says anything.

The silence feels soft and heavy. There's only the indiscriminate crackle of burning wood to break it up, here and there, in bursts. Maeve looks over and finds Karo focused on the front windows, staring out into the night. Neither wistful nor anxious, just a steady gaze. There's nothing out there that Maeve can see: the dark also soft, also heavy.

"I worried," Maeve says. "I wondered if they'd turn around and come back again before nightfall. But I guess not."

A drop of moisture, fat or just liquid, comes off the end of her skewer and hits the flame with a sizzle. She lifts it away from the fire.

"No, that wouldn't carry. Not for Dan," Karo says. She blinks, and the strain in her face is hard to ignore. "He'll be in it now. Until this thing is finished."

Karo's skewer flames up at one end and she gives it a shake, pulls it out to cool. But when she holds it up, the skewer keeps on shaking—the tremor, Maeve can see now, moving from Karo's elbow to her fingertips. She leans closer in case the other woman needs help.

"Are you all right?"

When Karo answers, it's matter-of-fact. All business.

"I have a great deal of pain. My stomach—my stomach hurts. It makes it hard to eat. And my bones, deep inside somewhere. I mean, not really the bones themselves, it can't be. It's just the nerves around them. The whole system is misfiring. That's all."

"You couldn't have gone with him," Maeve says. "You couldn't have made the trip the way he wanted you to. Dan, I mean."

Karo looks at her, misgiving in her eyes.

"On foot? No."

"Is it wise to live up here at all, then?"

"It's why I took the job." She takes a last survey of her half-burned skewer and lays it down on the ashy hearth. "I was diagnosed at forty—that's early onset, very strange. No one had thought to check for something like this, so I'd been through a terribly dark time. Unexplained pain will do that to you. You begin to look for a way out. But then I started seeing things, people, that weren't there—that's when I went back to the doctor. Because of the hallucinations. I thought I was going crazy." Her features stiffen, and something in her eyes changes, as though she is in a different place, a darker place, just revisiting the memory. "I mean, in a way, that's exactly it: I was."

She blinks slowly and takes a breath. "But on the upside, that early diagnosis—it means the drugs work very well. So a job like this, with reasonable hours, downtime, insurance that covers the medication—" She nods to herself, then to Maeve. "You can see that I couldn't continue painting. Not in any real way, not as my life, my living." She shifts, pulling up on the blanket, and the movement of her hips makes her wince. "I wish I could say I don't remember who she was, that Karolina. But I do remember. I still feel her inside me. This was, at least, a way to stay connected to that world," she says. "Making art is easier when you're well."

"Or wealthy," Maeve says. "Or you don't have children. Children come with a cost."

"I wouldn't know."

It occurs to Maeve that Karo must feel a certain amount of envy toward the constant parade of working artists who come through the center. More than envy—resentment.

For a moment, she wonders if it could have been Karo who locked Anna out. Anna, famous in her circle, both experimental and political in her way. Almost as quickly, she pushes the idea from her mind: *The woman is sick. She's struggling to toast a hot dog, Maeve.*

It couldn't have been her. In a way, what Karo has done here at the center mirrors Maeve's own plan. Trapped in a body she doesn't recognize, she's chosen to direct others instead.

"How long have the drugs been gone?"

"I took the last dose yesterday. I have a few sleeping pills left—" A sharp intake of breath as Karo reaches down to massage her foot, the arch curving painfully.

"You'll be glad of them, I expect."

There's a brief but noticeable silence, Karo looking at her rather strangely. Then: "I got complacent. My own fault." Her voice grows stronger, trying to resume her usual brisk pace. "But I'm sure they'll get a crew up here by tomorrow."

The day seems to have stretched on forever. Maeve's eyes are softly burning. She turns to lean on the arm of the couch so that she's facing Karo rather than the fire.

"You don't think it's dangerous, the four of them out there alone?"

"Of course it's dangerous. The conditions are dangerous. But it's dangerous to wait too long as well."

"That's not what I mean."

"I know exactly what you mean."

This time the silence is hard-edged. If Karo could easily get up and walk away, she would; Maeve can see it in her.

"She wasn't wearing shoes," Maeve says finally. "Anna."

Karo's face twitches.

"How much do you know about hypothermia?" she asks. Impatient, but resigned now to the conversation. When Maeve says nothing, she keeps on. "She probably threw them off herself. At the very end, before death—your body tries this last, wild solution. Your capillaries open wide. Blood rushes to the surface, to your skin. Suddenly it feels like you're burning up instead of freezing. You might strip off your clothes. Lots of people do," she says. "Don't think I haven't considered all the possibilities." She leans in sharply. "But I didn't see what happened to Anna. And neither did you."

Maeve pulls back, chastened.

"No," she says. "No, of course not. It's just—" She shakes her head, as though the action could dispel the tension in the room. It sometimes feels like the years she spent with Iain—and, later, hiding from him—have made her into a woman she doesn't like: anxious. Frightened, even. "I guess I'm thinking about her, that's all. She was so focused on those dreams, the bear dreams I had. Maybe they predicted something?" It's a naive thing to say, both flimsy and somehow very true. "She thought of them as transformative. Or, I mean, that's how she imagined them to be."

"Did she?" Karo blinks at her. "Anna was a filmmaker, not a spiritualist. She was interested in capturing those dreams, in using them herself—as images." She rolls her eyes. "Spiritualism." The change in tone suits her; she switches feet, working the cramp out of the other arch. "You'd have to believe that dreams find us, everything happens for a reason, blah-blah…do you really believe all that?" She looks down at her own hand, trembling there against her sock foot, then back to Maeve. "No.

185

Dreams are only fragments. Physical fragments in the brain. That's their value. We use them to work out what's past—and practice for the future. Practice! Not predictions. We say: *Trust your instinct,*" she says. "Instinct is what shows up when you've learned something over and over, from experience. You know more than you think, Maeve." There's a silence, and then that slightly hawkish look again. "In dreams, you always know what to do. Don't you?"

The question comes out low and serious, and they stare at each other for a long moment. Then the fire dims, and Maeve adds a little more kindling to it, shoring it up.

She doesn't answer.

There's a new brightness outside, the clouds thinning for long enough to let moonlight hit all that white, acres and acres of snow. They don't talk about whether to sleep or try waiting up in the hope that a dig-out crew might arrive in the night. They just watch as the light moves, the moon rising far above them, until the silence is too much to bear.

Karo slips a sleeping pill under her tongue and tucks in at one end of the couch, eyes closed, but Maeve eventually makes up a bed for herself on the floor, cushions from all the armchairs in a fat row and the duvet she rescued earlier in the day over the top. She can't sleep and lies there breathing. Listening to Karo breathe. There's no way to know what time it is. Midnight? Earlier? Later? By now the others will have reached the village, Maeve thinks. If the village is still there. If there is something or someone to reach. Above her on the couch, Karo twitches and murmurs, sinks further into her blankets, falls into sleep-breath. The fire keeps burning away and Maeve gets up and goes to the back door for more wood, then just stays there, staring out into the night.

It's snowing again, but only lightly. Fat, full flakes. Wind skims the trees, the promise of a new squall approaching. The moon hidden for the moment by clouds.

Standing in a dark window always gives Maeve the feeling she's being watched—even here, in the middle of nowhere, with no one else around, no one maybe for miles. Another leftover anxiety. She resents it.

Iain. Always Iain: in the grocery parking lot, or standing by the school's chain-link fence, or under the maple in Maeve's backyard. Iain at the window. On her porch. At her door.

Her neighbor, an old lady, telling her how charming he was: he'd left Maeve a bouquet, two dozen roses. Maeve broke down and filed a report. The police told her they'd speak to him.

But the problem, the cop said, calling back the next day, *is he's just not over you yet. He's still in love, he says.* Before hanging up, he reminds her: *It's hard for a man. You've taken his children.*

He waited outside her house the night before he died—the night before he got on a plane that put him in the wrong city at the wrong time. Maeve in the rocking chair at her kitchen window, keeping watch; Iain in a black rental car, parked at the curb.

July. High summer, a heat warning, and all of Maeve's windows and doors locked tight. She didn't dare to let the cat out. She didn't dare to open the door even for that. She'd signed for a registered letter early in the day, then opened it to find a court file number, a date.

He'd never get custody, her lawyer assured her. Almost certainly not.

So then why go to court?

Because fighting him would cost Maeve everything.

The children whining in their sleep, faces pink and slick with sweat. She'd given them ice packs to cool their pillows, a wet facecloth chilled in the freezer and laid across each hot belly. The cat yowled by the back door and woke them. Still she kept it locked.

He's just not over you.

Maeve in the rocking chair with a cushion in her lap. Under the cushion, a kitchen knife. She knew this was useless. Worse than useless:

the scar on her hand a constant reminder of how easily a weapon could be turned against you.

He wouldn't get it out of her hand this time.

It was easy to imagine him coming to the door. He'd done it before, stood on the step, pounding. Rattled her windows to see if they were locked. Maeve could see the dead bolt from where she sat, could picture, not a turning of the lock, but a crowbar splinter, the frame coming loose from the wall around it. One fist and then an arm breaking through. A boot, kicking its way in.

She'd go for his face first, the knife cleaving down the length of his nose, splitting him in two. He wouldn't expect that from her. He would expect something low down and lame, a few stabs to his soft parts. She didn't want to aim for his heart or his guts or even his balls. She wanted him gone.

After a few hours, she stopped waiting for him to come to the door but imagined instead circling the house herself. Going out the back entrance, along the high hedge, through the neighbor's yard, and down that way. Into the back seat behind him. Slicing his throat.

She's small and light and she knows how to move fast.

This is what she thought about during the whole long night. He stayed there in his car till the sun came up again. He stayed till other people started other cars, until the smell of coffee and bacon and gasoline began to move through the heavy air. She thought he'd never leave her alone.

Until he did, she tells herself now. He did go. He got on a plane and the plane took him so far away that he couldn't come back.

An accident. Kind of.

Sometimes she wonders if she willed it. The shooter. Can you do that? Can you wish someone dead so fiercely that your wish transmits? A child's question.

She is not a child.

Dreams, Karo said, are a way of working out the past. Not the future.

But Maeve is aware that she's still the same woman she was that night, with as much to fight for—even if the children aren't sleeping upstairs but waiting for her, far away, at home.

She closes her eyes now to expel the memory, to wash it clean.

When she opens them again, she blinks. Back in the trees, there's something moving. For a second, her heart skips—as though it could be Iain himself.

She peers out, thinking first that the others must have returned after all. But it's more defined than that. A shadow.

Perhaps not all of them. Perhaps just one.

Maeve shoves her feet into her boots and steps outside, holding the door safely open with one hand. But the shadow doesn't move. The darkness of the forest grows, lying in wait. No one shouts to her.

She does hear something, though. A huff. Is it? A low grunt?

Maeve pulls in, holds her breath—

But the clouds shift: the shadow disappears, swallowed up by the night. She scans the snow from her doorway out to the trees. Whatever it was—real or imagined—she can't see it now. The woods are silent. To each side, only the mountains loom in the dark.

She retreats back inside and locks the door.

The fire cracks and spits sparks, and Maeve shivers at the noise. She pads softly to her makeshift bed and lies down. Karo sleeping, and no one else in the whole place. She tries not to think of Anna lying on her shelf.

The building like an endless cavern around her. Maeve alone, exhausted and wired, all at once.

Sleep. She needs to sleep, that's all.

Her eyes finally close but even as she drifts off, she's unable to shake the sense that something is waiting, outside in the dark. Feeling it there.

The moonlight shifts again, then disappears. Dreaming now, Maeve slides her boots back on and steps outside into a storm. The snow is so thick she can't see—is that the building behind her? Or is that the forest, and the center is ahead? The ridge to one side and safety to the other, but which is which? Maeve gropes blindly for the door, the new snow stinging her face—but the door shuts, and now she's spinning in circles, desperate.

She realizes she is not alone. Something is out here with her. It grows darker, closer, pressing in. A new cold cuts through her wrists, the back of her neck. She knows it's there.

She cannot see it. She can't see her hand in front of her face.

In the lobby, Maeve opens her eyes with a start. Awake.

She turns over on her cushions, her breath coming short and broken. There's a creak back in the kitchen and she freezes—then again, somewhere else, lower down. She waits, counting the seconds between sounds the way you count in a storm between the flash and the crack of thunder. She can remember lying this same way, in the heat of that night, with Iain pacing on the sidewalk below. Willing herself to stay alert.

There's nothing out there now. Just a dream. She saw that for herself.

She closes her eyes, counts to ten, breathes. Allows the repetition to draw her gently back to sleep.

Another thump—the sounds are coming from the spa level. She's sure of it now. But this time, it's more like a slam. Heavy.

Maeve's head swims. She struggles to rouse herself, but it's too late, a new dream already taking over. She finds herself downstairs, in the lower hallway. She *is* dreaming again, isn't she? Or is she sleepwalking, like Anna?

It's dark, and she's feeling her way along the wall. This is where she was the night she saw Sadie crouched in a doorway. It must be; it's so much warmer here, the sudden change makes her shiver. On the other side of the wall she hears a groaning noise and another heavy thud, and she stops.

There's a room down here. Down in the basement. Did she know that? She peers in, squinting. On the far wall, she can just make out another door. A door to the outside.

That same sharp cold, stinging at the back of her neck.

A loud pop from the fire and Maeve bolts upright, fully awake this time. She is in her bed in the lobby, Karo asleep on the couch. She hugs her knees to her chest, recovering. The last dream image still burning in her mind:

In the strange room, the door's handle pumps up and down. The dead bolt grinds in its lock.

DAY 7

IN THE MORNING Maeve wakes by the fire, which is dead.

It's barely warm enough, even buried under the duvet, and the contrast where the air touches her skin is stark. The morning air is not just cool. It's crisp—frosty even. Bad dreams and a new blizzard swept in overnight, each of them waking her over and over. She burrows down inside the covers, relieved for the daylight. At least now she can stop trying to sleep.

In the light of morning, she pulls her hand from under the covers and places it on her cheek, her ear, and the sudden heat against her skin gives her a shiver. She twists in her makeshift bed to look out the window, but there's nothing new to see. It's snowing. Up on the couch, Karo is still sleeping; only the trim of her wool hat and her eyes show at the edge of her blankets.

Maeve keeps the duvet wrapped around her like a giant shawl and crouches by the hearth to rebuild the fire. The embers are there, black and ashy, and she builds a teepee of kindling first and lets it flame up before adding the bigger split logs, one by one. When the fire takes, she leaves it burning and, glancing back at Karo one last time, slips into her office and shuts the door.

Inside, Maeve scans the surfaces first, but the desk is spare and clean, the cabinets closed. She rolls a few drawers open and shut slowly, unsure what her excuse would be if Karo were to walk in. *I was just looking for an Advil,* Maeve practices in her mind. *I thought you might have some over-the-counter stuff in here.* The cabinets are stacked with hanging files; in the desk drawers, only office supplies.

Maeve looks to the window. Karo's day pack sits propped against an old painter's stool. She takes one last quick glance over her shoulder and opens up the pack.

There you are, she thinks.

She tucks Justin's camera bag under the wealth of duvet and opens the door.

Maeve passes through the lobby and goes up the stairs, duvet dragging, to her own room. The space is vacant and haunted now, bare sheets drawn up over the mattress, frost inside the windowpane. In the mirror, her reflection startles her. White-faced in white bedding, her own ghost. She needs to pee; in the bathroom, the water in the bowl with the first glassy sheen of ice forming along its surface. The porcelain burns cold against her thighs.

Safe in her privacy, she reaches into her pocket, pulls out the photo strip, and sobs, her thumb tracing the line of Talia's brow, as though she could tuck her long hair behind one ear or stroke Rudy's puffed-out cheeks. Maeve's own cheeks in the photo, a little gaunt but lifted in real glee. She wants to cry it out here, far away from Karo. Alone with it.

All the things this time was supposed to be. A rest, a reset, a way for Maeve to regain her spirit and come back a better artist—better, in fact, at everything. More able to care for her children. More able to care for herself. And every last moment of it turned to disaster. A punishment for wanting more than the world wants to offer women.

The snow and the cold and Anna frozen in it. *Punishment* seems the only possible word.

She gives herself five minutes—five minutes to wallow, she thinks— then wipes her nose with her sleeve and leaves again.

The common room at the end of the hall has the widest view of the grounds and a door with a manual lock. She stands at the window. She's so much higher here, the vantage so much better. She goes to crank the window open, thinking that it will shove the high-piled snow off the sill, but it's frozen shut. She has to push up onto her toes to see out. The open field to one side, and the new snow, always new snow, moving in.

Nothing else. No person, no vehicle, no rescue on the horizon.

There's a sudden flurry of movement by the forest border, and she pivots to catch it, but it's only a few elk. Separated from the herd? Charging out of the woods.

She freezes there, watching them, then turns back to look at the trees, expecting something else to appear behind them: wolves, or a bear, or even a moose. Something chasing them down. But there's nothing to explain it and Maeve watches them until they disappear from view. Spooked, and cutting through the snow.

When they're gone, she turns away from the window and unpacks Justin's bag, putting everything on the counter of the kitchenette: camera, hard drive, SDs. She goes to turn the camera on, but it's dead. Of course it's dead: she rummages through the bag's zipper compartments for an extra battery.

If nothing else, she knows Anna had the camera trained on her the night before she died, Maeve's last dance in the lobby. The footage is worth a look. But there's also whatever Sadie was doing with it. Secretly, with or without Sim. If Karo thought the thing was causing trouble, she must have had good reason. And that reason is likely on film.

There are two extra battery packs in the side pocket, one drained, one showing a 40 percent charge. Maeve slips the juiced battery into the camera and hits Play on the first card.

There's a blast of sound and she almost jumps out of her skin—the volume is way up. She hits Stop, looks all around, then takes a breath. Turns the sound down. Starts again.

The dance footage is the first thing she sees. It's the last thing that was recorded. The normalcy of watching herself dance on the little screen feels, at first, like a reprieve. But there's a strangeness to the way it's filmed—it goes in and out of focus, as though Anna were distracted, as though she were holding the camera but really watching something else. There's some ambient noise and Maeve nudges the volume up a little. She can see herself and also a shadow reflection in the window. There, it's not only Maeve in the frame but Sim too—his image growing larger in the glass until she sees the real Sim enter the shot, skirting the edge of Maeve's space. He disappears where the mezzanine stairs begin, and a moment later, Maeve watches herself fall.

The screen goes black.

Maeve removes the card and pockets it, like a souvenir she can take home. She plugs another one in. There are a million little files, all numbered, no names, and she sets them up to play through. The first few groups show a different High Water: full sun, leaves on the trees, people she doesn't know. A lecture, maybe, or a tour, outdoors in summer. The season changes. She's waiting to see the clip of Dan out in the snow, the one where he loses his temper and takes the camera from Justin's hands—but it's missing. Justin must have deleted that one, scrubbed it clean. She scrolls and tries again, scrolls and stops cold.

More and more, what she sees is Anna. It's like he tried to capture her in her worst moments, Maeve thinks. The ugliest angles, bad light, her face red with cold.

"Girl, he sure hated you," she murmurs aloud. She can almost feel

Justin's resentment in the clips. Once, he accidentally captures Dan walking into the moment, reaching out to prod teasingly at Anna's shoulder, to bug her, then suddenly taking her hand. He must have thought they were alone. The clip cuts off.

When she pulls out the card this time, a row of thumbnails pops up. Maeve realizes there are files temporarily saved to the camera itself. Scrolling back, she sees Anna again and hits Play.

Time-stamped only a few days ago: Anna, viewed through the slim crack of a doorway, left just barely ajar. She is in some kind of storeroom, Maeve thinks. The camera pans to the floor and up again, struggles to focus. A low murmur, a man's voice: she wasn't alone, someone was with her. Dan.

Maeve suddenly recognizes the basement hall.

It's not Justin behind the camera. These are Sadie's files.

The room comes back into view, zoomed closer now: Dan with Anna's hair taut in his hands, her throat arching. One hand moving over her mouth, then her eyes. Using his hold to direct how she can move. Folding her over a table.

For just a moment, Dan turns, and it's almost like he's looking into the camera. Then he turns away. Maeve rewinds, watches again.

Did Dan guess that Sadie was secretly filming them? Did Karo? They all had their twisted loyalties before she ever arrived.

A new thumbnail, and the image changes.

She leans closer. It's not Anna on-screen anymore, but Maeve.

Maeve in her room. When she thought she was alone. She watches herself cross from the bed to the window, rummage through a bag. Stand and pull her T-shirt off over her head; turn to the mirror, sweep a hand down along her own breasts, her waist. Examining her body before her morning warm-up.

A sudden cold feeling in her chest. Alone in the common room, Maeve looks over her shoulder despite herself.

How did Sadie get this? Why?

She pauses the video, trying to guess the vantage point. Was Sadie actually in the room with her? Or was she filming from the next room, silent and stealthy, that adjoining door just slightly ajar?

She scans forward, her heart starting to race. Maeve from overhead, from some high window, as she fights through the snow. A skip; static. Maeve in the lobby, lost in thought on the floor. Legs wide open, folding over into a stretch. Another skip. There's no rhyme or reason to the footage, and Maeve realizes they're almost incidental, hurriedly picked up whenever Sadie had the camera. Whenever she had a chance. Justin was so accustomed to his SD cards that he never noticed what Sadie was saving to the camera itself. Or he didn't care.

For a second, she wonders if she's wrong, if Justin took the videos himself the same way he took hate-footage of Anna.

On-screen, a door opens to a darkened room and the camera moves slowly inside. Everything is gray or dark gray. A streak of moonlight from the window lights the way; there's a muffled sound, movement. But then there's Sadie's black, bone-straight hair falling down her back, her slim shoulder, her hip—she's caught herself, accidentally, in the vanity mirror, camera in hand. A slow turn. Her lovely, strong cheekbones. Her lips.

The camera lifts and focuses on the mirror frame: Maeve's own little photo strip. Maeve and the kids. Across the room then, to Maeve herself, in bed. Asleep. She stirs as though a dream has disturbed her, and the screen goes black.

Sadie was in her room.

All those nights with Iain outside her window. Watching. Maeve feels like she might vomit. She thinks of herself, just a few moments ago, using the privacy of her assigned room to have a good cry. Privacy? It's as though she were onstage the whole time. Her every move before an audience; she just didn't know it. She scans forward, watching herself in fast motion: in the hall by her room, down in the lobby, walking in the snow. Once, the Minnie Mouse voice of someone talking, close to the mic. Maeve slows the film down to regular speed. It's Karo's voice she hears, at the very end of the clip: *What are you doing there? Be careful.*

Then another room. It's dark and hard to see, but Maeve's there, parading from end to end. Peeling away her clothes.

The lights come up, sudden and bright. She's standing naked, Sim crossing the room to meet her. It's his room the night of the party—the blank canvas leaned up against the wall reflecting light like a photographer's softbox. He reaches for her, a hand at her belly, her scar.

Looks into the camera, and winks.

Karo is sitting up when Maeve comes back downstairs, but she's wrapped tight in the bedclothes, a new dullness in her eyes.

"Good morning," Maeve says. She's left the camera upstairs. It doesn't matter to her now if Karo notices it's missing: she'd like to drop-kick it into the woods, bury it in snow, destroy it. She wonders if Karo has watched it all herself, if that's what she meant by *causing too much trouble.*

Maeve wonders if she always knew. If this is something Sim paid for, Sadie with a side hustle, she thinks. Or if it was merely Sadie doing favors. Sadie in love. Or Sadie, ambitious and eager to align herself with the most powerful man in the room.

Maeve shoves a foil tray of food into the hot ash at the edge of the fire.

"You should have some breakfast," she says.

Karo gives an odd smile.

"Imagine, this is what we've come to. The ballerina is going to make me eat."

Maeve bristles but doesn't respond. She turns the tray on the hearth, moving it with a careful hand.

"So, no rescue crew in the night, huh? Only more new snow." Karo shakes the blankets off her shoulders but stays where she is, slumped against the back of the couch. "And then there were two."

Her voice is low and cracks at the edges. A symptom of the dry air, but also something else.

Or is it? Maeve catches herself. Maybe it's just lack of sleep, or stress. How can you know if someone is behaving oddly when you've known her only a few days?

"I should melt some snow," she says, using the task as a cushion against Karolina's mood and her own. "We need water."

She gets to her feet and grabs the pot from its perch at one end of the hearth. Karo rocks a little in her seat.

"Any minute now," she says. "We should hear the purr of the plow engine. Isn't that right?" She leans her head against the back of the couch and laughs.

Maeve pauses, watching her, then throws on her coat and goes to the back entrance with the pot to scoop snow. She's careful to wedge herself firmly against the door, never breaking contact with it; there's no telling if the lock will jam should the door fall closed, leaving Maeve stranded outside.

She straightens up, squinting at the trees. It's the same view as the night before, although she's peering into daylight this time. There are no shadows now, no moonlight. No hint of a bear's huff or rough grunt.

She feels watched all the same.

Maeve sees the dusky room from Sadie's video form again in her mind, another kind of dreamscape. The camera over Maeve's bare shoulder. The light comes up, bleaching her skin. Sim crosses the room to meet her.

There is no sound at all outside of the wind, the creaking of the near tree branches, and the occasional rhythmic flap of an awning or a flag somewhere out of sight. The snow is falling heavier now.

Always snow.

There is no motor. No plow.

"You're beginning to wish you'd gone with them, aren't you?" Karo, still wrapped in her blanket, still unwilling to leave the couch.

Nothing, Maeve thinks, *could be further from the truth.* She doesn't want to be here at all.

Maeve wishes to God she had never come.

Karo seems off, in a deeper way. Paralyzed for the moment, biting at her thumb. She had high expectations for rescue by sunup; now the sun is up, and nothing has changed. Maeve has already mentioned the ice forming in the upstairs toilets and the news landed poorly.

"There's no reason to think we've been abandoned," Maeve says. But she's doing the math in her head—it's been eighteen hours since the others left.

She gets up to check the melting snow, pulling off the lid and giving the pot a violent shake.

What could have gone wrong? They got to the village and no one was there. There were other, bigger slides; the slides multiplied on each other. The trip from the empty village down to where people are did not go as well. Did not go at all.

She looks back to Karo, smaller and harder than ever where she's curled in place on the couch.

"I know Dan said—"

"Oh, fuck what Dan said." Karo's head snaps up. "If Dan doesn't show up with his rescue crew in another day or two, it'll be you on your own, trying your luck down the mountain," she says. "How much longer do you think we can really survive here?"

The speed of the turn throws Maeve for a loop. She can't quite respond.

"You say there's already water freezing in the bathrooms upstairs?" Karo keeps on. A half laugh. "The place is turning into an ice palace around us."

"Okay." Maeve sets the lid firmly back into place. "Maybe you need a little fresh air. I'll hold the door open for you. Might make you feel better—"

Karo just stares at her.

Maeve pauses, not sure whether to keep talking or just forget it. Karo leans forward and peels back the blanket, revealing her legs. Her feet in their wool socks are curled, cramped beyond any of Maeve's expectations. Each foot a crescent moon, a sickle, an exaggerated arching *pointe*.

"I can't."

Maeve wets her lip with her tongue, embarrassed. "I'm sorry. I didn't think—"

"It could get so bad so quickly?"

"I'm sorry," Maeve says again.

Karolina smooths the blanket back in place, then reaches down to massage her foot through the layers. Gingerly, as though it hurts to touch.

"I haven't been off the meds in five years. A lot can change in that time." She takes a breath and pushes it out, then looks at Maeve. "But you're right. It's my job, isn't it? To know what's out there?" There's a beat, and Maeve feels almost wary, as though Karo might be about to lose her composure or fly off the handle completely. Instead her face just hardens. "But I can't," she says. "So you're going to go for me. Outside." When Maeve starts to shake her head, Karo cuts it off quickly. "I need you to do a perimeter check, because I can't. I need to know if there's anyone coming for us."

Maeve feels her stomach drop, and she sinks onto the arm of the couch. She thinks of the shadow the night before, back where the trees begin. And in her dreams, that strange, dark presence, closing in. Maeve, outside, lost in a storm.

She knows it's irrational. She still doesn't want to go out there.

"In the toolbox in my office, you'll find some fluorescent ties—take those with you and use them as markers. The color will stand out against the snow." She means the markers will help Maeve orient herself, find her way back. She'll be out there alone this time. "Go down as far as the main gates, if you can," Karo says. "And as far again to the rear in case they're coming up the back road. You don't need to go all the way out along the ridge, not as far as we went together. Just to where it begins, to the break in the trees where the path used to be."

At the mention of the word *trees,* Maeve balks. She feels pushed into this, like she can't say no. Karo at her back, nudging her, urging her on.

"I don't think—" she begins. Is it even safe to leave Karo on her own?

"I need to know," Karo says, catching her look. She pauses, then says it again: "Maeve, I need to know. I can't bear this. Maybe you'll be able to see something, or hear them coming." She leans in, wincing. "You can flag them down. You can make sure they find us."

Her expression is less hard now. She looks like she might crumble. Even her voice has begun to shake. "You're a smart woman. And I'll be here—" She takes another breath. "I'll make sure you can get back inside." As she pulls up against the back of the couch, she winces again.

Maeve still doesn't move until Karo waves her away.

"Go on, get yourself ready. I need a moment to clear my head." But as she rises to her feet, Karo suddenly looks up. "And, Maeve—" She holds a hand out, as though she could catch Maeve's arm. "There's a cane, back in the closet in my office." She pauses, steadying herself. "I need to use the bathroom and I won't be able to walk without it."

The toolbox, plus whatever Karo salvaged as Dan loaded up his pack the day before, is tucked just inside her office door. *Toolbox* is a misnomer, Maeve finds. Not a toolbox at all but a large plastic storage container with a tight-fitting lid, the sort of thing Maeve herself uses to store Christmas decorations in the off-season, tucked away under her basement stairs.

Maeve cracks the box's lid and pulls it back.

On top, there's the tarp that Dan left behind, which Karo has folded up like a parcel: Maeve pulls this out first. Tucked inside, surplus flares and two cans of bear spray. In the tool bin proper there are a couple of cans of fire starter, a flashlight, six more flares, two neon safety vests, a small hacksaw, an ice pick, a camp stove. A bottle purifier plus two packs of tablets. A blue zip case for first aid containing latex gloves and bandages, disinfectant, a splint, a pharmacy bottle of penicillin. At the bottom of the tub, buried, she finds the fluorescent trail markers along with two rolls of duct tape.

But no snowshoes, not inside the tub or anywhere in the room. She swears under her breath: Dan has locked the extra pairs away. When she combs through the desk, she finds an envelope marked *storage keys*— but it's empty and she realizes he's taken the keys with him. The two women are not supposed to go outside, and this is another way for him to control that, even from a distance.

She pulls on a heavy coat she finds hanging on the back of the door and sinks her hands into the deep pockets. Her own boots, meant for city snow and warmer climes, will have to do.

She grabs a roll of duct tape instinctively—once, in an emergency, Maeve used half a roll to repair her pointe shoes; more than once, she's used it to wrap a sore ankle—then pulls out a handful of other items: the tie-on trail markers, a can of bear spray in a holster, a neon vest to strap over her coat. The blinding whiteout of her dream is still fresh in her mind. She can feel herself groping through it, as visceral as a real memory. She layers up, a pair of Karo's mittens over her own gloves, her hood pulled up over top of a wool hat, the safety vest as an extra measure. If things go sideways, she wants to be sure that Karo will see her from the door.

Her breath in the dream, coming sharp and frozen. She has to tell herself off, shake the feeling away.

"You're ready to head out on expedition," Karo says when she emerges, puffed up like a child in a snowsuit. Her tone is oddly suspicious.

"I enjoy expecting the worst," Maeve says. She adds some wood to the fire and shifts the waning pile a little closer to the hearth. Looking back at Karo, she tries to gauge her state of mind. "I'll be within sight of the center the whole time—you'll be able to track me in this beautiful vest." She offers a twirl, and the frown line at Karo's brow relaxes, at least a little bit.

Success, Maeve thinks. But she lingers, a piece of tinder in her hand, wondering if she should use it to wedge the door open. Just in case Karo can't manage it by the time she gets back.

Karo follows her eyes to the latch.

"Don't worry," she says. "I won't leave you stranded. We can't afford to lose any heat to an open door." Using the cane, she pulls herself across the lobby to see Maeve out the back way. It's a small reassurance.

Outside, Maeve feels less secure. Remembering the elk's sudden flight earlier in the day, she avoids the trees and walks around the building, following the route Anna must have forged between the doors, although there is no discernible path anymore. There's no evidence of Anna at all: she scans for the shoes Anna might have thrown off, the storm lantern she must have brought down with her, but any trace is long buried. New flurries dust her jacket and she shifts her weight, trying to keep her balance. She feels like she's sinking with every step.

At the front window, she waves and then checks to see if Karo is waving back, but the glare of daylight and all that white on the ground makes the window a mirror. All Maeve sees is a figure she knows must be herself, her face buried within her hood, the neon X of the vest across her chest. She leans in and visors her hands against the glass to look inside: Karo is nestled back on the couch, absently tending the fire with a long stick. Maeve knocks on the window and Karo glances up, lifts a hand in greeting. It's enough to allow Maeve to move on, the knowledge that Karo will at least be able to see and hear her when she needs to be let back inside.

She pushes forward in the direction of the road. The snow underfoot is denser now, hard-packed, and she tries to find a way to walk on top of it rather than forcing her way through, the frozen crust occasionally and suddenly breaking under her weight. Somewhere under here is the circular drive where the shuttle driver left her in the pouring rain—after telling her the rain itself was not to be trusted.

Can't predict nothing anymore, not around here.

Maeve squints up at the clouds. How could that have been only a week ago? Has she lost track completely? She tries to count back in her mind while plowing forward with her body through the drifts, hips tightening against it and her thighs starting to burn. She can see the trail the others made the day before already filling in, but it makes a deep enough cut through the white and she moves herself into it and shakes the snow off her legs. Turning back to see how far she's come, then pressing on, down to where the road used to lead, serpentine, to the main gates below. She pulls out her trail markers and reaches high to tie one on, then stops there, staring out. She tries to imagine the others on their trek: Dan out in front, Justin struggling to match his pace, Sadie keeping as close to Sim as she can.

And Anna gone, just gone. The curve of the bear claw in her pocket, hitched against her hip—a joke, in the end. It breaks her heart a little, the feel of it there. A memento, planted by a friend. Something to trigger a dream, and the dream just an image to record, to recycle, to make into something new.

All that time Maeve was sure it was a threat, evidence some man had been in her room—and the only real intruder had been Sadie. Sadie with her camera.

205

No wonder she's been dogged by a feeling of something there, looming over her. Somewhere in her subconscious, she knew.

But if Maeve was Sadie's main target, why did Anna's death have such an impact on the girl? Why did Sadie need to find that camera right away? Her first thought, her first opportunity. Because she was embarrassed or guilty—because she felt it incriminated her somehow?

The truth is, if not for the avalanche and everything that came after, Maeve would never have found out—and Anna herself would hardly have cared that she was being filmed. She might even have wanted to use the footage, a different angle to add to her own. The only person who really hates cameras is Dan.

Maeve stops on the thought. The first time she saw him lose his temper was out in the snow with Justin, ripping the camera from Justin's hands. In retrospect, it seems strange that he agreed to let Anna film him at all.

Almost unbelievable, in fact. She remembers Anna's halting response to the question. *He doesn't—he doesn't love it.*

But what if he didn't know? Or what if she was using that film in ways he didn't expect? What if Anna really did go and meet him that night, and there was an argument—

What if Sadie had caught something else on film, some other fight, something that might suggest the truth, only to discover after Anna's death that the camera was missing? She'd been mucking about with that camera for weeks; even Sim said as much. Maeve didn't watch every clip—she didn't look at every memory card. Shocked to find so much of herself on there, she'd switched the thing off.

She looks over her shoulder, a strange chill coming over her. How quickly Dan had found Anna's body—outside, from a window, when he should have been searching the rooms. She furrows her brow. How had he known where to look?

Dan, whose over-the-top CPR seemed even in the moment like some crazed display rather than the real thing.

It's a terrible theory.

And Sadie, who dove headfirst into this mess to try to gain Sim's favor, out there now, somewhere, with them both.

Snow catches on Maeve's eyelashes; a deep silence all around. There's no rip of civilization, no truck engine or snowmobile. No planes overhead. In fact, she can't think of the last time she heard the hum of an airplane making its way through the clouds.

No echo of a rescue plow burrowing up through the snow.

It's the kind of silence she used to covet: the way a travel brochure sells you peace and quiet.

Or an arts retreat. But that makes her think of Sim again, and she bites her lip.

If she ever gets home, she tells herself now, she'll take every vacation in a major metropolitan center. Nothing but Manhattan, Chicago, LA. Crowded cruises; Disney resorts with the kids. No Airbnb farmhouses in the townships. No more studio cabins in the woods. Nothing with fewer than two thousand loud, annoying people in her immediate vicinity at all times. Oh, to be surrounded by people. Imagine complaining about that.

It's a long moment before she catches herself.

Not *if* she ever gets home.

Not *if*.

When.

She gives the landscape one last good scan, a one-eighty-degree sweep of the eye, checking for any bit of motion, anything other than white. The fluorescent marker flutters where she tied it to the gate. She's farther out than she meant to go. The trail made the going easier, but it drops off ahead. She turns back toward the center, retracing her steps.

She can see herself approaching from a distance, a vague reflection: the puffy jacket, the neon X, chugging along, growing brighter, taller as she gets near. She's staring at the glass, trying to see beyond the mirror image and check on Karo, when something catches her eye.

She stops, alarmed. Over at the corner of the building, another reflection. Maybe? Some dark shape sweeping by.

Maeve waits. Alert, watching. There's nothing there now. Maybe it was a cloud in shadow. Or a bird. They haven't seen birds, it occurs to her now, for days. It's why the landscape is so quiet.

Not even a crow.

The shadow she saw last night, she reminds herself, was nothing.

She waits a moment longer, but the reflection or the sweep of wing doesn't recur. The silence seems to settle in around her in a new way, and she's aware of all her layers acting like insulation. A barrier between herself and the world. Her own pulse in her ears, a muffled swoosh. Suddenly anxious, she pulls back her hood, rips the hat off. Listening harder.

The building blinks back at her, windows silvery in the snow glare, reflecting the great expanse of white, the drifts stretching on and on. Her stomach tightens and she turns, slowly, to look behind her.

There is something out there after all.

Between Maeve and the gates, something skims across the snow. She leans back, straining to see in the weird brightness, trying to adjust her perspective. The thing whips and catches, then skates along farther. What is it? Some animal? What could be out in the open in this cold?

It skirts closer, and Maeve goes after it, even though the snow here is dense. It's not an animal, it can't be; the wind catches it up, and it twists and falls like a plait of long hair, like a skein of silk. Like rope.

It's red.

The second Maeve sees that, she recognizes it—she pulls off her gloves and sprawls ahead into the drift. It's Justin's scarf, his red cashmere. She pushes up to stand again in the wind. The scarf feels fine and damp in her hands, but as she turns it over, she notices the abrasion along one edge, and her finger splays through a new split in the fabric. As though it had been caught and torn, Maeve thinks. Not quite a hole. A wide fray.

She pulls her hand back and thumbs the damage anxiously. The finger thrusting through the hole seems carnal to her, almost gory. It makes her stomach turn. She has an impulse to dig the bear claw from her pocket and match it against the tear in the scarf.

Instead, her head snaps up, and she looks first over one shoulder, then back the other way, and again. The constant sheer of the wind against the empty landscape makes her feel as though she's caught in a tunnel. Anything could be right there, behind you, and you'd never know until it was too late. She has to close her hand tight around the torn scarf to keep it from shaking.

If something happened to Justin, it was before they got to the village. He must have been closer to the center than not when the scarf was lost. She thinks again of how she imagined him, struggling to keep up.

The wind rises, and a seam of snow ripples off the drifts and sprays across the horizon. There is snow coming down and snow going up, snow on the ground. Maeve pulls her hood up against the cold and turns and walks around the building, forcing herself to keep her eyes down, to keep her own path in sight.

A perimeter check, that's all. Three more trail markers left in her pocket: she needs to go only far enough to make some kind of report, to be sure that no one is out there coming for them. Or, she tells herself, to bring the good news if someone is.

She presses Justin's scarf down into her pocket. The scarf does not feel like good news.

Around back, there is at least a sense of shelter. The building acts as a windbreak and she cuts a trail to the edge of the woods, being firm with herself—*No backing out now*—one hand on the bear spray in its holster. The scattered few trees here and there are a reminder that there used to be walkways, little gardens marking the bend in each gravel path. She brushes the snow off a long, protruding branch and attaches another marker. She's smart about it, pausing to take a good sweep of the tree line and assure herself that nothing is there. When she's about fifty feet out, she calls in the direction of the woods.

"Justin?" Her voice doesn't echo but seems to whip away from her, instantly swallowed by the wind. She tries again: "Justin!"

There's no answer. Close to the edge of the forest now, Maeve casts around, looking for tracks. There's no sign of any other human, no animal's trail to follow. Nothing watching her from the woods.

She gauges the distance to the building, then allows herself a quick glance in all directions, just to be sure. Moving herself along—step-step-step, head down, turn, check right, over the shoulder and back—until it should feel casual, just another daily routine. Almost done now. But the white-on-white makes her head hurt. She squints and then widens her eyes; nothing works. She can't tell where one drift ends and another begins, and trying to see the nuance—what's light and what's shade, what's a dip caused by wind and what might have been made by something else—feels futile.

She's about to give up when a sudden drop takes her by surprise. The ground falls away: she trips and goes down hard, landing on one knee, then an elbow, her face in the snow.

Maeve pushes up to a crouch and brushes the cold from her cheek.

When she rises, she can see the depression all around her—not tracks, but a cleft in the snow where something heaved its body through. Some-one? No, it's far too big for a person. As deep and wide, easily, as the path cut through the snow out front by all the others on their way out.

For a moment she doesn't breathe at all. Her feeling the night before, that something was out here, watching her, comes heavy into her body. She fingers the scarf in her pocket and gets low again, looking more closely—for what? Some kind of hard proof. Red fibers, a trace of blood. But there's nothing like that.

Deep in the cleft, there are a few sharper marks, more discernible. More like tracks.

That's when she remembers the elk. Early that morning, only a few of them, three or four, charging out of the trees and off to the west.

Maeve steps back, her heartbeat calming. She can see how they came out through the trees, the branches snapped or swept clean where the animals brushed by them, the snow coming off in a spray. It's odd to see bare branches now, or the deep green of fir needles scattered against the white.

Back in the trees, a branch wavers in some current of air, as though something has caught it and let go. A moment later, even the branch is still.

She pushes her hood off again and glances around. Down at the front gates, the silence had been almost claustrophobic, but here, there's some kind of echo. Something whipping through the air.

Flapping. The same sound of a flag she heard earlier in the day.

But there is no flag, no awning, nothing on the building that she can see that would make that kind of noise, like the beating of a giant, distant wing. Her heart skips; she suddenly imagines the spinning blades of a propeller, a Search-and-Rescue plane. Maeve looks back a moment to the center. She's already been gone longer than anticipated. But isn't this the good news they were hoping for? A surge of adrenaline runs through her as she scans the area ahead, hyperalert. Impulsive, even. The echo must be coming off the ledge. The clear, open lip, high above the river and bare as tundra now, where she stood with Sadie that first day. An easy place to be seen, to signal for help.

She hesitates only a second before pressing on. Not right into the trees, not exactly, but along the edge, her gaze tracking deep into the woods. Just in case.

The building falls into the distance behind her. Karo, she tells herself, won't care—or not much. Karo will in fact be glad of Maeve's ingenuity if she's able to summon a rescue. The noise feels nearer now, echoing, cracking in the cold air. She splits off to the right, where the woods break apart, and pushes her way into the open, trying to get a better view.

Something flashes at her from high in the branches and she hears it, right overhead, sharper than ever—the sound she's been following all this time.

Just a sheet, whipping in the wind.

No, not a sheet. A tarp.

It's the dark green tarp, one of them, that Dan packed. But where Maeve is standing is the opposite direction of town.

She runs through all the things this could mean. That the tarp blew up in the high winds last night, all the way up the ridge from wherever they set up camp. Or that they chose some odd, circuitous route. Weren't they talking about that at one point? Going up to go down?

Or that the tarp somehow came free of the pack, or was taken out for some reason before they'd really left the property. Got caught by the wind and blew away.

Or that they never really left at all.

This last idea hits her like a blow to the chest and Maeve spins, checking behind her. There is no other sign of life, no equipment abandoned on the ground. Uneasy, she draws the red scarf from her pocket, scans the damage carefully. Next to the split, the fabric shreds away, the threads with an almost burned look and something else too— darker and gritty and somehow stiff. She fingers it.

Red on red. Dried blood.

Maeve looks up, then all around her, her heart pounding.

There was a disagreement of some kind. Another fight. The plan went wrong. Sadie, with her sharp, false loyalties, accused Dan of locking Anna out, and Justin retaliated, or maybe Justin knew about Sadie's footage and tried to use it against her, a blackmail scheme. That's why the video was still there, saved to the camera. Maybe Justin accused Dan himself or merely picked a fight out of jealousy. Anything was possible.

Or maybe this was always the plan. Maeve grows a little colder. If Anna's death was no accident—

She thinks of Dan loading his revolver and slipping it into the holster at his side.

Who else would target both Justin and Anna? What if this was a way to draw things to a quick end when Anna and Justin got too close? They'd all seen Dan's temper: with Justin, more than once.

She stuffs the scarf back into her pocket, then draws out its red tip once more, as though making sure she can trust herself, making sure it's really there. She remembers Dan's grip on Anna's hair, the way he turned, dead-eyed, to the camera. Above her, the tarp whips and cracks. This isn't what Maeve was hoping for. She was hoping to find—what? Search-and-Rescue, a helicopter. Someone she could flag down, like a woman with a flat tire at the side of the road.

Only there is no road. The sky is just sky. The truth of this starts to settle in and something colder runs through her again, a new desperation.

If Justin is dead, then it's possible that Maeve is out here in the woods with whoever killed him.

The tarp, like a bad omen, snaps again from overhead. She's standing in the emptiness when she hears something else. Louder, nearer. Everywhere at once. A shot? The crack of a gun.

Maeve's heart jumps. She ducks, crouching low to the ground, listening. It comes again, but this time the noise is deeper and vaguely familiar. Not a gun after all, she thinks: more like the echo of a frozen lake breaking apart in spring. A wave of sound. Rolling in almost like thunder.

Like the sound of a train.

That's when she knows.

Maeve turns and runs. Back along her own trail first, then off into the safer network of forest to the other side just as the ridge beyond where she was standing begins to cave in, down into the river valley below. The noise is there and then gone, enormous.

She spins in its wake, only a few hundred yards away. Watches as the ledge to the east collapses, then disappears.

Where there was land, there is no land now. Like the edge of the earth has fallen away.

But there was no earth there, she reminds herself. There was only snowpack, a cornice, a wide ledge. Impossible to know where the world ends under all this snow. Another hundred yards on, and Maeve would have gone with it.

The woods are quiet, her heart pounding in her ears.

She needs to get back to the center. Far out across the gap, she can see thicker clouds, the sky darkening again. The wind is sharper; it hurts her face.

Her own trail now seems too dangerous. Maeve turns to head back the other way, through the forest that surrounds the cabins. As far from the unstable edge as possible. There's a steep incline to one side and a kind of trough, a natural path leading down, and she takes this second route. Moving steadily, she walks with her head bare, despite the cold. It feels too vulnerable to keep the hood up, to have both her hearing and her vision restricted. The going is easier in the woods—less snow at her feet and more caught in the trees above.

There's the sound of snapping twigs, the odd *whump* of a clump of snow falling from branch to ground as she walks, and every time, she stops, frozen, listening to make sure there's nothing there. No one. It's only Maeve herself making the noise as she goes. It seems to take longer to get back than it did to come out—the snow is hardly as deep, but her clothes catch on the branches, and the woods here are thicker than before. The trees all start to look the same.

Sorry now that she didn't think to bring water. She stops a moment to get her bearings and bends down for a handful of snow.

That's the first time she sees the print.

It's not what she expected. It looks more like a foot—like a giant's footprint that has melted out at the edges and spread. She runs through any other possibilities, as though she could be making a mistake, but the print is real and bigger than her two feet together. The bear.

There are a few prints close in. They disappear again where tree roots break the surface and the snow turns to ice. The track is heading the same direction as Maeve.

She turns sharply left, moving away from the area as quickly as possible. Making calculations in her mind: if she's been walking in a straight line, the turn should spit her out back along the edge of the woods where she can see. But another twenty minutes of walking and she finds herself almost exactly where she started.

"Okay," Maeve says, and she startles at her own voice. What light there is in the woods is fading fast. She's been out far longer than she meant to be. There's a storm moving in and Maeve remembers the feeling of her dream the night before, trapped outside and blinded by blowing snow. Panic sets in and she struggles to keep her breathing even: lost is not an option.

Lost in the dark, even worse.

"Okay," she says again. Inhale, exhale. Trying to calm herself. "Okay."

If, instead of following the path, she climbs up higher, then what? She might gain a better vantage point—be able to see, for instance, the skylights of her studio cabin and from there get out of the woods and back to the center before she loses the light entirely. Angry with herself now for getting into this mess. What is she, a kid? She scrambles up an icy patch, smacking the snow from the lowest branches so she can use them as a grip. Her foot slips and she almost falls once, then again. A hazard, tree roots breaking the surface and the snow falling away between them. She reaches for the slim trunk of a sapling and pulls herself up the crest. On the other side, the ground falls away, rolling into a little gully. A ditch.

215

Maeve freezes.

Down in the ditch is an elk. What's left of an elk—ribs spread like fingers, the snow around it stained dark. Most of the meat ravaged away.

Most of it.

Her throat closes. This is no dream.

It's a cache. The bear's cache, what it's been eating. Maeve feels the burn of something watching her and slowly raises her head. There's the wind, vague and high above her, but in the woods nothing moves. If it's out there, it is stalking her. Silent.

All she knows is the bear from her dreams, the sound of it, its dark eyes. A threat bounding at the window. An image. A blur.

This is different, visceral. Just an animal, it will eat whatever it finds to stay alive.

It's a moment before she can bear to look down again. A tight fear coming through her body: the arc of the elk's antlers, the strange angle of its head, a ridge of exposed spine. A bull, a giant. Pelt peeled back, or torn away.

She blinks. There's something else down there, half hidden behind the mess. Some other kill? Something else the bear has dragged in, dark against the darkened snow. She moves cautiously to one side, eyes darting to scan the trees for any movement. A spray of black fur is wedged beneath the elk's hind leg. Odd-looking and damp.

Maeve stiffens. She already knows what's hidden there. Her head lightens, spins. For the space of a breath, she's nine years old again, her mother's hand at her back, nudging her forward, forcing her to look at what's caught in the fence. Forcing her to face it.

The dark ridge of fur is a fur-trimmed hood.

Sadie.

Maeve's stomach turns. It's Sadie, or what's left of her, tucked into the back end of the elk. Her slight frame in the snow the size of a child. The girl's hood drawn tight. Head thrown back.

Sadie's legs look bent and mechanical, broken where her body has been dragged, and Maeve thinks of Anna's frozen limbs pulsing stiffly under Dan's weight as he tried to revive her.

Sadie's face oddly torn at the temple. One eye open, the other eye destroyed.

She steps closer, sliding a little way down the slope. Shaking now. The wound at Sadie's forehead doesn't seem right. It's not the damage of claws or teeth. It looks more like a hole, a funnel blown clear through the back of her head to the front.

A gunshot. She can see the blast of it, the force.

Maeve's legs buckle and she lurches forward, catching herself. The bear didn't kill Sadie. It just scavenged her body from the woods.

She pulls up straight, her shoulders smacking against a tree and knocking her off balance; then she is gone, skidding down the little ridge, ice tearing at her hands as she tries to grab hold of something, anything. Her heart racing. She has to hold herself back from just running blind.

Sadie's body, lying there, flashes into her mind over and over. Her face. Maeve can't stop the image coming. Her leg, bent and broken, where the bear's jaws—

She stops, holding her hands to her mouth and rocking. Trying to stay quiet. She can feel herself falling apart.

She has to get away from here. If she goes out the way she came in, there's the danger of the unstable ledge. If she stays in the woods—

Maeve decides on the ledge. She wants the open lip, or what's left of it, to be in sight again; she wants to know where she is. She pulls up and keeps moving, the sound of her own sobbing breaking through even as she tries to swallow it down. Choking on it. She traces her own ragged path back to where she first ran into the trees, but it's farther than she thought. When she finally sees light between the branches ahead, she starts weeping openly.

This time she stays just inside the tree line, where she knows there must be ground beneath her feet. There's another noise back in the bush, far behind her, and Maeve freezes—someone tracking her through the woods. But when she turns, there's nothing there. She tells herself it's the wind coming up, another wave of the storm.

Maybe the bear dragged Sadie's body from far away. Bears can cover a lot of ground even in a few hours, can't they? Maybe there's no one out here but Maeve.

She tries to step more lightly, deliberately. As though that could help. When she hears another sharp crack, she spins and veers out of the woods.

The center is in sight now, although she is far across the clearing— Maeve forces her way through the snow, back to the path she forged on her way out, knowing it will be easier to run where the drifts have already been broken. But where she's left a trail, the snow is packed down hard. It's slippery underfoot and she struggles to keep going, faster, faster, struggles not to fall. She's almost at the building. She's almost there.

Another crash in the woods behind her and Maeve reels, turning in circles and stumbling backwards now.

She reaches back, grabs the door handle, and cranks it hard—only the door doesn't budge. It's locked.

Karo. She spins and bangs on the door with a fist, yelling out, "Karo! Karolina!"

There's no movement in the lobby. She pounds harder, screaming Karo's name, then spins again to scan the woods—

Her breath stops. The branches all bleed together, locking up like chain link. Maeve searches among them, panicked. All she can see is Sadie's blank staring eye, her hood stained and damp around her face. Some little movement catches at the corner of her vision, and she presses herself against the door, banging on it harder. The wind picks up, whipping across the open. Deep in the shadows, a branch cracks, then another. There's a spray of snow at the tree line.

Maeve stares.

But it's only a deer. Two of them. Suddenly they turn and bolt into the forest.

Spooked. Just like the elk she saw in the morning.

Maeve herself bolts, running around the other side of the building to the main doors, yelling for Karo.

This time when she grabs the handle, the door swings free, almost sending her reeling. A little piece of kindling is wedged in the hinge to prop it open—the very safeguard she had considered before leaving, but didn't actually put in place. Did she?

Maeve hammers at the wood to knock it loose, throws herself inside, and pulls the door shut.

"Karo!" She rushes into the room, adrenaline exploding. "Karolina!"

But the lobby is empty. Blankets sit in a heap on the couch where Maeve left Karo; there is nothing of the fire but embers. Maeve has been gone for hours, far longer than either of them expected. She scans the room, then spins to the door and back again. The air inside feels barely warmer than the air outside, although she doubts this can be true.

"Karolina?"

The call echoes off the high ceiling. The cane that Karo asked for in the morning is also missing, neither leaned up against the hearth where Karo was sitting, nor on the floor, nor anywhere.

Maybe she began to feel better after all. Maybe she massaged the cramp out of her feet, maybe she wanted to walk the circulation back into them. But where could she have gone?

Maeve tries again, louder, her voice breaking a little as it peaks. "Karo?"

Outside, twilight is turning to dusk. She can see her breath.

She skirts the room in the graying light, trying not to run, to stay calm—Karo's office, then back to the front desk, then the dining room and the kitchen beyond. The place is soundless apart from Maeve's own voice, her echoing footsteps.

"Karo!"

The pitch sharpening, higher and more desperate every time.

In the dining room there are two tables set with clean plates and folded napkins, coffee cups laid out—breakfast prep that was left ready long ago, the night before the avalanche. Caught in shadow, it looks like a tiny island of civilization in the sea of chairs stacked on tables, their angles almost skeletal, grotesque.

She crosses the lobby a second time, pushes the back stairwell door open, and calls up into the tunnel, but there's no response there either. A cold, shallow dread begins to work its way through Maeve's body. Karo left the front door wedged open for her—

But why?

Maeve casts a long look out the rear windows to where she crossed the field only moments ago. She can't see anything out there now, the darkening landscape hidden by blowing snow.

Is it possible that Karo went outside? The sound of her, her scent, the thing that spooked the deer. Maeve glances toward the hearth, the pile of blankets, the missing cane. She couldn't have. Not in her condition. Not by herself.

There's a shudder as a gust strikes hard at the glass.

This wasn't the plan.

She takes a sharp inhale and pushes it out, tries to pull herself together: *Don't jump to conclusions, Maeve.* But Justin's torn scarf burns in her mind. First Anna and now Sadie dead and half broken in the snow. And Karo…gone. Everyone else unaccounted for.

It's dark now, inside and out. The lobby growing vast around her. She needs to light a lamp. The building itself is so large and has so many rooms, Maeve thinks. Easy to hide in. Her throat tightens.

Stop it, she thinks. *You don't know. You don't know anything at all.*

Outside, the wind dips low, and she shivers. She's just bending to feed the fire when there's a creaking from behind her. Maeve pauses, turns around.

No, not behind her, not exactly. Overhead. Again—the ceiling joist trembles. As though something has fallen and hit the floor above. As though someone has misstepped, tripped, dropped something.

Someone.

Karolina. Maeve straightens, listening. *Karo.* Willing it to be true.

There's another creak, and then another, more distant. Fainter, farther on. Is it really the ceiling? Or just the walls themselves groaning in the wind?

A hard smack against the windows, and Maeve jumps. The storm moving in fast. The glass shudders again in the dark.

Maeve lights the lamp and carries it to the back window. She can barely see the snow blowing out there, only her own reflection as she draws near, her face, sharp and white, her eyes just dark hollows. She's waiting to hear the wind swirl around again, pick up its howl. Strong enough, a moment ago, to thunder at the glass. It's too quiet now. But something catches at her. She turns slowly, trying to focus.

The locked back door Maeve banged at. She watches now as the handle trembles.

Her dream comes back to her in a wave: a door in the basement, the dead bolt grinding in the lock. Outside, the snow is falling in thick, heavy lines. If someone was close enough to turn the door handle, she would be able to see who it was. Wouldn't she?

For a moment she sees Sadie again out in the snow, her one intact eye, the pupil full and black and frozen. She leans into the window, peering closer.

There's a crash, and the whole door frame shakes.

Maeve jumps back, the lamp in her hand swinging. She sets it down and grabs the closest thing—an armchair—and shoves it against the door, then pushes another chair against that, irrational now, kicking the logs from the pile to fill the cracks.

Leaving the lamp behind, she rushes across the lobby to the front door and pushes the couch up against it, struggling with its weight. A blockade. The wind; it must be the wind. But Maeve scrabbles at her waist for the can of bear spray and gets under the front desk, breathing hard. She can still hear pounding at the back window.

Sadie lying in the woods, over and over, her body broken.

"Karolina!"

She tilts her head back and screams Karo's name, but the sound just echoes.

A can of bear spray is not going to help her. She doesn't even really know how to use it. Karo is not going to help her either. Karo, limping on contorted muscles. If she is there at all. Maeve needs to be able to defend herself.

"Karo!"

She crawls out and skims across the lobby to Karo's office. The tool bin is in there; there were sharp things, not weapons exactly—but wasn't there an ice pick? A saw? But she pushes back the lid to find the box in disarray: all that's left is a single neon vest, a couple of flares, the first-aid kit. The tools are gone.

"What the fuck. What the fuck—"

She's whispering out loud. What's happened here? She shoves the two flares and a box of long matches into her coat pocket, then suddenly re-members the freezer. In the deep freeze, in the kitchen—the emergency hatchet on the wall. A hatchet is better than nothing.

She runs back across the lobby in the dark. The space feels wide open now, furniture piled up against the entrances to either side. As she hits the dining room, something grabs at her, catching her foot—a chair leg, the chair toppled from where it had been stacked. Her foot is wrenched out from under her and Maeve goes down hard, taking two more chairs with her. There's a crack as her head smacks the edge of a table; when she pushes up, the world spins. *Jesus, Maeve!* She winces at the pain. *Why can't you be more careful?* It takes a moment for her head to clear, and she staggers up, listening for the sound of breaking glass from the lobby. She picks up a dining chair and holds it against her body as a shield.

Why. Can't. You. Be. More. Careful.

There are no windows in the kitchen, the only light a dim glow that follows her in from the main hall. At the freezer door, she fumbles to disengage the latch. The door swings open. Inside, pure black.

Maeve sets her chair against the door to hold it open. It's still powerfully cold inside the room; she can feel the sudden change in her fingers, her ears, her cheeks, and works faster. She gropes along the wall for the emergency release button and the hatchet, then remembers the matches in her pocket. She draws them out and sparks a light. Her corner of the room warms to life—the emergency button practically at her fingertips.

The ax is there, right where she remembered it. A glorious little shiny blade. She springs it from its holder and slides it deep into her coat pocket.

The flame plays its way along the match's wooden shaft. Maeve lets her hand drop. She knows Anna is in there, Anna on her shelf. She doesn't want to see her.

As she turns to the door, her boot kicks something in the dark, and she trips, almost losing her balance. The sound makes her jump, some metal frame ringing out against the concrete floor. *Be careful.* She tries to kick the thing aside, but it's heavy; it barely scrapes along the ground when her boot hits it.

That's not what stops her. As she lurches to keep from falling, some-thing bumps, gently, against her shoulder.

Something else there, a shadow wavering in the dark. Maeve steps back, half tripping again. Her match burns out and she throws it down, fumbles to draw the next one, and strikes it. The new flame sputters to life. Down on the ground is the shelf ladder; that's what she keeps tripping on. She looks up.

Feet.

Who would have moved Anna's body, hung it up like this? Maeve raises the hand with the match a little higher. The ankles are rigid. Toes and arches curled tight. Sharp as sickles.

It's not Anna. It's Karo.

Hanging by her neck. She's dead, her eyes frozen wide, and a trickle of dark blood, thick somehow, at her nostril.

Maeve stumbles back, out of the freezer. She can feel her breath coming faster, too fast, and she pitches forward and vomits on the ground. She drops the match and heaves again, leaning on her knees in the dark.

When she goes back out to the lobby, she doesn't even try to take shelter. The space is vast and open now and she stands in the center of it, alone. The only light comes from the lantern she left lying on the ground by the back door; in the hearth, just a leftover glow. It's cold.

Maeve sinks to her knees, staring into the emptiness.

She brings a hand up to the pocket over her heart. She can feel the outline of the little photo strip there but doesn't draw it out. She doesn't want to see them—no. It's the opposite: She doesn't want them to see her. Not like this. The cold of the floor seeps into her bones. Her knees and shins are aching with it.

She doesn't have to stay here. She can climb higher, where the water has frozen to ice, where there is frost like lace trim on the bedspreads, snow lining the inner window frames. Lie down there. Strip off her warm clothes. Go to sleep.

Let this be over.

Is this what Karo went through? With Maeve's long absence, she weighed the odds and gave in. Maeve bites her lip, fighting tears. Fighting her rage—damn Karo for just leaving her here, leaving her all alone.

She is there on her knees when the wind drops, and in the silence, she hears it again. A sound overhead. First, the same creaking as before. Maeve freezes, perfectly still, listening. For a moment there's a new and deeper silence. Then, from somewhere far away, bells.

Slight and chiming, like a child's music box being opened, the mechanical ballerina beginning her slow twirl. Maeve's head tilts slowly up.

Above her, the crystal beads of the chandelier tremble against each other. Ringing. A cold draft rises from the floor.

There's a gunshot, and the sound propels Maeve to her feet.

The strike of metal on metal and a cascade of noise, footsteps, or something dropped and bouncing along the floor directly above her. A jangle of glass rings out from the chandelier.

Karo? Maeve thinks automatically. But no. Something cold and heavy plummets inside of her. If not Karo, then—

Another shot rings out and she spins to the window.

A streak of fire surges through the air and hits the snow. It feels as though she cannot breathe at all; there's only the slightest puff of fine mist from her lips. Her chest hurts.

She struggles to catch up: not a gunshot but a flare, fired from a second-floor window.

She scans the room—a cavern, the entrances blocked off. Only Maeve, alone, at the center of it. At the gallery door, there's a yawning shadow. A crack, a deep V. The door is unlocked.

Outside, another flare streaks to the ground, and then silence.

Far above her, at the top of the stairs, the sound of footsteps.

"Maeve!"

The ring of his boots against the open stairs. Maeve turns to see

Sim coming down from the mezzanine. As soon as he sees her, he starts to run.

Her legs bow. She wants to weep.

"Thank God you're okay—" He has the flare gun in his hand. "I've been up there for ages. I've been looking—" He seems to need to catch his breath; his breathing as rapid as her own. "I searched the whole building twice. Finally thought I'd light a few flares, just in case you were outside."

Maeve stares at him—only a flare gun, only Sim upstairs. She's trying not to cry.

He pauses where he is, halfway down the steps. A little uncertain now.

"Maeve. You okay? Do you hear me?"

His face looks battered; he comes down into the dim lamplight and she can see the dark shadow of a bruise around one eye, a fresh lesion at his eyebrow. He reaches for her, hand over hand, pulls her in toward him. Maeve works to hold herself up: she feels like she might collapse.

"I was outside," she says. Her voice sounds thin, even to herself. Sadie lying in the cache, the splay of her black hair, the black trim of her hood against the snow, the elk's dark fur.

Only Sim. Only a flare.

He strokes her face, temple to jaw, as if he's making sure she's real.

"Jesus, Maeve. I'm so glad you're safe." He glances around at the furniture stacked up against both doors. "You must have been scared," he says. "Come here, come here."

He's wearing his coat, but it's unzipped, and her brow rubs up against his collarbone where his sweater is fraying. Her face pressed into him. The hood of the coat damp at the trim, but not wet. Not snowy.

She steps away to get some air. Recalibrate.

"What were you doing outside?"

"I found—" she starts, but then stops again. Her breath catches.

"Maeve, what's going on?" He comes in toward her again, leaning to set the flare gun down softly on a coffee table, the only untouched piece of furniture in the room.

"Karo's dead," Maeve says finally. She can't bring herself to describe what she found in the woods.

He blinks, and there's a pause before he answers.

"Is she?"

Maeve's shoulders stiffen against her back. She can feel the throb at her temple where she slipped and struck her head. Her body is tight with fear, hours of it now, but she can't seem to let it go. There's still a little space between them, but if he reached his hand out, he could touch her. She's sorry now that she pulled away.

"She hung herself," she says finally.

He just nods. Then:

"She didn't seem the type."

"No," Maeve says. "She didn't."

But Maeve had been gone for so long. The guilt of that thought: Karo lost hope.

She can see that his hand is shaking too as he reaches out to her.

"When I got back here, I found the door wedged open. I figured you two went out together and left it like that for safety."

"She stayed behind," Maeve says. "She wasn't well. She was sick."

She's got both hands sunk into her coat pockets for warmth, one fist still curled tight around the handle of the hatchet inside. She has to work to let it go, the hand cramped around it.

He leans in.

"If Karolina—" He stops, taking stock, and tries again: "What can I do? Do you want to show me?"

Maeve lets her eyes move around the room. The doors, front and back, sealed off with heavy furniture. She has to keep reminding herself to breathe, to let her body relax. Not Dan who was upstairs, but Sim. Sim who raided the tools.

She shakes her head. She doesn't want to go back to the freezer, not for anything. An ugly death. But strangely in keeping with Karo's character too—she did everything on her own terms. And wasting away, trapped in her own body, would not be her terms.

"How did you get back here?" she says.

Sim looks at her. He lowers his head a little, trying to maintain eye contact, keep her conscious, connected. She must look like she's in shock.

"I should never have gone. I knew it was a bad idea. Come here—" He reaches for her again, trying to draw her toward the stone hearth, but she can't seem to make her feet move and he stops. Neither of them says anything. Then: "It's not good news, Maeve."

"What do you mean?"

"There's nothing down there. In the village. They evacuated; the place is empty. There's no one there."

"And?"

"And what?"

Maeve finally manages to step in closer.

"And—what happened?" Her eyes are burning and her head hurts so much where she banged it; her temple with a stabbing pain, sharp as a needle. "I found Sadie. I found her out in the woods." The words burst out of her.

"Sadie?" He steps back, confused.

"What happened to her out there? What happened to Justin? And Dan? Why are you back here on your own?"

"I came back for you, Maeve. I was scared that—" He swallows his words and starts over. "What do you mean, *you found Sadie?* Where did you see her?"

"You were supposed to send a rescue crew. All of you. Why didn't you go on? Wasn't that the plan? Find help?"

He tries to take her face in his hands. She knows she must look wild. She feels hysterical.

"Maeve. What do you mean, you found Sadie?"

Maeve pulls away. "She's dead. She's dead, Sim. She's dead like Anna and now Karo—"

Sim drops his hands, helpless. His eyes changing somehow. He rocks a little on his feet, anxious, then walks away, circling back toward the fire.

"We get down there and there's nothing. Nobody." His voice is starting to crack now. "I didn't want to tell you this, Maeve." He sits down at the edge of the hearth, his head hanging low, his body rocking back and forth. It takes a moment but he finally manages to meet her eye. "The whole thing was a mistake," he says. "You were right. If there had been people in that village, they would have sent someone for us."

Maeve feels her heart speed up, feels a flip in the base of her throat. She doesn't want to be right about this. It was their best real hope.

"But it's still the plan we agreed on," she says again. "The plan was you find someone."

"Yeah, well, you had a plan too, Maeve—" His voice thinning out, tired. "You were supposed to stay the fuck inside where it's safe." He pokes some tinder into the fire, jamming it until there's a spark, before turning back to face her again. "I just risked my life to climb back up here and make sure you're okay, and I get here and you're nowhere to be found. Where were you? Out in the woods? Fucking brilliant. That's not what you were supposed to do either. Is it."

Maeve backs up a step. The change of tone is confusing. And if the village was evacuated, they should all have come back together. Shouldn't they?

"Sorry, I'm sorry, I'm just—" Sim stands up but, watching her reaction, doesn't move closer. Instead, he folds his hands together. "I was so worried about you, Maeve. So fucking scared. I get back here and the place is just...empty."

"It's okay," she says, and he steps up to meet her.

"But where's everyone else, then?" she says. It's the second time she's asked the question. He looks over his shoulder, and she wonders if he has the same fear, that someone has followed him, someone is lurking outside. When he turns back, he looks her right in the eye.

"Where did you find Sadie," he says quietly.

"The bear..." Maeve falters, unsure how to describe it.

Sim shakes his head. "No. There's more than a bear to be worried about here. Dan—"

"Fuck Dan." She's whispering now, fierce. She feels somehow more anxious, watching him look over his shoulder, and has to fight against it. "Fuck Dan—where's Justin? Where's Justin, Sim?" The scarf in her pocket.

Sim backs up a little. His voice pleading: "That's what I'm trying to tell you. Justin's dead, Maeve." There's a beat. He drops his head into his hand and rubs the bruise at his temple. When he looks up, he has to take a breath and start over. "Justin and, yeah, Sadie too. They're both dead. Dan—he lost it out there."

Maeve feels her stomach lurch, as though she might vomit again. Instead, she finds herself staggering toward him.

"What do you mean?" She doesn't know if she wants to cry or punch him.

He takes a shaky breath.

"Just listen." He's speaking low and even, working to steady his voice. "There was a fight." He holds a hand up to his own battered face. "Christ, look at me. The whole thing was a mess, okay? Starting right away, from the word *go*." He takes another breath and exhales. "We're barely past the gates, and Justin opens up the pack. Half of what's in there comes flying out in the wind. We lost it all, half of everything. Shit blew away. Flares, everything, gone. Sank into the snow." Sim shakes his head. "I thought Dan was going to kill him right then. You know what he's like. I had to pull him off Justin."

Maeve thinks of the scarf, how it was whipping along in the wind. Justin's missing tooth, his split lip still fresh.

"But you said you got down there—"

"I just put myself between them the whole way. Stay on track, right? Follow the plan. Hours of it. I did my best, Maeve—I swear. We finally get down there in the dark, it's fucking cold, and the village is empty. We got nothing—no signal. No flares. Nothing. Two in the morning. God-damn snow blowing everywhere." He presses his lips together and rocks in place, trying to find the words. "And Dan cannot get over how fucked we are, how we are fucked specifically because Justin lost half our shit." Sim's voice comes up stronger now, but his eyes look hurt. *No—terrified*, Maeve thinks. He looks scared, like he's reliving it, the same way she can't un-see Sadie's body in the snow. "So he's railing, and he's railing," he says. "And suddenly Justin just goes at him. We can't even see anything, it's just dark and wind and snow, and I'm trying to grab Dan to hold him back. And Sadie, Jesus—" His voice cracks and he has to look away from her to keep on. "I can hear Sadie running around, screaming for them to stop—and then suddenly Dan's waving his gun." He drops his head. "He didn't mean to shoot Sadie too. That was an accident. I'm—I don't know. I'm almost positive of it."

Maeve feels her jaw tense. It's not far off the narrative she told herself out in the woods, the tarp cracking in the wind above her. The cold and the dark and the stress of it all too much. Justin pushing, and Dan pushing back.

"Then he takes off, boom," Sim says. "I tried to follow, to track him, but the snow was too much. I lost the trail. I got worried he'd come back here, and you girls here alone." He pauses a moment, looking at her. Searching. "Did you see—" It's like he's trying to figure out what to say or how to say it. "Did you see anything strange when you were out there?"

He steps in to touch her and she can feel the tremble in his fingers and it reminds her of Karo. Anything strange? Her own hands start to shake. The scarf in her pocket, the deer that spooked and scattered at the forest's edge. The elk's body in the cache, and Sadie lying dead beside it. The constant sense of something, something out there, trying to get in.

And Sim turning up here alone, his face bruised and bloody.

Anna and, now, Karo dead in the deep freeze. If Dan snapped out in the storm, could he also have locked Anna out?

He seemed half crazed when he found her: manic, going at her body with his violent, failed CPR.

Unless that was just part of the show.

"I saw the video," she says. Her voice is dull. "Sadie's video. I saw what she was filming for you."

Sim backs up—just a half step, not even that. Surprised. Serious.

"I'm sorry," he says. The apology trips out of his mouth easily, as though he's embarrassed, caught stealing something he can afford. "That was her idea. Her thing. I shouldn't have played along."

Maeve's brow furrows. She remembers Karo's description: *Sadie's a pleaser.*

"Did you pay her?" she says. "I mean, what was it even for?"

He has a way of holding her in his sight, those hurt eyes again. She can't bring herself to look away.

"I said I'm sorry. I'm sorry you saw that. I can understand why you'd be upset—"

It's not an answer, not really, but Maeve nods.

"Maeve?"

But she still doesn't respond, and he takes on a more serious look.

"What I asked her to shoot was Anna and Dan. I promise. Anna was always trying to sneak in and see what I was working on, and I knew she was rotoscoping some sexy wolfman scene. So I wanted to scoop her, take some footage of her and Dan and run it under my own installation, on the floor, a thing you walk on. My project is—" He's reluctant to talk about it, as though it could still be important. "It's about bodies too." He gives a final nod. "Sadie made some bad decisions of her own. That's not on me."

But Maeve is thinking of the wink. He had to have known.

"It just—it makes everything weird, Sim. I don't know—" She falters a little, rocking back on a heel. "I don't know how to feel with you, I guess—"

"Maeve." He's looking her steady in the eye. A sharp intake of breath. "I came back for you," he says again. "I know you're scared, but I need you to stay focused. Dan—"

He seems to lose his words. Before she can react, he's already crossing over to where she is. His hands on her face. "There's no one in the village. You understand? No one else is coming. I couldn't leave you here alone. I just couldn't." Maeve feels her body tense, the surprise of it, so fast— but he pulls back just enough and lets his hands slide from her face to her shoulders. Gives her a little bit of space. "We're safe here. Bar the doors, keep a lookout. If Dan is still out there, he won't survive another night. Not even with his experience," he says. "We can wait it out. Just us, alone. Me and you."

Dan, the first day she was here, watching her in the woods at night, silently. Tracking her. And the way he'd been with Anna—barely looking at her in public, a weird, controlling vibe. But almost eager to fight with Justin, aggressive more than once. In both cases, it seemed to work— Anna and Justin trying harder to win him over, not less.

He likes to feel in control, Sadie told her. He likes to make others feel dependent. Top gun.

The elk this morning, and the deer, spooked, chased off by something outside: is it possible he came back, has been stalking around the center the whole day?

Watching her from the woods as she stared down at Sadie in the bear's cache, as she tripped and stumbled through the deep snow, terrified and flailing, banging at the center's back door for Karo.

For Karo, who was already dead.

Inside her, a kind of stitch, a needle pulling tight.

What does she really think happened here—in her heart of hearts, in her gut? Maeve thinks back to what Karo told her the night before: *In dreams, you always know what to do.*

But she didn't. In her dreams that night, she'd been lost, turned around in a storm, or watching, powerless, as something unknown fought its way in. She shuts her eyes, trying to refocus. Breathes in, opens them again.

"What about Karo?"

She means what should they do about Karo's body. They'll need to go back into the freezer, take her down, cover her with another white sheet, lay her out on a shelf of her own. But Sim braces, defensive.

"I don't know anything about that."

This comes out clipped, almost angry, as though she asked the question to provoke him. Maeve feels a renewed strangeness, something cold, something pricking at her temples.

His hands drop away from her body and he rolls back his shoulders; there's a change in his face, his way of looking at her. Like some kind of electricity, some charge has run through it.

"Maeve, things are bad right now. In a week, two weeks, you'll be home with your kids and you'll see how crazy this was. I didn't hurt anyone. Why would I hurt Karo? Or Anna? I care about you. That's why I'm here. Okay?"

Her head throbs. Behind him, she can see the furniture still shoved tight against the back door. It's cold in the room. Maeve wants to pull her hood up, pull her coat tighter. She's working to go back in time, to replay everything she has said to him since he came down the stairs. She goes over and over the conversation in her mind: *Why would I hurt Karo? Or Anna? I care about you—*

She is sure, quite sure, that she didn't accuse him of hurting Anna, of locking Anna out. Maeve has hardly mentioned Anna at all.

Sim lifts a hand to her chin, tips it up so that she'll look at him. She's expecting anger, but he looks only confused and scared. The same as Maeve, just the same.

There is no road. There is no rescue. There is no one else here.

"Okay?" he says again.

But she takes too long to answer. When he leans in to kiss her, she can't even move. She just lets him.

The new heat lasts for an hour or so, and then the fire dwindles and the room begins to grow cold again.

"There's not much left," Maeve says. She's standing at the back door where they had stacked wood for the duration, but the pile is now almost totally gone. No one expected to be here for so long. Waiting.

Sim loads up an armful of what's left, more sticks than logs, and points out at the dark.

"Over there," he says. He means Dan's woodpile against the side of the building, now frosted over if not buried in snow. He builds up the fire one last time. They've moved all the furniture back into place now, more or less. As though nothing ever happened.

There's a wide snow shovel by each door, meant for clearing the walkways rather than true digging. Maeve watches as Sim zips up his coat, reaches into the pockets for his thick black gloves.

"Just stay inside, stay warm," he says, but Maeve feels too strange propping the door with the little wedge Karo left and instead she holds the door herself, keeping her back against it while Sim tries to use the plastic shovel as a tool. It takes a long time; the new storm has laid down a layer of ice over the top of any snow and he's forced to chisel at it, the ice slick and smooth, before he can even begin to burrow after new wood.

Wet wood, frozen wood. Maeve searches the tree line, squinting to try and make out some kind of horizon, but there's too much cloud and she can't see anything in the dark.

Dan has not come back.

"What will happen to him now?" Maeve's voice is grim.

Sim pauses, turns his head in her direction. "Who?"

"Dan. Will he just freeze to death?"

"I don't know," he says. He hauls the new wood inside. "Probably."

She jars a little. It doesn't seem the right response.

Maeve checks the door once, twice, to make sure it's locked. Then again.

"He can't get in," Sim says. He leans into the hearth, working.

"It's not that—" she starts. Although it is, mostly. "Last night, when Karo was sleeping, I had the strangest feeling that something was watching me." She tips her chin out at the dark. "First, out there. But then I couldn't shake it. I kept thinking I could hear a door somewhere, like a hatch, I don't know. In the basement, maybe. A door opening. Something coming in." She turns away, but her fingers still play at the latch to one side. Worrying at it. "I know it sounds crazy, but I dreamed there was a door to the outside. Another door."

Sim listens but doesn't say anything for a moment, waiting for the new fire to catch. Then: "There is a door, downstairs."

Maeve turns to look at him, her body tensing.

"There's a storage hall, for equipment. They keep a few ATVs down there in winter," he says. "You can see it from the outside when there's no snow. It's like a little slope down to a steel door." He looks pensive. "What did you hear?"

"I don't know if I heard anything," Maeve says quickly. But she can feel it, the way she lay there last night, fighting to stay awake. "It's just— every time I fell asleep, I thought I heard it again."

"But heard what again?" He sounds a little impatient now.

"A creak, I guess. The sound of a door or someone moving."

He nods, thinking.

"We should go take a look."

"No—" Maeve actually steps back. She remembers her dream too vividly: the dark hallway and unknown room, the door handle moving. Someone on the other side; something coming in. "No, I'm sure it was nothing. I don't want to go down there."

"Come on, I'll show you where it is. There's a steel door and a dead bolt—no one can get in that way. But you'll feel better if you see it."

"I really won't."

"Besides." He's on his feet now. "It's so warm and steamy in the spa. It's the last warm place on earth."

Maeve stiffens. She almost feels like he might force her, drag her down there. She can't really explain why she doesn't want to go except that it's dark and cold in the corridors, and the humidity of the spa will not warm her up, she's sure. It will only make everything feel worse— damp, clammy, like a cave. Like a tomb.

There's a beat of silence, and then he sighs.

"Okay, no problem. You stay up here on your own and I'll go check it out. That way I can tell you for sure there's nothing down there. Okay?"

But Maeve balks at this plan, too; she doesn't want to be left in the darkness of the lobby by herself. The ceiling with its high chandelier looms over her, the glass beads now hanging still and silent.

"Maeve—okay?"

"Sure."

Her hands are cold and she sinks them into the pockets of her coat. Hours, now, since she came back indoors, but she still can't get warm. He gives her one last look before he disappears.

Once the door shuts, she regrets not going along. That same feeling— something dark and heavy, inescapable—seems to grow stronger at once. Stalking her. She closes her eyes to try a calm-breathing technique, but the sudden blindness scares her and she blinks them open right away. Stands by the fire instead, trying to warm herself, trying to shake it off. Shake off the fear.

That doesn't work, of course. She knows that: with Iain, she wished her fear gone many times. Hard to break that kind of training, no matter how much you want to. She pulls out Anna's bear claw and strokes the smooth bone. It's soothing, in a strange way. Her breath and the soft crackle of the fire the only sound.

Iain left and didn't come back only the one time, and she was at home when it happened, thousands of miles away. Wishing had nothing to do with it. *Just another shooting among many.*

No one meant to kill him. The bar was crowded; he simply got in the way. Maeve heard about the shooting on the morning news before she heard Iain was dead. The phone call had come later in the day.

She said all the right things—that she was shocked, that it was a shame. A tragedy.

It's true that she was shocked. She wandered through the rest of the day in a kind of fog, deep in her own memory, her vivid imagining of killing him herself. But Maeve hadn't killed Iain.

It briefly felt unbelievable. Not that he was dead: that someone else got there first.

On the six o'clock broadcast, the whole story came out. It wasn't a random shooting, whatever that means. It was a murder-suicide gone wrong: the shooter's real target was the hotel barmaid. His girlfriend.

His ex-girlfriend—she'd left him two weeks before. Maeve, alone in her kitchen with the radio, wanted to laugh.

There's a burst from the fire and she jumps, startled out of the memory. Above her, the barest tinkle from the chandelier. She looks up. The heat from the fire slowly rising, shifting things around. She thrusts the bear claw down into her coat pocket and bites her lip.

Sim is still not back yet. No sound from the stairwell.

If he's telling the truth, he was in the building for hours—arriving while Maeve was out in the woods, searching the rooms, watching for her out the mezzanine windows. But wouldn't he have checked the basement storage area then? If he knew there was a door to the outside? Wouldn't he have checked the spa?

Maeve pauses, thinking that over.

Perhaps not.

But if he found the door wedged open and got in that way himself— wouldn't he wonder who else was inside?

Who might be down there now.

She shivers, still not over her chill. It feels strange, ominous that he's been gone for so long.

She wonders, briefly, if she should go after him. Or at least call down the stairwell? But the idea gives her another chill and she has to breathe through it. She's just letting her anxiety get the best of her; there's nothing down there, no one. No one could have come in the secret service door. No one could be hiding there or lying in wait. He's only checking every room, carefully, one by one. That takes time.

The service door is locked, she reminds herself. Locked.

But Dan, of course, would have the key. Karo's words come back to her: *He'll be in it now. Until this thing is finished.*

She steps closer to the fire. A few yards away, the door to Sim's gallery sits half open. He's been so careful with it before. How many times in the past days has she watched him lock that door? Protective of the space and whatever he's doing in there. The great mystery installation.

She could go in now. He'd never know.

Still no sound from the stairwell. She looks over her shoulder. The windows along the back of the building reflect the darkness of the room, the darkness outside. Only in one panel can she see the glow of the fire, a bright heart near the bottom of the pane, fading as the light reaches higher. And she sees herself, of course, her own outline standing near it, her legs and shoulders and breasts and head in a kind of firelit silhouette.

Maeve steps back quickly, trying to douse the reflection. Anyone watching from outside would see the fire, would see Maeve standing alone. She refocuses, but her shadow is still there in the slim light and she has the impulse to run, to get out of the fishbowl of the lobby. Only where would she go?

She looks over at the gallery again, at the tall, heavy door standing open.

Maeve shoves her way in. It's dark in the gallery but there's a flashlight hanging from a peg on the wall and she flips it on, then shuts the door and leans against it. The room smells of sawdust and adhesive, a chemical smell. It's colder in here than in the lobby. She takes a breath and the air is sharp against her nostrils.

She doesn't want to think of the kitchen, the dark freezer. She aims the light ahead.

The gallery is just a mirror of the lobby, vast and high-ceilinged with its own curving staircase—the rails now covered in drop cloths— winding up to a mirror mezzanine above. Just as vacant. Maeve just as small within it.

She moves slowly, aware of the sound of each footstep and the odd, jutting piles of leftover materials, shards strewn around on the floor.

Her light follows the curving staircase to where the ceiling stretches high above. In the top corner of the room, the plaster rosettes have been covered over with plank wood—to support the installation, she realizes. The light plays along the ceiling and she trips slightly as she walks. Some piece of plaster underfoot.

Only it's not plaster he's been sawing through. *The smallest rib of a great blue whale.* What's underfoot is real bone, a skeleton, the pieces jagged and polished and clean. She lets the light sweep along the ceiling until it hits a weird kind of shadow. She stares.

The thing he's been working on all this time.

Here, there is no crystal chandelier. The installation hangs directly above, spider-like. Long, curving segments radiate out from a central hub, falling away from one another almost like flowers in a vase. Bound by a neat coil of wire.

She climbs the first few steps almost unconsciously, adjusting her angle, the shadow of the thing on the wide blank wall beside her. Maeve suddenly recognizes the shape.

A hand. The whale's rib bones curving and spreading apart, not like flower stalks, but like claws, like fingers. Looming over her, inescapable. Maeve feels trapped, pinned to the floor beneath it. The very feeling she's been fighting for days, a darkness pressing in on her. She brings the light down fast, and the change is disorienting: she stumbles, trying to navigate the staircase. The sweep of the light along the floor reminds her of the video Sadie took—this is what he meant it for. She can imagine the hand hovering over the projection, Anna and Dan moving together under its shadow; Dan grasping Anna's hair, her head tipping back, taut.

Maeve's stomach lurches. At the foot of the stairs she trips again and falls, her flashlight spinning on the floor—but it's not whalebone underfoot, it's something soft. The pack Sim took on the hike down the mountain, now spilled out. She moves through the contents with a light hand, trying to stuff it all back inside—a headlamp, a few power bars, the remaining tarp.

Then something smooth, cold to the touch.

There's a creak and Maeve jerks her head up. She grabs for her light: "Who's there?"

She stands up quickly enough to make her head spin in the dark. He's back by the door, a bleached silhouette in the flashlight's beam—and then suddenly he's there beside her. He pulls the pack out of her hands.

"You have the gun," she says. "Dan's gun." She had it in her fingers. Another moment and it would have been tucked away in her own coat pocket.

She doesn't say anything else and he roots through the pack, checking to see that the gun's still there.

"I told you," Sim says. "He flipped out. He took off."

Maeve steps back against the rail.

"You never mentioned you got the gun away from him," she says.

He pulls his hand out suddenly, and she startles—but when he opens his palm, there's only a handful of loose bullets chinking against one another.

"It's not loaded." He pockets the rounds. "I took the ammunition out to make sure there wouldn't be another accident. Doesn't explain what you're doing. Just looking through my stuff? Is this why you sent me downstairs, so you could sneak in here?"

It's dark and cold and the fragments of white whalebone scattered on the ground make the room feel like a grave. Maeve wishes she'd had more time with the pack. She wishes she had found the bullets instead of the gun so she could count how many were left.

"What really happened out there?"

"I told you."

She reaches into her coat pocket, draws out the red scarf, holds it out to him. Sim takes it, hesitating. Then:

"I already told you," he says.

"Tell me again."

"They fought. Down at the gates, and then on and on." He leans closer. "Dan has an ugly temper. You saw it. You know."

"So Dan just shot him?"

"No." Sim seals up the pack but he doesn't let go of it; he keeps a hand on the strap. "You want to know exactly? Fine. They're fighting, it's dark, it's a storm. We can't see each other. We can barely hear each other. I only knew Dan pulled out the gun because it went off. Maybe he meant it like a warning shot, I don't know, but he hits Justin. Justin's down in the snow, and I get on his back—Dan's—trying to get the gun away from him. Sadie's on the ground screaming. You know like she did with Anna, after we found Anna's body? She's down there, and I'm on Dan, and he just keeps firing. And suddenly it goes real quiet." Sim's voice is cutting here; he's almost spitting the words. "And he just drops the fucking thing. He saw what he'd done. And he starts running," Sim says. "Why do you think I have the gun? He took off."

Maeve shakes her head slowly.

"I didn't want to scare you, Maeve. I didn't want to upset you even more—"

"And then—"

"He's out there. Somewhere. I came back here."

"No," she says. "Justin and Sadie. You just left them there."

There's a silence.

"I didn't have a choice."

The story is almost the same. The story about the fight is the same, Justin and Dan, but the first time he told it, Dan was waving the gun, Sadie was running around, and Justin started it. This time, Justin gets hit right away, Sadie gets on the ground with him, Sim hears the sound of the gun before he sees it. She gives it a moment to sink in.

Trauma makes it hard to remember details. Maeve knows that from experience. But it's not the details that make her doubt the story, it's the tone. It's like he's going through the motions. Like he's angry at Maeve for even asking.

Maeve hesitates, trying to put her finger on which part of it bothers her most. What she knows is this: every minute she spends here feels more like a threat.

The best thing would be to defuse the tension. This, too, Maeve knows from experience. Avoid conflict. Just pretend. Be nicer, smile, don't say what you really think. There's a name for this, a therapy name. What do they call it?

Sim slings the bag onto one shoulder. "Don't go getting into things that don't belong to you, Maeve."

"I'm not—I don't want to get into anything," she says. Steady now.

Tend and befriend.

Not forever. Just long enough to get away.

"I know you knew him for a few days, Maeve, but sometimes people are good at hiding who they really are." He takes the light from her hand and aims it at the shadows above. "Do you like it?"

There's a silence.

"It's a hand," she says finally. "Isn't it? Made of whalebone." She's dizzy, still imagining Anna there, projected on the floor.

Or not Anna. Maeve, the video of Maeve. Her skin, the scar at her belly gleaming.

"A puppet hand," she says.

"It's my hand," Sim says, and he holds one up, spread flat, and lets it hang there in the air. "This is where I wanted you dancing. You and your coil of rope." He looks up almost wistfully. "I wonder who'll see it now."

He nods to the door, inviting her to leave.

Years of ballet training taught her one thing: get up.

She left Iain while he was away on tour. Packed the children's things and her own in twenty-four hours, left the furniture and the car, moved house silently and secretly and almost totally on her own. He was supposed to be gone for a week. The next day, she went to the studio for the first time in a year. To feel grounded, at home in her skin. To work. To try and reclaim something of herself, what career she had left.

Get up or you'll lose your spot. Get up or some other girl will get your place, and there is always some other girl, waiting.

Iain was supposed to be gone for a week, but she should have known.

If the music hadn't been on so loud or if there hadn't been construction outside, she would have heard him coming. His footsteps or the key in the lock. Instead, there was only a sudden brilliant flash as the door flew open. A flood of light, hitting all the mirrors at once, and Maeve, blinded, came flying out of a turn and missed her landing. She hit the ground hard, hip first, then knee, shoulder, wrenching her neck to save herself.

Get up.

He'd gotten home and found the house half empty. Someone had told him she was here, some assistant or junior corps dancer. Or else he just guessed.

Or else he followed her. He'd done it before.

The music swelled louder and Maeve, dazed, tried to get her bearings on the floor. She could taste blood already; her tooth tearing through her lip as she fell. She could still feel herself spinning. For a moment, her eyes focused on the mirror and she saw someone else there. A woman. Another dancer, stretched out on the ground.

She should get up, Maeve thought. *She needs to stand up now, get up and save herself.*

The image blurred and then came back before Maeve realized what she was looking at. The woman was just herself. Her own reflection.

By that time, it was too late. He'd shut the door behind him. Not some other dancer but Maeve who was on the floor. She got up, and he knocked her down again. And again. But she'd had that spotlight moment, the clarity of seeing herself, finally, from outside. When he kicked the mirror in and it shattered, she grabbed her shard of glass and held on, even as he ripped it from her hand.

She didn't save herself. The studio manager heard the noise of the fight from the hall, came in and pulled Iain out of the room. Talked him down.

They were old friends. He was used to it.

Without that interruption, Maeve is sure he would have killed her. Just lucky? The broken bit of mirror, bloodied, lying on the ground beside her. She picked it up and saved it, a reminder, a promise to herself that she would never allow anyone to do that to her again.

Like beach glass, a souvenir, locked safe in her childhood jewelry box. Wedged beneath the tiny dancer who pirouettes on cue whenever the box is opened.

"I'm all right on my own," she says when they're back in the warmth of the lobby. "If you want to stay in there. If you want to work."

She's trying to buy time, but Sim's eyes change and she stumbles on, too quick to grasp at an opportunity.

"What if we both do? What if we run this retreat ourselves—come on, you said it—" She's bright and airy, as though none of this matters, as though she is simply trying to please him, that's all. "Complete seclusion, right? You do your thing and I'll do mine, and I'll meet you back here later."

She can feel herself flushing with relief. The studio cabin is still there, the key in her coat pocket; if she can get out to the studio, she can lock the door. Her mind is moving fast. There's still days' worth of food in the kitchenette. No power, but that cast-iron pot could be made into a kind of heater, a firepit, a stove. There are blankets and a first-aid kit in the cupboard. She can be safe out there, alone, waiting for help to arrive.

"Work? You mean out there, in the cabins? It's the middle of the night."

"It must be almost morning."

"No. What? Maeve, that's crazy—it's dark and there's no heat in that place. Hasn't been for days. It's unusable." He comes closer. "If you want to dance, you can dance for me." When she doesn't answer, he says it again: "Dance for me. I like watching you."

Maeve nods.

"I know. That's why you sent Sadie into my room, isn't it? So that you could watch me."

He says nothing, and she turns toward the door.

"You can't go outside." His voice rising behind her. "I won't let you." His hand on her shoulder now; she stumbles, spinning back.

"What happened to 'We're not animals'?"

She realizes she's forgotten to smile.

"You're so different. Like something changed," he says. "I can't figure out what you want. I mean, what?" He gives her hair a flick, but gently, off her shoulder. "What do you want? Do you even know?"

"I just—I don't want to be cornered, okay?"

"Cornered?" He works the word in his mouth like it's some other language. "Look, Maeve—" She starts to back away, but he's already reaching for her again, his hand closing around her arm.

For a second, she's back at the freezer door: the shine of Karo's hair, slick as an oil spill, when Maeve bumped against her. How dark it must be inside when the door closes and locks.

Karo wedged the door open for her. Karo, in pain and perhaps delusional, made a choice to kill herself. There's desperation in that story, but dignity too.

His grip on her arm tightens.

"Just come here, listen to me." He pulls her in; he's got her by both shoulders now. She turns her head away, or tries to. "Maeve, come on."

His thumb in the soft place just under her collarbone, the hard tip of it pushing in. She brings her elbows up, adrenaline surging.

"Don't—" Maeve pushes him off, hard. "Don't ever touch me like that again."

The force of it surprises him; he almost laughs. He grabs at her arm, her wrist. As she twists away, her palm splays, the long scar across it shining in the low light. She holds it up.

247

"My husband did that," she says. "My ex. So do not touch me like that again. Get it?" She shakes him off.

"Maeve! Okay, I'm—"

He steps in again, and this time she backs up without tripping.

"I can't stay here with you."

His expression changes: slowly, like he's only now realizing that she's serious.

"Don't be like this. Don't!" With every step she takes away from him, he follows her. She's not funny to him anymore. "Don't do this."

"You're scaring me."

"No, I'm not." The words come so quickly she can't respond. "Why are you trying to ruin this?"

He won't slow down and she lifts an arm to protect herself. But then something changes—he closes the gap too fast. She catches him hard on the jaw.

The surprise of it throws him off and when he springs up, it's with a backhand. More force than she was expecting: there's the scrape of wood on wood as the table behind her skitters and Maeve hits the floor.

There's a breath, her hand to her face. He lets his arm fall.

"Maeve—"

"No—"

She's already pushing herself back along the floor, trying to get away.

"Wait. Wait. I'm sorry—" Sim drops to his knees. "Maeve. That is not me. That's not what I'm like. I am so sorry. We've all been through a lot. Look at me."

He's crawling toward her. He's still trying to get close. Maeve glances over her shoulder, trying to keep from getting trapped against a wall. She's aiming for the lobby's back door.

"Just stay with me here. Okay? Stay with me."

She scrambles to her feet, backs farther away.

"No—"

But he's on his knees in front of her and just keeps coming.

"I need some space," she says. She's closer to the back door with every step. "Don't worry about it. Just—now we're even," she says. "Right?"

Maeve can feel herself start to shake. The tremor exploding inside her, a freight train trapped at her chest. Everything moving at once.

Outside it's still dark. She can make it to the studio cabin in fifteen minutes, even in deep snow. At worst, in bad weather and against the wind, twenty. But if she tries to run, will he follow?

She still has her coat on—that's how cold it is indoors—and she roots around inside the deep pockets. The two flares are there, and the cold can of bear spray. There's the hatchet with its smooth blade, the box of matches, the roll of duct tape. And down under that, what she needs most: the studio key. She scoops it smoothly into her palm, the bear claw hooked neatly into the key ring. She pauses, the tip of it pricking at her own thumb. Anna's claw.

Her lucky claw.

"Maeve, I want to start this over—"

He's on his feet again. He's so much taller than she is, and his stride is so long.

"Maeve—"

She's almost got her hand on the door. He moves toward her, and his foot slides against something on the floor. Maeve looks down, squinting. It's some little bit of paper.

She slides a hand inside her coat, to her breast pocket. The photo is gone. It's somehow fallen out in the moment her body hit the ground. Her breath catches.

He moves just a single step back, but it's enough for him to see what she wants. He bends and peels the photo strip off the floor. Looks down at the images, then back at her.

"Yours?"

She knows she should go, start running, but somehow she can't. Not without that photo. She can't leave them behind.

"Maeve."

He's holding it close, like a lure.

Maeve steps in, haltingly, her hand out. She can see the pictures, the faces upside down from where she is. Distant now. The paper has gotten wet at one corner, and in the bottom photo the image wavers, as though the children are floating away.

She can't do this on her own.

"Give it here," she says.

He presses the thin strip against his chest.

"Can we do that? Start today over."

She wants to punch him. She wants him to understand this kind of powerlessness, how it feels to comply only because you're afraid not to.

"Just fucking give me my photo." She lurches forward and grabs the strip out of his hand; the corner tearing as she spins away.

"Maeve, did you hear me—"

She's almost out when he catches up again. His body suddenly between her and the door.

"Maeve. Listen—"

"No." She holds up a hand. "You listen. I am asking you: Do not come closer. Please. Do not."

She heaves a chair between them. Waiting for the right moment. In case she has to fight her way through.

"Maeve—"

Maeve—

Iain, his open hand knocking her back, her brow smacking the mirror behind her. Maeve, he says. Maeve. Just look what you've done to yourself.

That one time, the only time she ever raised a hand back at him.

Sim shoves the chair and grabs for her shoulder. She spins, trying to wrest herself away; when he hauls her in, she bites his arm, hard. He yells out and grabs at her hair, her neck. Maeve tries for the hatchet, grasping, but it's deep in her coat pocket, blade up; it slips and she can feel it slice her palm before she can get purchase.

She pulls it out, the pain of the gash shocking enough to make her gasp and fumble. The handle catches on the edge of the pocket, and in an instant it flips away, steel blade ringing against the stone of the hearth. He's swearing at her or swearing with the effort of trying to fight her.

She gets her fingers around the can of bear spray instead, bringing it up and slamming it into the side of his face like a weapon until he goes stumbling back.

When he lifts his head again, he's bleeding—the edge of the can has cut him at the brow. Blood runs down over his eye and he dabs at it with his arm to clear his vision. Like he can't believe what he's seeing, the blood staining his sleeve.

Iain looked up, his cheek cut and bleeding. She'd caught him with the edge of her ring. He came at her then for real. Threw her back against the mirror, then kicked it in.

She's on the ground with a long silver shard hidden in her fist. Waiting. Just a moment too long.

She jams her hand back into her pocket, searching again for the key inside. There's no room in the center that's safe enough, no door that can't be kicked down. But the studio is there for her. It locks tight: he can't get in, can't even watch her from outside. It kept her safe from a bear; it can keep her safe from a man.

Maeve shoves the last chair in Sim's path and goes for the door.

She skids across the ice, then falls, landing hard; a layer of frozen crust forces its way down into her coat at the collar. Snow everywhere. At her neck, in her ears. Inside her sweater, her boots, her bra. A night of new weather, ice pellets and freezing rain, has made the terrain that much more hazardous. Maeve takes a long inhale. The air is so sharp it hurts; the pain gives her something to focus on. She gets back on her feet, trying to brace herself against the wind, and scrambles to a small clump of trees, the only place she can't be seen from the building.

The photo is still in her fist, snow-covered and sodden. The other hand a bloody mess. She spreads her fingers, and the new wound softens, filling with blood, the length of her palm and running the line of her old scar almost exactly. Her head spins. Everything from her pockets now spilled out on the frozen ground. She gropes through the snow with the bloody hand, and the cold feels good.

The studio key is there, still hooked to the bear claw, a shadow against all the white.

A moment later, she hears the whine of the back door yawning open against the wind. Sim's voice, caught and lifting away through the blowing snow. Yelling her name.

"Maeve—Maeve!" A pause. Then: "You know Dan is out there somewhere. No one knows the terrain better than him. Not you. Not me. He can survive out there, Maeve—you can't."

The wind comes up and it's suddenly no different than her dream— the howl of it, the snow, all just the same. Only a crazy person would follow her through this.

Her injured hand stings and she rips a strip of duct tape off the roll and wraps the wound, but she's bleeding freely now, the palm washed in blood, warm and copper-scented, every time she flexes. The tape won't hold on her damp skin. She needs to get inside fast.

Another bang as the back door opens up and falls shut again. A light arcs through the blowing snow—the beam from his flashlight. Then a flicker from the woods. Maeve snaps to focus on it: a triangle, the fluorescent trailhead marker that points the way to the cabins. A beacon, a sign.

She jams the bleeding hand inside her pocket and starts running.

* * *

She knows when he hits the woods behind her by the sheer sound of it: the sharp crack of falling ice, frozen branches splintering, his voice coming throaty and harsh. She can't make out the words anymore. It all sounds like heavy breath, something forcing its way through. But it's not an animal; the sweep of his flashlight is still there. She can tell he's moving fast, the beam surging and flickering ahead. He must have guessed where she's going.

She moves from marker to marker, searching for her own trail, whatever path between the center and the cabin she tramped down herself over the past days. The solar lights are buried now: the new storm has coated everything in ice, and she slides when she hits the clearing around the studio, has to kick and dig in with her heels to break through the heavy crust.

At the studio door, she slams her good hand against the lock.

The lock, the handle, the door itself—all immovable. All frozen, iced over, buried. The ice is clear and solid and an inch thick. She looks over her shoulder, frantically presses the warmth of her body against the door, thinking maybe she can melt it. The flicker of his light from the woods—she knows she has to move again.

But there is nowhere else to run now.

She could try to make it to the village herself. Or burrow into the snow and hope, at least, to last till morning. The only real possibility is to somehow backtrack and lock him out of the main building, but Maeve knows immediately it won't work; he'd smash a window in before he froze to death. The thing that made the studio cabin so secure—no windows at all.

Wind whips at her ears, her fingers. She realizes she's shaking. Back in the woods, he calls her name again. *He's never going to give up.* She starts going over contingencies the way she used to with Iain. Ways to talk him down, ways to protect herself. Keep space between the two of you, look around for anything that can be used as—not a weapon, per se, but in self-defense. She wishes the shovel were still hanging over the studio's front door.

The binding around her hand gapes, and Maeve looks down to see a dark stain spreading in the snow at her feet. Her palm slick with it. She knows what the scent of warm blood can attract out here: in the woods, there's the man, but there's also the bear. The thought makes her gag a little bit, but she holds it in her mind.

All this time, she's let others build her fear of the bear. Anna with the violence of her *rougarou* dreamscape, Karo with her dismissals. Dan more than anyone with his locked doors and bear spray and rules. But Maeve is the only one who dreamed of the bear, night after night. She's the only one who now knows where it lives. And the dark terror she'd felt for days, the feeling of something there, watching, waiting at her door— it wasn't an animal at all. She thinks of Sim's spiny hand looming from the gallery ceiling, the way it seemed to pin her to the floor. Paralyzed. Unable to protect herself.

She fingers the claw in her pocket, remembering the dream moment, like this one, at the cabin door when it grew right onto her hand. Are dreams predictions or practice?

From deep in the trees, she hears the gun go off. A warning shot.

He is never going to let you go, she thinks again.

No. But she can use that against him. She squeezes her fist shut and counts to five, waiting to see the stutter of the flashlight beam one more time. Then she runs.

She is small and light and she knows how to move fast.

She's going to lead him to the bear.

In the sky, there's the barest hint of the coming day. The wind brings new snow with it, picks up the light top layer at Maeve's feet, making the ground in front of her sway and dance. She strains to make out the horizon, squinting to where she knows the ridge begins and beyond that.

Beyond that, just glitter.

In the clearing there was just enough light to guide her, but back in the woods, it's still too dark to see. Maeve skirts the edge of the tree line, trying to keep the brighter open lip in sight. Her injured hand has gone numb, and she's glad of it—glad to be rid of the distraction, even though she knows it's probably a bad sign. It can't be long until morning now. Can it? She glances up at the branches, willing some little bit of brightness to break through.

But the mesh of trees seems endless here, getting thicker rather than thinning out. She turns and heads deeper into the canopy. The woods all look the same now. The same darkness, the same reach of limbs, the same stillness. The farther she goes from the open wind tunnels around the center, the quieter it is. The sound of being swallowed.

Somewhere in the distance she hears the crack of a branch and she stops, frozen. The sound coming, not from behind her, but somewhere far ahead—someone or something moving through the forest. For a second, she thinks of Sim's story and her stomach tightens as she imagines Dan out there, waiting. Then she immediately throws the image out again. Sim was lying, he's a liar, the story just a diversion, and now it's slowing her down. If anything is out there, it's an animal. The bear—and that means she needs to move faster, not freeze up.

She's banking on finding the bear before Sim finds her.

Maeve waits a moment longer for another noise, some kind of confirmation—that huff, or the familiar musky smell—but nothing comes. Then another crack, behind her now.

She hears her name again.

"Maeve! Maeve, don't be a fool! You're not alone out here."

She whirls around, looking in all directions, but she can't see Sim anywhere, can't tell exactly where the voice is coming from. Then, far to her left, a swoop of light.

She can hear him getting nearer, moving fast, panting as he speaks.

"It was always Dan, Maeve. Dan shot Justin on the trail. Dan came knocking on Anna's door that night, then pushed her outside in the cold—"

The words cut through the night air. Maeve stumbles, stunned and alone. Her stomach rising into her throat.

Dan didn't know where Anna was sleeping the night she died. None of the others did. Only Sim had seen her there. Only Sim could have known which door to knock on.

She starts moving again, close enough to keep him in sight.

"I'm trying to protect you, goddamn it. You need me." Sim's voice growing strained.

The trees here are needled and snow-covered; Maeve feels like she's cutting her way through a maze that springs back and re-forms around her, sprays and pricks at her face. Her hood catches and pulls away—for a moment she thinks it's him, he's there, but no, it's only another branch. She tugs it off, angry, and yanks the hood right down.

She comes, finally, to a break in the woods. Not quite a clearing, but at least some breathing space, the forest floor hard between iced-over roots. Maeve looks down. She's found it, the path she followed the day before. The woods here carry sound differently and she can hear, again, a trace of the world outside the tree line. The wind moving off now, the skies beginning to clear.

She can hear, too, the faint, constant thwack of the tarp somewhere far ahead on the ridge. Guiding her.

Then, close behind, almost not even yelling: "Maeve—"

She takes off at a run. She's leaping now to stay just ahead of his beam without tripping and she can hear him swearing whenever he falls behind, unused to the trail, the knots of ice-covered roots and powder bluffs that Maeve herself learned only the day before. The key is to stay light and, above all, stay on your feet. She's using the bloody hand now, and it's no longer numb, the pain of it screaming high into her arm every time she wraps her fingers around another rough branch and hauls her body along. Where the woods grow darker again, she can still follow the sound of the tarp, caught in its tree, beating against the wind.

Ahead of her there's the root-gnarled crest that leads to the cache, rough now with new ice, and she slips, almost falls, clambers higher.

At the top she leans hard on a bare trunk, gripping it for balance and trying to catch her breath. Day is coming. There's an openness to the trees here, a spare feeling to the branches—they're thinner, somehow—and the first real light makes the woods seem gray and dim but no longer black. The wind comes spiraling in and cuts through the gully. She can let him catch up now. She only has to wait.

Down in the ditch, the elk, or what's left of it, is still there. The cage of its ribs raw and filling with new snow. And tucked behind it, the ridge of dark fur she knows is Sadie's hood.

But no bear.

Maeve listens for it—it must be somewhere close by. It must be. She can feel her connection to it now, as though the claw in her pocket were throbbing.

This was the reason for the dreams. Wasn't it?

Down near the elk, she can see where the bear has made a bed, branches torn and piled into a deeper rut in the snow. But not just that—something else, some softer stuff. Grassy. Like the ragged edge of a blanket, like frayed yarn, with more of it caught around the icy roots at her feet. Maeve reaches forward and pulls a handful closer.

It's the tarp. The green tarp. Shredded.

But that doesn't make sense.

If the tarp has blown out of the tree, then the noise she hears from the ridge—

It means something else is making that sound. Something else is up there, beating in the wind. Her breath catches.

An engine. A propeller.

"Maeve!"

The beam of light cuts through the trees. In an instant, the forest floor around her burns with it, the glare off the snow making her squint, the elk's black eye gaudy and rotten.

And Sadie, half buried beneath it, her hair matted into the fur around her hood.

She spins to see Sim closing in on her now, back in the shadows. She brought him here, hoping to lead him into a trap.

Another frantic scan of the forest. She can feel her confidence slipping. There's no bear.

He glances down at his footing, and she marks the moment when he sees the cache, the sweep of his light catching it from twenty feet away.

She rises to her feet, her voice wavering:

"What did you do." It's not a question.

"Maeve—"

He's trying not to yell, not to draw attention. It's almost a whisper. He stops moving, then slowly raises his head again. His eyes change. There's a new, grim look to him, a commitment.

Sim's light holding on Sadie.

If Sadie wasn't shot accidentally, down in the village, if Dan didn't kill her, then what happened? Maeve can imagine her trailing behind Sim, dogging him, trying to find her way back to the safety of the center through the long, cold night. The elk early that morning, spooked and rushing out of the woods—because someone was there after all. Maybe this was the place Sadie caught up to him, Sim reeling in surprise. Tired of her persistence. Angry.

Or afraid of what she knew. Whatever really happened on the trip down the mountain, Sadie was a witness.

Maeve takes a step back, then again, checking over her shoulder, but the gap between them stays unchanged. Sim picks his way toward her, the beam of light aimed low at his feet.

There is still no bear. She turns her focus, desperate; the rhythmic sound is there, and under the wind, there's another noise now, a hum, soft and growing. Something up there, hidden by cloud or darkness. Someone up there, looking down. Looking for survivors. It's what she hoped for yesterday. A helicopter. Someone searching for them. Searching for Maeve.

The bear, or the woods, drew her here for a reason.

"Maeve. Come on!" More urgent than a whisper. A snarl. "Don't be stupid. You'll die out here. Come with me! Come back with me."

She needs to get her bearings. She can't stay here, invisible, lost in the trees. She looks over her shoulder, judging the distance to the open, from here to where the ledge leans out over the valley and the frozen river below. The ledge she saw shift and fall just a day before.

But the highest point is not the ridge. The highest point is farther on: the SkyLift.

Daylight rises all around them and she scours the forest ahead. New growth sweeps along the gully to a rocky outcrop just beyond, a rock wall that leads up to the same ridge where it wraps around on the other side.

That's the fastest way to the lift. Not along the unstable ledge but down through the ditch, past the bear bed, and up the outcrop beyond. A shortcut. Over the wall, the rock covered in ice and snow.

This is her only chance. Now.

She pushes off, leaping down into the woods ahead. Her heavy boots kicking at bone left in the snow.

"Maeve—"

He's still calling, but the voice is far behind her now, distant. She twists to check as she's running—she can see him there, fearful, unwilling to go down into what is obviously the bear's territory—and then moves on again. The muscles in her legs are dragging with exhaustion, her bones weighing her down. But when she turns back a second time, he's gone, and she makes a mistake.

She pauses, afraid. Looking for him before she gets there.

It's only a moment.

She scans the cache, the woods to either side of it, the day growing brighter now, it seems, with every passing breath. Sim has disappeared. The waning hum above her, circling, but the pulse of it still strong. There's a vague crackling higher in the trees, the sound of friction or wind moving through the rimy branches over her head. She's alone.

And then she turns.

She can smell the thing before she sees it, before she hears it even— then it's there. As if the forest simply opened to it.

The bear. Maybe a hundred yards back, maybe more. Deep in the woods. Its massive head trained on Maeve, a dust of snow on the shaggy fur of its shoulder. A grizzly: she can tell by the shape of it, its humped back. The sheer size. Its snout, lifting; it squints back at her.

A male. That much is obvious, even at this distance: six hundred pounds, at least. She can hear it huffing at her, or barking. Maeve's breath caught in her throat. She tries to hold steady, tries not to show her fear, but when it charges a few yards—Maeve jumps back.

It was never waiting for her. It's just defending the cache.

Head up, ears up, alert. It pounds a paw against the ground, and snow sprays up in a mist.

There's no other sound. The woods and the wide white belt between Maeve and the bear are silent.

She can no longer picture the bear from her dream. This bear seems bigger, more sharply outlined by the snow, its eyes hidden, shadowed by fur. It is completely dark. There is no reason to it.

She thumbs the claw in her pocket, thinking of Anna, Anna's words. Suddenly realizing her mistake: *Nature turns to chaos. The problem is you can't control it.* The sign in the road: ALL WILDLIFE IS DANGEROUS.

The grizzly paws the ground, huffs again.

Sim is gone. Only Maeve stands alone in the bear's home. Its cache.

She needs to get away from the elk, get out of the area, but she's afraid to take her eyes off the bear. It stays focused on her, its gaze never changing. Now padding forward again. Stalking her. Closing in.

Maeve starts moving backward, her arms stretched out wide both for balance and in the hope that this will somehow make her look bigger. The bear doesn't charge again but keeps coming the same way. Starting and stopping.

Her knees are shaking and she tries to still them. She's no threat to the bear: she's prey. Her only chance is to get to the wall and climb.

Light filters through the trees but the bear's fur seems to absorb it. It is just a mass of darkness, moving ahead. Then it halts. Head low. Watching her.

Maeve spins and sprints the last stretch to the wall.

Her fingers dig into the ice; she finds a toehold and begins to climb. The outcrop goes up, not quite vertical but at a slim angle. Fifteen or twenty feet to the top. Where the ice dips and gathers snow, the wall looks pockmarked. Each spot another rough ledge she can—maybe—jam her boot into, maybe push higher. She can hear the bear's huff as it closes in. The wound on her palm leaving a mark, a streak of blood wherever she puts it down.

Near the top, there are no more rough patches: a thick layer of ice pours over the edge toward Maeve, snowless, as smooth as if someone had held a hose to its lip. Her hand slips and she slides back, boots scraping to stop the fall. She's four or five feet down before she catches herself, finds her footing, tries again. Her fingernails useless against the slick of ice above.

The air around her changes. Maeve reels. The smell of the animal is overpowering, musk and rot cutting through the cold air. The bear's rough grunt, below her now. She looks down to see it raise its head, its eyes black and dull. Black claws gripping the ice. It barks, jaws open: the smell of it choking her.

Her own breath coming in thrusts. She jams her boot hard into a crevice, kicking and kicking to get purchase. Then she pulls a hand away and goes for her pocket.

When she brings it out again, she's got Anna's claw tight in her fist. Her arm swings at the shoulder and she hammers the claw like an ice pick into the sheet above.

It sticks.

Maeve torques her shoulder again to pull herself up over the lip, but something goes wrong—it doesn't work. She grasps the claw tighter and heaves to keep from falling back, pushing up with her legs from below—but only one leg swings free.

The toe of her right boot is trapped in its hold. Stuck fast where she slammed it in so hard. She tugs again, then tries bearing down through her heel and kicking up, but it's no good: the boot is locked in place.

The bear huffs at her, pawing low down against the snow, before it stands up for the first time.

The problem is you can't control it.

The jolt of the first swipe knocks her sideways. The bear's paw hits the rubber heel of the stuck boot; her ankle spirals as Maeve hits the rock wall, shoulder on, her bloody fingers shearing across the ice, the other hand tight on the sunken claw. The bear drops down and then comes at her again.

Her ankle is suddenly useless and numb with pain, her foot loose and scraping at the tongue of her boot. The bear comes up again and she swings to the side, propelling herself with her good leg and then kicking down, trying to loosen a chunk of rock or ice to deter it. Her ankle somehow floating as it twists this time, light and detached. A claw sinks into the wall just beside her, but the animal's weight is too much: the ice breaks away and it falls back. The bear drops to all fours again, raises its snout and makes a few throaty barks.

Maeve keeps it in sight and gives a last jolt to free herself. The action of pulling up against the trapped boot makes her head swim. She reaches down with her bad arm to release the foot, wrenching up on her own thigh as though it were made of scrap wood.

The foot slides free just as the bear rears up again, and a searing pain tears through her calf.

She pulls her thigh in to her chest, but her foot just dangles—the ankle almost certainly broken, the leg useless now below the knee. She brings her other foot up and catapults herself over the lip, landing roughly on her side and rolling quickly away from the edge. Maeve draws herself to a crawl and punches at chunks of ice and exposed rock along the rim, sending them hurtling below like warning shots. The bear is still down there, trying its luck against the ice. The lift terminal behind her, a hundred feet away.

She's on her knees, trying to stand, when she hears something scrabbling up the ridge from the other side. She listens for the rumble, for the ledge to collapse—but this time it holds. The injured leg drags behind her as she heaves up, crying out as she wrenches the claw out of the ice, then throwing her arms out high and wide and bellowing as loud as she can. Blood soaks her jeans where the bear has ripped her open at the calf.

But it's not the grizzly that comes bounding up along the ridge.

It's Sim.

Her leg suddenly gives and she's back down again on one knee.

She looks up to see him already bearing down. Maeve braces her good leg. She's holding the claw tight between her fingers, like a set of keys. A weapon.

Above them, the mechanical hum grows in strength, and for just a second she tilts her head to the sky, squinting through the cloud cover to see what's there.

"You hear that?" Her voice surprises her, low and used up.

But the distraction is enough: his eyes flick away from her, and Maeve rises, quiet, her sock foot gingerly on the snow. As though she is standing on it. She doesn't want him to know the ankle is broken, the leg ruined. Maeve can stay silent through just about anything. She needs him to think she can still fight.

There's another crash from the woods below.

Sim jerks his head: it's the second time she's seen him look scared. She takes her chance and starts to move away toward the polished steel girders of the SkyLift terminal, the cables extending out dull in the gray light—but he catches her by the shoulder and she stumbles back. The bad ankle like a tether, holding her in place.

She pushes him off and he catches her again.

"Maeve, there's nowhere to go. Come on with me."

She pushes him off again, but he won't let go and the effort knocks her back. She lands down on one knee. Beneath them, the ice shelf groans. The combined weight of two people, too much.

"Careful, now." He steps in closer, like he wants to help. But when he reaches out a hand for her, his coat swings open: there's a flash of black, a leather strap. The gun, there in its holster.

Her leg is gone at the hip, she can't feel anything anymore. She looks down at her slashed hand, almost surprised to see it still bleeding.

Her voice is low and calm. "Go back to the center, Sim."

He steps in again. Another creak in the ice shelf; they're on a weak spot of some kind. Maeve tries to shift her body slowly away to where the shelf feels more stable. He's standing over her now, so close that his belt buckle could almost brush her hairline. Wind comes howling up the ridge, bringing a shower of frozen snow with it, and for a moment she can't see or hear anything else.

"Listen to it down there, Maeve—you won't survive. Come with me instead."

Down in the woods, the bear heaves against the wall another time, and the ice covering it cracks, breaks away, and falls to the ground below. Eventually the bear will hit rock. And climb.

Sim jolts again at the noise of it, and this time Maeve springs onto her good leg, reaching for the gun. Her hand on the gun and his, too, and the holster wet and slick with snow and sweat. Maeve's hand bleeding, her bad hand. He's grabbing at it, trying to pry her off, when she comes at him with the claw. Not at his face or neck, but where it's most useful: the razor tip tearing through the soft place between his thumb and forefinger. His hand flashes open in reaction—enough time for Maeve to close her fingers around the revolver and wrench it free.

The gun goes off with a blast and she's knocked back, a terrifying spasm through her hand as she locks it around the grip, but this time he's charging at her. She fumbles with it, down on the ground, her fingers slick against the trigger. She pulls it again—the pain of using the bad hand is exquisite and the thing kicks up in her grasp, the force of it surprising her. The shot takes out a branch overhead.

He stumbles forward to avoid the falling limb and slips against the smooth lip, his legs scissoring before he rights himself on the ice. His hand now torn and bleeding too.

"Stay there," Maeve says. She's easing herself slowly back to standing. First on one knee, then a half hop to her feet. Her hand seizing up, the hand with the gun in it. She works to keep it steady, trained on him.

He shakes his head.

"No." He moves toward her, deliberate. "This isn't the plan, Maeve. Give me the gun."

Maeve fires, on purpose this time, but the action of pulling the trigger sends a new explosion of pain through her hand. The gun kicks again and she hits the ice at his feet. The power of the revolver is too hard to control and she reaches out to try and steady it with her left hand.

There's a fault down in the ice, taking a beating. Grinding now, any time he shifts his weight.

He steps forward, then back. Weighing the risk.

"Maeve, don't be stupid. Think of how good we are together. Don't waste that. Don't throw it away." He keeps coming and she fires another round between them, this time aiming for the weakness in the ice shelf. Pain flares from her palm to her shoulder and she almost cries out.

The ice cracks and breaks away between them, a long furrow running through the lip, and Sim jumps back, his voice rising in anger and panic.

"You don't even fucking know how to use it! Give me the gun."

There's the deferred, echoey sound of ice and loose rock ricocheting down the outcrop to the forest floor. She's got the gun out in front of her and presses her arms tighter into the sides of her body to stop them shaking. He's working to keep his voice low and steady.

"That thing is coming up here to kill us both and it will be your fault."

"Get back, Sim," she says. "I mean it. Get away from me. Go back to the center."

Her hand is locked in spasm now and she doesn't know if she can pull the trigger again, if she can even make her fingers work—or how many bullets are left.

She tries to listen for the huffing, the throaty bark of the bear below them, but the wind drowns everything out now. What's coming down is not even snow but sleet, ice pellets, something she can barely see through. Sim stiffens; the silhouette she knows is him moving toward her again.

"You're being crazy." He rallies, taking a few quick breaths. "Listen—"

"Listen? What are you going to tell me this time, Sim? Sadie shot herself? That's how she died? Anna had a terrible accident and locked herself—"

"Maeve, I don't want to do this here. This is what I'm saying! You're in shock. I want to go back to the center. To the gallery. They won't find us here."

"You used Sadie to get to me and then you threw her away. And Justin, what did Justin do wrong? Every time someone gets in your way, they end up dead." She brings the gun up a little higher. "Not me." She backs away from him, toward the lift terminal again. She's reduced to a kind of limping hop, the snow around her staining red.

He follows her steadily, though. His voice coming lower, down in his throat. "They won't find us here, Maeve, and I need them to find us. You'll ruin everything. Give me the gun."

"How many times do I have to tell you no? What is it going to take for you to understand? You need to leave. Go."

All at once, there's a rush of sound up the escarpment. They both wheel to face it, Maeve with the gun jackknifing out in front of her. She fires, and it goes wild, the force of it sending her flying back. The smooth lip at the edge of the outcrop reverberates this time, and she can see the stress fractures webbing through the ice.

From the ridge, a voice breaks through the air.

Maeve grips the gun. She can feel the tremor rising through her body as she tries to understand.

"Stop!"

A figure emerges from the far side of the ridge, through the trees. His hood pulled tight around his face, his pack still on his back.

Dan.

Uninjured. Not frozen to death overnight, after all.

Alive.

Maeve hears herself gasp, a sob caught in her throat. She's not alone. Dan moves slowly and carefully through the snow, his hands raised.

He yells again: "Stop! Put it down!"

Maeve realizes, suddenly, that Dan is yelling at her. The gun in her hands is still trained on him. She had assumed everything Sim told her was a lie. She thought Dan was dead, frozen like Anna or shot with his own gun, somewhere down the mountain. But if he followed Sim back up here through the night—

She shifts, suddenly unsure of whom to keep in her sight.

"Maeve!" Sim spins to face her. The two men flanking her and Maeve left swiveling to try and keep an eye on them both.

Dan comes closer.

"Maeve, put it down." He's still got his hands out so she can see them, but he's approaching her sidelong, eyes trained on Sim. "I need you to give me the gun and get behind me. He's dangerous—"

"The gun stays with me." Maeve's voice has fallen a little lower, harsher. She's starting to have a hard time getting breath into her body and it shows.

But Dan keeps coming. He moves in, focused now only on Sim.

"I followed you," he says. "I knew you'd come back here."

He cracks his jaw slightly, and Maeve can see the dark bruise at one eye, a strange angle to his face—as though something is off. She realizes his nose is broken.

Sim watches him rigidly, then turns back to Maeve. Surprised, but recovering fast.

"Maeve. You can't trust him, Maeve. Give the gun up. Give it to me."

Maeve begins to edge back, toward the lift. If she can just get farther away, she can keep both of them in sight at once. Her hand has fully seized now; she moves the gun between them, first on Dan, then Sim, but the pain of trying to hold it steady makes her arm shudder.

"Stay where you are," Maeve says again. Imperative that they don't know that the weapon is almost useless.

Dan still moving closer.

"Maeve," Sim says, matching him, moving in on the other side. "I didn't kill Sadie. He did. That's why he's tracked me back here. He knows I know. Maeve—"

She wheels to train the gun on Dan and he stops dead, hands up.

"Where's Justin?" she says. When he doesn't answer, she brings her voice up louder, but it cracks as she tries to speak: "Karo is dead, Dan. She killed herself." He flinches at the words but Maeve pushes on, working to keep from crying. "Sadie is dead too. Where is Justin, Dan? I want to know what happened to Justin. What happened out there?"

"I'll tell you when you give me the gun, Maeve. Put it down." Dan's voice is steady and as soon as she stops moving, he comes closer again. "If Sadie is dead, then Sim killed her, not me. Just put it down. I don't want any more of this—"

Maeve pulls back, thrown by his choice of words. *If Sadie is dead...*

"There's no *if*. I'm telling you she's dead. Sadie—"

Sim moves up behind her, and she pivots to face him.

"It's not true, Maeve. Don't listen. He killed Justin out there on the trail. That's why he won't tell you what happened. He would have killed me too."

The two of them closing in, one on either side. Sim losing patience, his voice echoing.

"Give it here, Maeve. Give it to me!"

There's a crack, the sound of ice splitting on a pond, and Maeve pulls up. Then a shudder down below: the ice tearing away from the rock this time in a sheet, the bear's rough bark rising up around them.

"Stay back, please—" Maeve says. Her voice is breaking and she realizes that she's lost, she is crying. She's going to die out here, bleed to death while a rescue chopper circles overhead. She will never get back to Talia and Rudy. She pictures them, their faces at the wide bay window, watching the driveway, waiting and waiting for her to come home.

Dan is almost near enough to touch her now, she knows that. Maeve freezes, willing her hand to start working again, but it's twisted and burning, locked around the gun's grip. She can feel her shoulders sagging. She just wants him to take the gun away, to let her go. He steps in, reaching for her.

"I didn't kill anyone, Maeve." His voice peels along smoothly, the trained, steady tone of negotiation. "Nielssen jumped me for that gun

269

and disappeared back up the trail—and then Sadie was gone too. She followed him." He steps in again. "You know you believe me, Maeve. She would do anything to stay close to him. He had her scared of me, filled her with stories—"

"He's lying, Maeve. Look at him. Remember? Always in charge, holding everyone else down. Top gun—"

Maeve looks from one to the other, reeling. *Top gun*. Not Sadie's phrase originally, then, but the other way around: words that Sim had fed her. A way of setting her against Dan.

Dan shouts over him. "Maeve! I told Justin to go get help. To keep going down till he found someone."

Her stomach flips.

"Justin's alive?"

She glances up into the steel-gray sky, listening again for the engine hum. If Justin somehow survived, made it down far enough to find help—

There's a flicker in her peripheral vision, Dan moving in, and she spins back, hanging on, her bloody hand trembling.

She doesn't care what happened anymore. She just wants that helicopter to see her and she wants Dan and Sim gone.

Dan steps in one more time.

Suddenly Maeve feels herself fly forward, Sim lunging into her from behind. She lands hard on her knees and then they are both on her, Maeve in the middle as the two men grab at her, rip at her frozen hand. There's a dull thud as Dan's fist connects and Sim is thrown back. Maeve seizes the moment to push away, but Dan catches her elbow and wrenches it back, holding her there—then Sim's hand closes tight on her wrist, twisting.

He's trying to aim the gun, Maeve realizes suddenly, his fingers over hers; she braces herself with her good leg, fighting him, trying to force the muzzle to the ground as Sim works to slide the gun out of her damaged hand. When Dan lunges in again, his fingernails tearing at her arm, she screams and brings her teeth down into his hand and there's a blast.

Dan pitches forward into the snow.

Maeve, suddenly free, reels back; the gun hits the ice and skids away. She is shaking, her bloody hand flat and open now. Her own ragged breath, her heart pounding in her ears.

Sim, still on his feet, stares down at her from above. Then he leans in and grabs the weapon and fires. But it only clicks. Empty.

"Maeve—" There's a moment of silence as he looks at the gun, lying inert in his own hand now, then at Dan on the ground.

His whole face changing.

"Maeve," he says again. "What did you do?"

Maeve slides back along the ice.

For a moment, she really doesn't understand. "What do you mean?"

She shifts again and the ice sheet underneath her slips; she can see all the places where it's cracked and broken now, the long furrow widening as Sim moves carefully around on top of it, edging his way toward her. When Maeve moves, it shifts again.

"That wasn't me, Maeve."

Maeve looks over to where Dan slumps, a wide, dark stain moving out from his broken torso. Close range, the blast has blown his chest open.

"You—you wouldn't let go," Sim says.

Maeve looks at Dan again and her head spins. It's hard to focus. There's so much white.

"But it's okay. No one will ever know. I promise. It's over now." Sim crouches down, watching her as she tries to slide away from him. "We're not getting out of here alive, Maeve. Don't you see? This is the end of our story. Come with me now—don't ruin it. They'll never find us here, in the snow. We'll be buried. But back at the lodge, in the gallery—think of it. Think of their faces. They'll find us in the gallery. That will be our legacy."

There's a beat as the horror of what he's saying sinks in. *This is the end of our story.* Maeve sees the whole narrative spooling out like rope. First his quiet attention, then a growing obsession. Now, stranded for days, he's devised a way to make them both immortal.

Her hands are shaking. Blood from her ripped palm runs down her wrist.

They'll find us in the gallery.

He leans in to grab her and she kicks out in self-defense—there's a sharp crack from the ice shelf underneath them, the sound ricocheting and echoing in the morning air. Below, the noise of it seems to rouse the bear, and it charges against the rock wall; the ground shakes beneath them. Sim lurches back. But then he pushes slowly up onto his feet, moves toward her again.

The cracked shelf around him rumbles. *Like a train,* Maeve thinks. *It feels like a train.*

She heaves herself back. There's a rolling clap as a fissure in the shelf moves between them. A chunk of ice breaks and falls away from the lip beside him. Sim freezes.

"Maeve—" It comes out throaty, a whisper, as though the sound of his voice will be enough to cause the ice shelf to break away, dragging him with it. His face goes slack with fear, eyes wide. He looks just like a child.

Then he reaches for her, his palm upturned. "Maeve—"

He wants her to save him.

Instinct is what shows up when you've learned something over and over, from experience. Karo's voice in her head. Maeve looks at him pleading there, and wants to laugh. It finally makes sense. Every dream. She thought she could somehow control the bear—not understanding, in those dreams, there was no bear. The moment of transformation—there was only Maeve.

She looks down at the claw in her hand and lunges back, anchoring it deep into the safe ice behind her. She throws her good leg high, then brings the heel down with full power into the widening crevice in the shelf.

Sim drops to his knees just as the long fracture in the ice comes apart, lurching, grabbing for solid ground. Maeve grips the claw like an ice pick and kicks again, hammering into the shelf with all her strength twice, three times. There's a deep groan as the lip breaks apart under them; she pitches her body back up where it's safe just as the weak layer begins to slide.

"Maeve!"

His arm flails, grasping for her.

Then he's gone. The forest below like a hand, closing around him.

Maeve stares after him, breathless; the empty space where his body was. There's a long and blinding howl from below. A shudder runs through her, every muscle quaking, and for a moment there is nothing beyond that.

The scar on her hand now matched by a newer wound. It's stopped bleeding. Finally. Maeve closes her other hand over it, protecting it, trembling with effort.

Wind sweeps along the ridge. Her ears are ringing and it's hard to concentrate. She can hear her own breath, but can't seem to get enough air. She knows what this is: shock setting in. She needs to keep moving while she can.

She pushes up to standing. Dan is lying only a few yards off, his body blown apart in the cold.

Maeve turns away, dragging her bad leg. There's a new scent in the air, a stronger, heavier musk rising up from the forest. Metallic. She doesn't look back.

Somewhere in the clouds above, the hum of the chopper grows louder. She can hear it; she's following that sound only. It's hard to see anything through the gray morning. Black spots, like the missing pieces of a puzzle, drop into her view. Like a bad connection. Pixelated. She cannot seem to stop shaking.

To the east, the sun is rising, stronger and stronger every minute. She lifts her eyes, following the light. The steady blink of a searchlight still skims the morning haze.

At the lift terminal base, she eases herself up onto the ledge and tries sliding out into the open, then stops and sinks a hand into her coat's deep pocket instead. She can't climb out onto the lift. Not now, not the way she wanted to.

But she's already imagining how her dancers will look. How to make these movements, this broken body, into something beautiful.

The bear is behind her now. Maeve reaches down and lights a flare.

ACKNOWLEDGMENTS

A very big thank-you to the teams at HarperCollins in Canada and Mulholland Books in the United States, and extra-specially to my wonderful editors, Iris Tupholme and Helen O'Hare, who helped me in a million ways but mostly by loving this story as much as I do and sharpening it at every turn. To my agent, Samantha Haywood: You make it possible for me to do my dream job! Early readers and excerpt readers who held my hand: Sharon Bala, Miranda Hill, and Bianca Spence (to whom this book is dedicated and who also talked endlessly with me about dance and helped me to better understand it). For bear knowledge, resources, and advice, Jay Butler and Claire Cameron. For sharing her process and her story and many helpful videos of her own practice time, my childhood friend Allison Cummings (and, by extension, her company, Sore for Punching You). The Banff Centre for Arts and Creativity, for providing inspiration and elk (but, thankfully, no bears). Caroline Clarke, who worked patiently with me to create the map of the High Water Center for the Arts. ArtsNL for financial support that made working on *The Retreat* so much easier.

Most of all, to my family, who are kind and fun and funny and take my mind off murder. And especially George Murray, who reads every draft, listens to every worry, and to whom every book should be dedicated, forever.

ABOUT THE AUTHOR

Elisabeth de Mariaffi is the critically acclaimed author of *The Devil You Know*—which was named a *Globe and Mail* Best Book and a *National Post* Top 100 of the year, shortlisted for the prestigious Thomas Raddall Atlantic Fiction Award, and longlisted for the 2017 International Dublin Literary Award—as well as two other books published in Canada: *Hysteria* and the Giller-nominated *How to Get Along with Women*. Her original horror-comedy *Fly Girls* was a WIFTV From Our Dark Side winner and is currently in development as a feature film. She has taught fiction and screenwriting at UBC, Memorial University, and the Humber School for Writers in Toronto. Elisabeth makes her home on an island in the North Atlantic—in St. John's, Canada.

MULHOLLAND BOOKS

You won't be able to put down these Mulholland books.

THE QUIET BOY *by Ben H. Winters*

CITY ON THE EDGE *by David Swinson*

MOON LAKE *by Joe R. Lansdale*

THE RETREAT *by Elisabeth de Mariaffi*

ROVERS *by Richard Lange*

GETAWAY *by Zoje Stage*

THE LAST GUESTS *by J. P. Pomare*

Visit mulhollandbooks.com for
your daily suspense fix.